The Island without Seasons

Bartolomeo Veneto (c. 1470–1531), *Ritratto di Gentiluomo*

Robert Lazu Kmita

The Island
without Seasons

*Translated from the Romanian
by James Christian Brown*

Os Justi Press

Lincoln, Nebraska

Originally published as *Insula fără anotimpuri*, Târgu Lăpuş, "Galaxia Gutenberg" Publishing House, 2019

Os Justi Press
P.O. Box 21814
Lincoln, NE 68542
https://osjustipress.com/

Inquiries to
info@osjustipress.com

Hardcover ISBN 978-1-960711-03-8
Paperback ISBN 978-1-960711-04-5
eBook ISBN 978-1-960711-05-2

Cover design: Julian Kwasniewski

On the cover: Claude-Joseph Vernet, *A Landscape at Sunset* (1773)

Interior layout: Nora Malone

There occurred violent earthquakes and floods; and in a single day
and night of misfortune all your warlike men in a body sank into
the earth, and the island of Atlantis in like manner disappeared
in the depths of the sea. For which reason the sea in those parts
is impassable and impenetrable, because there is a shoal of mud
in the way; and this was caused by the subsidence of the island.

—Plato

There is something splendid about everything that is unknown; and
here the mystery concerns an island-continent which has vanished
forever. Moreover, Atlantis was an island which enshrined human
ideals, so that its mystery is fused with a sense of longing.

—John Gwyn Griffiths

Others, following Augustine, say that "just as the deluge resulted
from an outpouring of the waters of the world, so the fashion of this
world will perish by a burning of worldly flames." This burning is
nothing else but the assembly of all those lower and higher causes
that by their nature have a kindling virtue: and this assembly will
take place not in the ordinary course of things, but by the Divine
power: and from all these causes thus assembled, the fire that will
burn the surface of this world will result.

—Saint Thomas Aquinas

Contents

Chapter 1

Prologue: In the Storm

The waves battered against the ship with a terrible roar. In the cabin, the swaying lamp projected quivering shadows that made the objects around seem mere phantasms lacking any solidity. As the waves became more and more agitated, the roll of the ship forced me to bend my knees and shift my weight from one foot to the other. It was the only way I could keep my balance. The thunderclaps, spokesmen of the storm that battered the vessel with all its force, were growing louder. It was one of those long sleepless nights in which you would have considered loss of hearing to be a blessing. Haunted by the auditory memories that woke them in the middle of the night, the sailors of those daring times, when the marine chronometer was yet to be invented, yearned for the one thing worth wishing for in the midst of a storm: quiet. You can get used to the sight of mountains of water rising like colossi over a storm-tossed ship, but you will never withstand for long the piercing myriad-voiced howl of the west wind. Its dodecaphonic concert is hard for any mortal to bear. Some say that the excesses of noise can drive you mad even if you desperately plug your ears, pursued relentlessly by the voice of this spirit as unforgiving as the voice of a guilty conscience. As majestic as it is terrible, the wind of the west wants to prove its supremacy over the vast aquatic territory that lies under its command. Once unleashed, it attacks you honestly, fair and square, threatening to overturn your vessel if you do not prove man enough. It does not tear the sails of your ship, as its cunning eastern brother prefers to do, but throws itself at you with such force that it is ready to snatch them away, masts and all. Such a catastrophe can occur when the order to furl the sails is not given in time. As involuntary witnesses to that wind's assaults, we must acknowledge the truth of the ancient saying learned by all apprentices of the oceans: "It's blowing like cannon fire." The test to which the crew of a ship faced with this merciless winged spirit is subjected may be passed only by those destined for a place on the bridge: those, that is, who have not only identified their calling to be sailors, but also follow it faithfully.

A circle of light, sharply defined and large enough to take in the only chair in the cabin, fell upon the desk—an old *secrétaire* with a multitude of drawers—at which I could see the hunched figure of the captain. From his uniform it was plain to see that the man before my eyes was the commander of the ship, a brigantine that had traversed the seas and oceans of the Early Modern period. To my disappointment, there was no clue to reveal his identity. His dark blue tunic had wide sleeves and turned-back cuffs, trimmed with gold thread that gave a fresh shine to the worn fabric. Gold too was the narrow band sewn on either side of the split in his coat tails, which hung on either side of the chair. A simple black tricorne hat, its brim edged with silver braid, lay on top of the books on the shelf above his desk. Hanging from the strip of wood between the cabin's two windows was a cross of walnut bearing the body of Our Savior, His face expressive at once of suffering and compassion. Although the captain's legs were bent back slightly under the chair, from the angle at which I stood I could see both his black shoes, with heavily worn soles and large buckles that reflected the white of his stockings, and his beige breeches, fastened under the knee with round ivory buttons. White and grey mingled in the few short locks of hair that fell over the collar of his coat, showing that the man that I was studying with boundless curiosity was somewhat advanced in years. Having no powdered wig or queue tied with a ribbon, he seemed to fall short of the stereotypes in my mind—the mind of a modern person lost in another age. I could not see the insignia of rank on his collar tabs. Only the shining cord tied to the hilt of the sword that stood in a rack to the left of the desk gave an indication of the status of this man whose face

I so desperately wished to see. Driven by an irresistible impulse, I began to move, as silently as I could: I was convinced that the slightest noise would bring an end to the extraordinary experience that had projected me into an age long past. I watched the movements of the captain's hand. He dipped the point of his quill in the silver inkpot with a restrained motion, so as not to splash drops of ink on the paper that his left palm pressed down upon the wooden surface. The scratching sound as he wrote could be heard only in the short pauses between thunderclaps. With a calm that could only have been achieved after long years spent out on the oceans, he was fully absorbed in an activity utterly remote from the raging deluge. Imperceptibly, I continued to move. I slipped along the wall of thick horizontally-placed boards, blackened by the passage of the years since the vessel had first been launched. The woolen carpet helped me to avoid making unwelcome sounds, and the thunderclaps, frequent and long-drawn-out, rendered inaudible any creaking of the floorboards as they bent under the weight of my body. I stopped an arm's length behind the captain. An intense emotion perceptible in the form of a dryness that turned the roof of my mouth into a desert of unrelieved aridity held me paralyzed. I was conscious that I had only to reach out my hand and I would touch him. I was content, however, to let my greedy eyes scour the surface of the desk where, along with a closed volume, lay the page that the mysterious individual seemed to have just finished writing. Beside it was another, similarly covered with writing on one side only. The captain sprinkled a fine powder over both pages, in order to hasten the drying of the black ink.

Suddenly the roll of the ship became more pronounced, while its pitch took on catastrophic proportions. Consequently, at the extremes of its irregular swinging, the circle of light from the lamp reached into hitherto dark corners. The Nameless One looked at the crucifix. He listened anxiously to the noise outside. After a few minutes, he opened a drawer and rummaged hurriedly in it. From its dark recesses he took out a piece of charcoal, which he gripped tightly in his left hand. He pulled the book on his desk toward him, and began to write, in bold block capitals, two words, which took shape letter by letter before my wide-open eyes: "IN MENSA." He had barely finished writing when, with a tremendous crash, the ship rolled violently, almost smashing me against the right-hand wall of the cabin. I found myself pressed to the ceiling as the wood creaked and crackled in a long groan. The world had turned upside down. Before the light of the lamp breathed its last, a brief glimmer permitted me to decipher the words on the pages of the volume, which had taken flight like an albatross with outspread wings: "PLATONIS, AUGUSTISS. PHILOSOPHI . . ." Thrown into darkness, what I felt in my astonished heart was not so much fear as an overwhelming regret: I would have given anything to know the identity of the captain and to gaze, even if only for a moment, on the face of the one I had been seeking for so many years. Who was he? No answer came to my unspoken question, only the enveloping silence of the darkness.

I woke up in a sweat, shivering yet overheated at the same time, lying on one side by the wooden wall of the hermitage where I found myself assailed by the storm. When I opened my eyes, the explosion of a thunderclap, which sounded like the roar of an avalanche in a massive stone quarry, was fading like the last breath of a dying person. Through the cracks in the little building I could make out flashes of lightning, and their light helped me to recall where I was. Not in a ship in any case. Fully restored to my senses, I realized that after countless hours keeping watch I had dropped off to sleep, in spite of the raging hurricane. The presence of the man I had seen so clearly, so vividly in my dream had left in my soul the scent of a world obscure and remote, yet no less tangible than the world in which I was now, at over two hundred years' distance. Deep in thought, I tried to recall all the details of the scene I had contemplated in my oneiric reverie. A sort of unease took hold of me as I remembered the two words the captain had written in charcoal: "IN MENSA." In a feverish state, I withdrew to the driest corner of the hermitage so that I could open my rucksack without the rainwater touching it.

I took out the black leather folder protecting the volume containing the eighth tetralogy of the dialogues of Plato.[†] Ever since I had discovered it

---

[†] Thrasyllus of Alexandria (first century A.D.) divided the thirty-six writings left by Plato into nine tetralogies, each consisting of four dialogues. The ninth tetralogy also includes Plato's letters. The dialogues in the eighth

in the chapel, I had carried the precious little book everywhere with me. I looked at the title page as though I were seeing it for the first time. Emptied of all thought, I turned the pages with the sole aim of carrying out what was most likely a pointless check. Toward the end of the book, after the index, I found the page where strange signs, such as only a hand lacking the guidance of reason could have scribbled, surrounded a circle in which the yellowish white of the centuries-old paper was left unmarked. It all bore a striking resemblance to a nocturnal landscape in which the full moon was immersed in the indigo ocean of the sky. Dominating the header of the page, two words written in charcoal defied my reluctance to make any connection with my extraordinary experience: "IN MENSA." I gave a sigh of resignation. Here in the middle of the hermitage island, over which I had wandered not knowing whether I was awake or dreaming, I should already have become accustomed to accepting all that transcended my power of understanding. I was, however, too much of a novice to manage such an ascetic performance. I could only note the presence, in this world, of these words inscribed in the book by an anonymous figure, the inhabitant of the strange dream out of which I had woken in confusion. The frontier between "here" and "there," between "now" and "then," the boundary between the visible world, that of the living, and the world beyond, that of spirits, had turned into a volatile demarcation line that might, at times, be crossed.

My restless mind questioned the possible links between the man in my dream, the story of Atlantis in the dialogue *Critias*, and Father Francisco López de Gómara, the faithful secretary of the famous conquistador Hernán Cortés. All that I had experienced had awakened in my conscious mind the desire to communicate the mysterious story that had been uncovered with so much effort. After the tedious waste of so many years of life simply going with the flow, now I was alive! The two Latin words—"IN MENSA"—rose before my eyes like a new test of the labyrinth. Almost constrained, I began decisively to consider the possibility of passing on

---

tetralogy are *Cleitophon*, *Politeia*, *Timaeus*, and *Critias*. The story of Atlantis is told in the last two of these.

all these things that I had discovered in a forgotten corner of the world. It seemed inconceivable that all that I had begun to bring to light concerning Plato's story of the disappearance of the island of the Atlanteans should perish, once again, and perhaps forever, under the waves. I had to do something, anything, to record the lessons of an unsolved mystery. And that is why today, on this 15th day of August in the year 2003, I am starting to write the testimony that you are now reading.

My name is Alexander Jacob Wills, and I have a Ph.D. in the history of ancient Greek philosophy, that wondrous Elysian field that I frequented assiduously in my youth, only to abandon it some years after crossing the threshold of adulthood in a fancied protest against a world in which I could not find my place. I am considered by my few friends to be a teacher of philosophy, and by others a specialist in classical studies or a historian of the ancient and medieval worlds, but I must confess that I cannot truly say what I am. I have often deciphered difficult texts and obscure pages, but I have never managed to decipher the enigma of my own vocation. A plant without deep roots, I had barely reached the age of thirty when I came to work in a digital content company, after turning down the chance of a path, insecure as it might be, through the world of academia.

It is true that my mother, Francesca Wills, fed with all the affective ruses of discrete motherly love the professional hesitations of her only son. She had always had reservations about my wish to follow the path of her father, my grandfather and my guide into the arcana of ancient history, Dr. Paolo Paltini. She knew, most likely, from her own childhood days, the difficulties lying before those who choose a path founded on vocation and not on trivial pragmatic considerations. Worried about my future, my mother would sigh from the depths of her soul every time we got caught up in interminable discussions about the theory of the correlation between the micro- and the macro-cosmos, the existence of Atlantis, or the mystery of the channels in the Great Pyramid of Giza. It is no wonder that when she sensed the extent of the soul-searching to which I had fallen prey, she took every opportunity to encourage me in my decision to turn my back on the world of academia for good. For my part, however, I regarded her attitude with gentle condescension. I knew very well that it was not her little stratagems, springing from an admirable maternal instinct, that had led me to this decision.

As an outsider to the behind-the-scenes politicking that went on in the departments of Ancient History of the universities where I completed my studies, I understood all too well that I was destined to pendulate endlessly between the post of assistant professor and the modest grants that might come the way of a researcher in an unfashionable field. It was not so much perpetual poverty that frightened me as the certainty that my ideas and the interpretations I proposed for texts, in which I brought to light other senses than my fellow scholars, made it a safe bet that I would always occupy a marginal position in my own field of enquiry. And thus it was that when a friend, who knew of my spare-time interest in digital graphics, proposed a complete change in my professional prospects, I accepted. It is true that I had not for a moment anticipated the consequences of such a decision.

But what is the point of all these lines about the past? I only want to underline the boredom of a dull, minor existence, into the midst of which the rare flower of a crucial change revealed itself in all its glory. I cannot repress, after the days I have spent in the middle of the ocean, the overwhelming feelings that come over me as I find myself in another world. A voluntary Crusoe on this little island that is itself no more than a small outlier of the island that conceals the key to the mystery of Atlantis, I am caught in the middle of the greatest storm that I could ever have imagined. And yet here, surrounded by furious waves and devastating winds, forty years into my life, I know the peace, unexpected though always sought, that I lost long ago, back in my childhood, when I committed my first sin. I have passed through the eye of the vortex.

The roar of the deluge outside and my own complete inner peace are ample proof of this. Before I crossed through the whirlpool of my own existence things were quite the opposite. The outside was calm, while my inner world, hidden behind the gates of perception, was battered by a storm that never abated. Until I arrived on this minuscule dot on the map of the Atlantic ocean, my life was no more than a chute down which I rolled, inevitably but providentially, toward the narrow neck of the funnel in which I was totally absorbed at the moment when I accepted the Duke of Kirkwell's proposal. It is about all this that I want to write for as long as the torrents do not swallow up this little hermitage, which is trembling at every joint under the assault of a hurricane that is turning the very air into a barely breathable watery paste. Will anyone ever read these lines, I wonder?

I stubbornly insist on using the pen and diary of my grandfather, Dr. Paolo Paltini. The generous flaps of its leather cover have protected it from the omnipresent water and damp. It comes as a real comfort to me to look at its dry, rustling pages, slightly yellowed by the passage of the years, only a few of which are covered with the notes made by the man who was my true, my only teacher. I read again and again the last sentence written in his hand:

Nella lontana isola dove regna una sola stagione . . .[†]

I murmur the words, sensing through them the enveloping aroma of the language of my childhood, the language of Dante, of the tiny Italian hill-towns to which I escaped with my bicycle in the sunlight of immortal Umbria. A sentence that quite possibly had not been written for any particular reason, but merely to delight a soul that loved the music of a better world. I remember my grandfather as if I'd seen him yesterday. He would listened carefully to baroque compositions, sitting, somewhat awkwardly, on the edge of a large leather-covered armchair, his gaze lost in the green of the fir trees on the slopes of the low mountains of Ussita. He could sit like that for hours on end, with his back straight and his hands resting on his knees, interrupted in his contemplation only by the finale of the elegant music of Domenico Zipoli, his favorite composer.

As memories drift through me, I sit with a blanket pulled over my head and continue, imperturbably, to write by torch-light. I feel in the hermitage of the Nameless One like Jonah in the belly of the great whale. It is a dark place, cramped and fragile, a place where the noises of the tumult outside resound as if through a huge wall of damp ice. I say "damp ice" because of the walls red with decay, drenched in water and slippery,

---

† "In the distant island where reigns a single season . . ."

leaning to one side, firmly supported only by the rocky base of this secret place of shelter provided by the tiny island where no one suspected that a human dwelling place could lie concealed. When I pause from writing, I sit hunched up, my arms wrapped tightly round my knees, shifting my weight from side to side to stop my legs from going numb.

A prisoner in this old building, which dates back more than two and a half centuries, I am surrounded by a huge mass of liquid, like a tiny person hidden in his mother's womb. Returned to the state of an embryo, I cannot exclude the possibility that a new birth may be possible only by passing first through death—the insistent gateway that leads to unsuspected realities. The labyrinth through which the Duke's enigmas led me has given me an understanding of this. After years of silence, lit by the calm wisdom of Paolo Paltini who was the soul of the expedition that His Grace supported with great generosity, I can now speak, moved by the eager desire to pass on a vision, the treasure of any mind for which truth is not just an outmoded notion. It is clear to you, I believe, that hope still flickers in the obscure depths of a soul remote from the agitation of the raging elements outside.

I shudder at each new clap of the thunder that resounds unceasingly. The light of my torch is fading. I am determined to continue this letter to no one in particular in order to set down, in as much detail as possible, my incredible experiences of the last few days. I feel the need to enter into a dialogue with myself while I struggle, one more time, fully to convince myself of the reality of the improbable occurrences.

I get up stiffly. Keeping the blanket on my freezing back—it is the only useful thing that I was inspired to take with me when, only yesterday, I left the island of the library to row out to this little islet—, I enter the chamber of the Nameless One. Here lie his bones, bleached by the passage of more than two centuries. Hunched before a *prie-dieu* whose rotting wood has lost its luster, they are clad in an antiquated costume that would disintegrate immediately if I were to touch it. Behold the anonymous explorer whose name I will most likely never know! The man whose remains my grandfather, Paolo Paltini, and his friend, Gilbert Newman, Duke of Kirkwell, sought for years with firm, calm determination. As I look at them, I am troubled by the thought that neither of these two men will ever know that my search bore fruit in the end.

I am attracted by the unnatural peace of this place. The sound of the storm is muted here, so muted that it might be going on some hundreds of yards away. It seems to me that this effect is due to the privileged space occupied by the little room, whose timber walls have been built as an extension of a shallow cave, dug by unseen powers out of the only rocky outcrop on this tiny Atlantic isle. I look at the table, now sloping because one of its legs is broken; I look at the book, with its worm-eaten pages, covered by a thick layer of dust, which, in the most natural way imaginable, still lies open. A single thing catches my eye, glimmering faintly like the glow of an ember under the ash of a cosmic fire: the glint of gold and the shimmer of moon-colored pearls—the beads of the rosary twisted between the fleshless finger bones of my praying host. Although I am shivering to the very marrow, I still run the light of the lantern around the room, but I cannot penetrate the mystery of a life that came to its end on this invisible dot in the midst of the vast ocean.

Repeatedly seized by fits of shivering, I pull the blanket around me, but it can scarcely dry the dampness of a feverish body. I listen powerless to the howling of the raging elements. Everything around me is shaken. The conviction that the end is near is becoming firmly planted in my overexcited mind. The island of the Nameless One's hermitage, the island of the library, even the whole world might perish in this devastating storm. Will I ever see the light of another day? Will this tiny island survive amidst the furious downpour? It seems hardly possible. Back in the other room, without the slightest shade of pessimism or despair, I repeat my verdict, curled up on the fine sand in the furthest corner of the hermitage where I found the remains of the illustrious unknown.

After repeatedly resolving to face the onslaught of torrential rain, desperate to find the boat I abandoned in a small refuge on the eastern side of the island, I am finally resigned to my fate. All is lost. In the first hours of the hurricane an animal fear made me rise, time and time again, ready to dash out on the pretext of securing the boat. I realized later that this was the reaction of a claustrophobe desperately seeking salvation from a too constricting space. Later I became resigned: only by a miracle could a boat left on the shore, not tied fast, have stood up to the raging wind and the endless deluge of water. No connection to the outside world was now possible. No one would find out all that I had discovered at the end of two weeks of searching, added to the years dedicated to this investigation by my predecessors.

Covered by a mist of cobwebs, the Nameless One's tricorne hat held a troubling fascination for me. Already in my childhood I learned to discover the unaccustomed sensations that were triggered by the contemplation of ancient artifacts in the museums to which I was taken by my grandfather, himself a passionate scrutinizer of the vestiges of the distant past. I spent hours on end in the underground chapel of the Church of Saint Benedict in Norcia, where I tried to capture the faded whispers of those who had lived there more than a millennium and a half before. The mere idea that an object had been used centuries before by anonymous inhabitants of other ages was the occasion for a deep descent within myself. With my face glued to the protective glass I spent long minutes seeking to fill myself with the simple thought that I turned around endlessly in my innocent mind: "The thing I am looking at was touched by someone all those centuries ago . . ." However it is only here, in the boundless Atlantic, with the memories of my childhood far behind me, that I have realized that when I contemplated the remains of past ages I was in fact seeking to escape the fatal meanders of time in order to taste the joy of eternity.

The evocation of the past, either by inwardly going over one's own memories or by confronting what remains from the inhabitants of other times, seems to permit the intuition of a dimension of existence situated above the ceaseless flow of the liquid of temporality in which we live immersed. Memory is nothing other than the reflection, distorted, of a capacity of the intellect that, in our present state, has become alien to us: that of living in a continuous present, untouched by the confusion generated by participation in the illusion of the past and the future.

I would have liked to have had a time machine to transport me to the gardens of the Academy, that grove outside the walls of Athens where Plato conversed with his disciples, or to the library of the Northumbrian abbey of Monkwearmouth–Jarrow, where Bede, known as the Venerable, wrote the history of the Anglo-Saxon people and yet still found time to unveil the lessons of the unseen world of the Book of Revelation. And lo and behold, I find myself projected into just such a timeless place right now, as I gaze on the tricorne hat that was worn by the Nameless One more than two centuries ago. Unseen, the time machine has transported me, without my seeking such a thing, into a corner of the world that has remained unchanged since the middle of the eighteenth century.

Made of black felt, simple in design, without any feathers or other accessories, with a low crown, the upper edge of its triangular brim hemmed with a narrow ribbon of silver thread, the tricorne rests on a crumbling chair of roughly cut wood. It is as though it had been placed there yesterday, negligently, hurriedly, in a quite natural way. Were it not for the remains of cobwebs that whiten it, I might expect someone to turn up and put it on his head. Adopted particularly by commanders in the British and French royal navies, and popular in the eighteenth century, when it adorned the heads of such illustrious figures as Captain James Cook, Field Marshal Richard Molesworth, General Thomas Gage, and Admiral Augustus Keppel, the tricorne was a priceless clue to the identity of the Nameless One. Moreover his whole costume recalled the style of uniform worn by French naval captains. The closer I looked the clearer it became: blackened as it now appeared, this was not the garb of a cleric.

For many years, Gilbert Newman was convinced, as was Paolo Paltini, that somewhere on the island lay the remains of the author of the mysterious pages about Atlantis in the *Historia general de las Indias*, Father Francisco López de Gómara. The empty sarcophagus in the chapel, decorated with the arms of the family of his protector Hernán Cortés, seemed to confirm the hypothesis. Now, however, the evidence in the hermitage shows that this man cannot be a Spanish cleric of the sixteenth century. The year, deeply scratched in Roman numerals—MDCCXLVIII—on the door of the shelter where I now find myself leaves no room for doubt. By that year, 1748, when the anonymous French captain renounced any connection with the mother island to live out his last years in the hermitage,

Father Gómara had been gone from this transient world of earthly cares for more than 150 years.

My overwhelming experiences of the last few days trouble me so much that I have begun to talk about things, people, and happenings that call for much more careful advance preparation—I mean a much better documented introduction to the exposition of facts that might easily shock the unprepared reader. I have made up my mind to close this diary entry and to start setting down on paper, while I await the conclusion of the hurricane that is ravaging the lost island, the story of the seeking and discovery not only of the mystery of Atlantis, but also of the treasure that gave me back my life. A life that not even death can take from me . . .

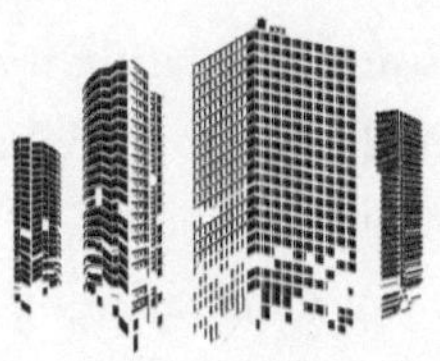

Chapter 2

Lost in London

When I began my usual preparations for another day at work, I did not in the least suspect that I was approaching a turning point in my existence. The variations of my life so far were woven together chaotically, ready to be sucked into the funnel of an unpredictable whirlpool. Beyond the numerous repetitive activities that characterize the life of a software tester, beneath the thin film of appearances—quiet, polite, and formal—, the contradictory waves of a veritable subterranean ocean were pounding against each other. Like the first tremors caused by an undersea volcano, certain presentiments of the coming moment of grace, the *kairos*, as the ancient Greeks called it, were already in evidence. One of these signs, unfamiliar and diaphanous, was music.

It was July 7, 2003. A Monday, just as frustrating as the first day of a new week usually is, banal, dull, monotonous, void of enthusiasm. Always with a sour taste, always unfolding under the sign of the inevitable question, "How much longer?" Newly awakened out of a deep sleep, I discovered, with no small surprise, that the ears of my memory were resounding with the old Gregorian melody that I had learned in my Italian childhood, the Creed: "*Credo in unum Deum, Patrem omnipotentem, factorem cœli et terrae, visibilium omnium et invisibilium . . .*" Somewhat discomfited, I tried to clear my head of this musical reverie, whose content might be perfectly appropriate in the Tridentine Mass that I attended in Corpus Christi Chapel on Maiden Lane, but right now seemed rather disturbing.

I switched on the radio, I turned to my favorite news channel, I selected a CD and inserted it into the player, I even tried to hum something remembered from my teenage years. None of these was able to drown out the ancient hymn that was sounding within me. On the contrary, all they achieved was to give it more definition, as when you set the volume of a hi-fi system to give precisely the amplification you want. I resigned myself.

With a cup of coffee in my hand, leaning on the frame of the huge living-room window, I looked at the morning sky, letting my gaze wander among clouds colored by the light of the sun. But can we call it light? Or shall I reveal its profound nature and say that in fact it is a light that is darkness? I do not exaggerate when I state that this was the plain truth of the life of an adult male, well into middle age, by the name of Alexander Jacob Wills. I lived submerged in the false light of the dominant darkness.

Always tired, I was unable to forget the disappointment that resulted from my change of direction after I finished my doctoral studies. Back then, conscious of the lack of any prospects that would have made it possible for me to fulfill my true vocation, I had taken the decision to leave academia in return for a relatively well-paid job in the software industry. I was unsure whether this amounted to a shipwreck, or simply a disembarkation in a foreign port. Sometimes I acknowledged my inadequacy in such a transparent manner that my colleagues raised their eyebrows at my unpredictable and not always intelligible confessions. As my outbursts displayed nothing but my own hostility toward myself and my incapacity to find my "place," no one paid me any attention. And so it was that the years passed and I found myself bound by inertia to the same job, to the same routine. Without glory, without fruits, without meaning. Contrary to my own surname, I seemed to lack the will to change anything in my own life.

As I have already said, on the morning of that day, I was content to look at the clouds, whose colors were extraordinarily attuned to the sounds of the sacred music. I had no desire to emerge from those moments of quiet that preceded my descent into the urban chaos. And, also as usual, I began the process of immersion in the everyday by fixing my gaze on my black rucksack. I wondered if all my accessories were in their places.

In fact it only remained for me to slide my phone into a side pocket and there I was, ready to go. One last sip of coffee, and, unable to repress a sigh coming from the depths of my being, I left the peace of my living room. I glanced in passing at the thick volumes of the Septuagint lined up on a bookshelf in the hall—a dusty reminder of my former preoccupations—and then I shut the door and set out, unarmed, to face the world. The grey world.

The ancient Gregorian hymn still refused to leave me. I was surprised to notice its persistence at the crossing of Tottenham Court Road and New Oxford Street. Once I had reached this point on my route, surrounded by the barbarous noises of countless vehicles, I had an acute sense of the unseen musical soundtrack of the *Credo*. It was like a wall of sound that dampened the impact of the auditory shocks to which I was subjected. A timid pedestrian, I navigated a route carefully chosen to avoid crowded areas—but above all to allow my eyes, so abused by the dull mass of concrete, glass, and metal, to rest on the last remains of that London in which classical architecture still had something to say. If I were to describe it in all its concreteness, my bold effort consisted in a continuous detour, in the form of a sophisticated zigzag, marked at intervals by buildings whose age could be numbered in centuries. As soon as one of these architectural survivors came into my field of view, I gripped it with my gaze and gluttonously drank in its forms, feeling its lines, delighting in an austere beauty that stood in radical discontinuity with the unaesthetic functional architecture round about.

The first part of my route took me by a few undistinguished streets on which the rare buildings erected more than a century before were indecently intermixed with edifices of glass and concrete. The crossing of Mortimer Street and Wells Street, on the other hand, offered an opportunity to escape from the architectural jungle by contemplating the patch of sky that was more visible from here. Motorcycles and bicycles were lined up on either side of the tarmac, waiting like boats at the quayside, caressed by the waves of the river of humanity endlessly circulating through the arteries of the city center. The shop windows of a building that still bore the inscription of its year of opening, 1924, offered passers-by not only the reading material in the Carlton bookshop but also the mutant fruits of post-Darwinian imaginary in the form of "fighting dinosaurs." After passing through an area abundantly sprinkled with cafés, estate agencies, clothes shops, and small restaurants, I headed toward Whitfield Street, to the spot where I could delight in an encounter with the oasis of greenery opposite the Transport Police. Known as Crabtree Fields, the little park reminded me every time of happy days spent in North Carolina, where I once lived in a district that was also called Crabtree. I was soon back on Tottenham Court Road, and briskly made my way past the various bank headquarters, where no one can walk at a relaxed pace. I slowed down only when I turned into Bayley Street, to prepare myself for the most beautiful part of the walk. For all that I have never found Georgian architecture particularly attractive, the park there, which bears the name of the Duke of Bedford, offered me those moments of peace that all urban castaways so avidly seek. I continued slowly along Montague Place, past the massive buildings of the British Museum. In this part of my route, I recalled hundreds of hours over the last few years spent in the intimacy of its inexhaustible collections of antiquities. When I reached the park in Russell Square, I went in by one of the side entrances, intending to prolong my walk in a refreshing way, as I did every Monday. I had only taken a few steps along the alley when an unexpected occurrence—the *extraordinary event*, I might say—presented itself as a fresh sign of the uniqueness of the day.

I suddenly found myself in the midst of a huge flow of people whose lips were moving insistently without producing any vibration, any sound wave, any voice. I contemplated the image of a crowd of deaf people, a real crowd that was visibly communicating without transmitting any audible message. I walked among clusters of speakers who were gesticulating energetically, enveloped in an impenetrable silence. I had to take care neither to bump into nor to be bumped into by some group absorbed in conversation without the element of sound to fill the interstices between the spaces occupied by the participants. In spite of the gestures exchanged by the interlocutors, I could hear nothing. All was submerged in a silence that could not have been more palpable . . . An uncomprehending participant in this unprecedented colloquy, like a pioneer of cinematography in some unknown silent movie, I realized that absolutely all sounds, including those of the heavy morning traffic, were scattered like smoke dispersed by the wind. The noises of the street reached me as though I were contained in an unseen sphere produced by the loquacious gestures of the people surrounding me. Only the gentle caress of the Gregorian hymn accompanied the deafening silence that had come over Russell Square. I advanced with slow steps, slower and slower.

Unexpectedly, I found myself being addressed by a small group who had not yet grasped my alienation. Their expressive faces looked at me with complete seriousness and they gesticulated. They were striving to transmit to me a message whose point utterly escaped me. Obviously they had confused me with some new member of their community. If you want to understand the situation in which I found myself, you need only imagine a person addressing you, with perfect diction—as you deduce from the movements of their lips—and facial expression to match, while not allowing the slightest sound to burst forth from the larder of phonemes from which words are articulated. You would observe that person moving his lips, you would note the expressiveness and liveliness of his eyes, but, at the same time, you would have to acknowledge, with perplexity, that you could hear nothing. I assure you that I felt like the interlocutor subjected to such an experiment. I smiled awkwardly, waiting for the denouement that would result from my exposure as an illiterate in the language of signs. On the other hand, encouraged by the gesturing of those without the power of speech, I wanted to give them at least a small gesture of authentic, sincere solidarity. I raised my arms and brought them together above my head in a semicircle, in a clumsy attempt to suggest the embrace of the sky on a truly beautiful day. After a few seconds, I pointed my right arm toward the sun, toward the tops of the trees, and then I concluded my ad-hoc message with a slight tilt of my head, doubled by a wide smile. Right from the start of my little mime act, all those in front of me instantaneously stopped their gesticulations, and began to scrutinize me with maximum suspicion. They looked at one another, shook their heads in consternation, and then moved away as one. I was disconcerted, but I shrugged my shoulders and continued on my way through Russell Square.

Although the solemn music continued to caress the inner sense of hearing in my heart, my thoughts had become far too intense to be silenced. The meeting with the crowd of deaf people had revealed to me, mercilessly, the truth about my precarious condition, about my incapacity to make myself understood and my lack of ability to understand those whom I met every day. I was thus not at all surprised to realize that I had tears in my eyes—perhaps because of the strong breeze where Bedford Way opened onto the park, or perhaps because I was becoming aware of the perpetual failure of my day-to-day life. I gritted my teeth and continued along the street toward the point where, at last, I would let myself be sucked into the formless throat of the concrete, metal, and glass colossus that was home to that awful tyrant, the great god Job.

Seeing a group of colleagues idly chatting as they waited for the lift, I granted myself one last delay. I opted for the fire escape stair, little used by others but often by me, that gave access to each of the sixteen floors of the building. I only had to climb to the seventh. I left behind me the bustle of the street to face the torments of my daily work. There was nothing heroic in the ascent, although the zigzag of the stairs might very well have represented the contorted path through the innards of an all-devouring beast. What this dragon burned up was no less than the energy of my hopes, the fragments of a wreck that lacked the courage to confront a world hostile to aspirations incapable of satisfaction by the schemes of bureaucracy or the illusions of consumer society. And yet I consumed and allowed myself, without much resistance, to be consumed. Under the sway of such a state of mind, I was not surprised by the indifference of the almost inaudible words with which the secretary at the reception desk greeted me. I turned to the right, along the corridor where my office was situated, greeting with a degree of affability the various coworkers that I met on the way. The Gregorian music had increased its intensity again. I was involuntarily murmuring the words of the Creed. It was this very activity that prevented me from grasping the third and last of the premonitory signs.

Entering my office, I politely greeted the heads bent over monitors, and then hurried to take possession of my place. In front of me, the co-ordinator of the team in which I worked, Alroy, an Irishman with blue eyes and white hair, in decided contradiction to his name,[†] turned toward me a face on which you could never detect the slightest expression that would allow you to decipher his state of mind. He made a quick sign to let me know that in five minutes we would be having a short team meeting in the kitchen at which each of us would give a report on our various tasks for the week that had just begun. I hung my coat on the hook, started my computer, took my phone from my rucksack, and hurried to the appointed place. The other nine members of the team were already present, talking quietly without missing the chance to savor the aroma of their morning coffee. The appearance of the boss put a stop to the conversations, which immediately metamorphosed into progress reports and various technical discussions. As soon as they started to speak, I finally grasped the extraordinary event.

The third sign, strange and at the same time frightening, might very well be considered a mere predictable prolongation of my meeting with the soundless speakers. I watched in amazement the mouths of my interlocutors and listened with all the concentration of which I was capable. I could hear almost nothing. The sounds, coming from a distance, were dampened as if the intervening space were stuffed with cotton wool. Their gestures enabled me to understand a little of what was under discussion, but all I could actually hear were vague echoes in which I could make out only isolated words that made no sense. Squinting and tensed like a spring, I tried to follow the faces and lips of the others with the same despair with which I had sought to understand the signs addressed to me in the park. When it was my turn to speak, I gave a resumé of the main points of the activities I had in hand, greatly distressed at the prospect of being interrupted with questions that would be inaudible to me. Without blinking, Alroy said something to me in which I could with difficulty make out only the words "transitions," "compositive," "behaviors," and

---

[†]   From the Irish *rua*, "red-haired."

"menu." I would have been overcome with panic had I not immediately realized that he was not expecting me to give any answer. He turned to another member of the team and paid no more attention to me. Sunk in my deafness, I continued to look on with resignation.

In spite of the presence of the whole range of gestures that accompany the act of communication, the content of the discussions had become, practically, inaccessible to me. Once the meeting was over, I took stock of my situation, just for myself, in no uncertain terms: my presence here had no sense. Meaning, any meaning, was absent. I was left only with the exterior carcass of the act of communication. On that day, Monday, July 7, 2003, the bonds between me and the great god Job had lost all their substance. I could record the event with the precision of a medieval chronicler. I continued to carry out my work by a sort of inertia, sending and receiving messages through the usual chat program. Otherwise, without any regret, I experienced the presence of the soundproof wall that separated me from my colleagues. No explanation seemed necessary, apart from the simple recognition of the effect that the encounter in Russell Square had had on me. I was sure that all that I was now experiencing was merely a prolongation of what had happened to me there. The rupture between me and the environment into which I had integrated myself more than seven years before could no longer be hidden. I was beaten.

For years I had striven, I had hoped, I had labored to cultivate my mind with the aim of passing on an exceptional body of knowledge. When the path that I had followed came to nothing, my resources of passion and ability had not disappeared; they had simply been camouflaged, more or less skillfully, under the unconvincing façade of my new career. Rendered speechless in the face of what was now evident, I found myself forced to admit that just as you cannot change your nature, neither can you change those gifts with which your soul has been endowed to serve a pre-defined calling. Invisible, but no less omnipotent, God, the Maker of all things, has provided each of us with our own abilities, directed toward a purpose whose call continues to make itself heard in spite of all our efforts to hide it, to forget it. Foreign to the mercantile, opportunist, and pragmatic spirit of recent times, the word that designates this purpose, "vocation," was taking revenge for the obstinacy with which I had strained all those years to escape it. Fool that I was, perhaps even coward, I had forced myself to believe that it was sufficient to forget a few words in order to cancel the reality that they denoted. The response of reality had been overpowering. Confused, isolated in the oppressive silence within which resounded, more and more quietly, only the sounds of the sacred music, I carried on in my perplexity with the ritual of my usual life, while at the same time being absorbed by the most unusual situation imaginable. I wondered what to do next.

As I was, in general, quiet and reserved by nature, probably no one noticed anything out of the ordinary in my suddenly behaving as if deaf. Messages continued to appear one after another on the screen of my computer, and software tests proceeded in the standard manner, but I was no longer the same person. The thought of handing in my notice became more and more insistent, but equally insistently I kept repeating to myself that I had no alternative prospects for the immediate future. As I floundered in the whirlpool of uncertainty unleashed by the situation in which I found myself, a message from the secretary's office stopped, at least for the moment, my slide into the abyss of my own inner emptiness. Simple and banal, the three lines sent by e-mail requested that I confirm receipt of a letter that I knew nothing about. Without thinking, without hesitating, without knowing what I was doing, I confirmed. I would have thought no more about the matter, had it not come back to me toward the end of the day in the form of a question regarding this letter. For the sake of something to do with my last minutes in the office before going home, I started looking through the piles of papers and files on my desk for the so far unidentified envelope. There was no trace. Puzzled, I leaned back in my chair wondering where this letter addressed to me could have ended up. With my hands clasped behind my neck, I tilted my head back. For a few moments, I shut my eyes, weary as they were of the endless ballet of pixels and the composed and recomposed simulacra of reality on the surface of the monitors. When I opened them again, my gaze fell on the portion of the floor that was partially hidden under the wide desk. A yellowish corner sticking out from the shadows under the utility cupboard caught my attention. With an approving smile, as though I had discovered it by my own efforts, I leaned down and picked up the letter.

When I read the few lines, my expression became serious again, indeed even solemn. Although, at first glance, the contorted script seemed incomprehensible, I could make out the name of the addressee without any difficulty: "Mr. Alexander Jacob Wills." A little further down, my address was written in the same hand. When I turned the envelope over to see if there was any indication of the sender, the temperature of my whole body changed palpably. Printed in black ink and made up of double lines, the letters here had an elegance that set them apart. More than their form, however, their content crushed with a single blow any resistance I might have put up in the face of my destiny, or—who knows?—maybe even the mysteries of Providence. "Gilbert Newman, Kirkwell, Oxfordshire." The illustrious name opened the floodgates to a wave of intense emotion, welling up from the zone of my solar plexus and raising a question mark over my ability to control myself. I remembered perfectly the morning, long years before, when I had received a telephone call from my mother, eager to tell me, among other things, how my grandfather had just been employed as librarian by an eccentric aristocrat. When he sold a good part of his family's art collection to buy an island in the Atlantic Ocean, Gilbert Newman, Duke of Kirkwell, had been at the center of numerous controversies, not all of them stirred up by environmental campaigners. Immune to sensational news, my mother, Francesca Wills, would not have bothered to mention such matters, had it not been on this same Atlantic isle that the Duke's library was now located.

For days on end I wondered how a collection of books deposited on a patch of dry land somewhere far out in the ocean ought to look. You may have wished, at least once in your life, that you lived in a castle or, perhaps, in the virgin forests of an island in the middle of nowhere. In my case, though I did not in any way anticipate the possible fulfillment of such a fantastical desire, nothing prevented me from imagining the halls of the library and my grandfather's work in an oceanic temple of knowledge. There, surrounded by books, Dr. Paolo Paltini had spent the last years of his working life, until the onset of illness forced him to return to his native Ussita. Only my reticence had prevented an amplification of our correspondence beyond the usual Christmas-time letters. Although I would not readily have admitted it, I was afraid of once again falling under the sway of my old passion for study. My dreams, however, often carried me along the corridors of a library whose mere imagining kept awake in me an incurable curiosity.

All this passed through my mind as I turned the envelope in all directions. Without any hurry, I introduced the point of a plastic set square under one of the corners of the epistle, to tear open its upper edge. Once the meticulous operation was complete, I extracted a sheet of yellow paper, folded in two, bearing the coat of arms of the Duke and a message as short as it was implacable:

Dear Mr. Wills,

The memory of your late grandfather, Dr. Paolo Paltini, impels me to address to you this invitation. I shall be at your disposal on Wednesday, 16 July, at 11.00 a.m. in the principal salon of my ancestral home in Kirkwell, Oxfordshire.

With full confidence,

Gilbert Kirkwell

Concise, to the point, and yet evocative, the tone of the message suggested the sort of firmness that comes across as unusual to someone accustomed to living in an age that has long forgotten the forms of politeness. It would have been hard for me to imagine such elegantly expressed constraint. Clearly the writer had intended, within the limits of decency, to forestall any possible refusal on my part. The closing words communicated the same message.

Troubled by the unsuspected prospects that I could perceive in forms resembling the shadows of evening settling over London, I left the company building with an acute feeling of imminent parting. The fact that I had just one week until my meeting with the owner of the library island had brought into my life something fresh and mysterious, like the wind that made the leaves of the trees in Russell Square gently rustle. I did not know why, nor did I know the source of the unexpected joy that, mixed with waves of melancholy, was irrigating the dried-up channels of my heart, which had not known for a long time the enthusiasm aroused by the simple, the austere passion for knowledge.

In the days that followed, I lived within the undefined horizon opened up by the Duke of Kirkwell's message. Marked by the transitional character of my imminent journey, I prepared for the visit with the greatest of care. I made a note, on paper purchased exclusively for this purpose, of all the possible routes to the Duke's residence at Kirkwell, and then I chose the best road connecting the park in front of the house to the nearest town. As is the case in England with almost all historic buildings, I expected to find that it was the pole around which the neighboring settlements and roads were orientated. To my surprise, neither the park, nor the nearby lake, nor the chapel, dating back at least seven hundred years, were classed as tourist attractions and honored with large and easily recognizable signs. On the contrary, the house was hard to find, and the district did not offer much accommodation for visitors. I came to the inevitable conclusion that the Newman family valued their privacy more than the income they might obtain from tourism. In the end, after smiling awkwardly and gesticulating pointlessly through a telephone conversation with a retired couple who owned a B&B in a little hamlet by the name of Fordsall, I managed to secure the only accommodation currently available locally. It was a room deprived of all means of communication: no wireless signal, no TV, no other facilities. Just a little bedroom and a bathroom. It was, however, all I needed. As was my usual practice, I intended to arrive the day before, so as to have time to get to know the surroundings, to estimate distances and make calculations, and to plan the schedule of my visit down to the smallest detail.

Since I had received the message, everything around me had changed. I was floating in the tumult of life, drawn into an unstoppable vortex that was carrying me toward the neck of the funnel through which I was going to tumble into the abyss of actions and events belonging to the uncertain territory of adventure. Since my encounter in Russell Square, I had become incapable of fully hearing my colleagues. No matter how hard I tried, I could perceive more clearly than ever the wall of crystal that muffled my contacts with their world and that of my few acquaintances in the field in which I had been working for the past seven years. Objectively speaking, nothing had changed in the style of my communication, which in any case was reduced to the minimum. However, my inexplicable deafness had granted me an honest awareness of how unsuited I was to a field into which I had wandered, lost, lacking the compass of vocation. At the end of the day, what would a physicist be among confectioners, or a shoemaker among electrical engineers? I knew *who* I was, but I was completely ignorant regarding *what* I was.

When I was a child, my father, Ailbeart Wills, an officer in the Royal Scots, repeatedly gave me a warning that every time aroused an immediate reaction. "Keep to your place!" he would say, with a firm tone, whenever I overstepped the limits prescribed by a rigid upbringing. Paralyzed, for a few seconds, by the steady and penetrating timbre of his voice, I could never manage to understand what this "place" was to which I was supposed to keep. After my experiences of the last few days, memories of my Scottish childhood had flooded back and my confusion was amplified. The only point of stability consisted in my unswerving confidence in the total rightness of my father's judgement. Categorically, I had not found my "place." What it might be, I could not say now, just as I had been unable to say then, more than thirty years before. I was left with my hope in the unforeseeable fruits of the coming meeting and the comfort of the question: "*Et quid amabo nisi quod aenigma est?*"[†]

[†] "And what shall I love, if not that which is an enigma?"

Chapter 3

The Art of Conversation

The day of my departure came round. Reluctant as I was to leave the comfort of the apartment where I had spent seven years of my life, I slipped out hurriedly and went down the stairs without a backward look. After a monotonous journey by Underground, swaying under the impersonal neon light, I arrived at Victoria Bus Station. At 9 a.m., I was to leave for Oxford by coach, and from there I would catch the bus toward my final destination, Kirkwell.

The bustle of passengers, more numerous than I had expected, was dizzying. Sinking in the rapids of the urban crowd, I found myself deprived of any stable point of reference to cling to. Even at Upper Crust and Burger King, the places where you can take a frugal breakfast or a crisp croissant, sitting at table was no guarantee against the sense of endless flux. In the end I found my support in the only element that remained stable in the midst of the perpetual oscillation of passengers: the electronic panel that displayed the schedule of arrivals and departures.

A few minutes later, having taken my place in the ranks of those who were awaiting the coach for Oxford, I was dozing with my eyes open and involuntarily taking in the indefinite range of sounds around me. Determined to find some activity that would diminish the sound pollution that was flooding my ears, I began to detect, at a level deeper than the layers that the ambient noise could touch, fear. The same fear that had almost always accompanied the inevitable confrontation with the unpredictable prospects that opened before me. I was afraid. There was no way I could stop myself questioning the motives that had led me to accept such an unusual invitation. What could I gain from setting out toward an uncertain destination? Every time I had started on a journey, regardless of its nature, the same questions had raised doubts, usually short-lived, about the period of transition spent waiting for the plane, the train, or the car that was to carry me to my destination. Being of a sedentary spirit, though accidentally traversed by a vague longing for change, I had regretted every occasion on which I had plunged imprudently into the unknown.

Stirred into action again for a few minutes by all the agitation of boarding the Oxford Bus Company coach, I was soon nodding off in my ample seat as we set off without delay along the M40 motorway. Dominated as it was by the industrial areas around London, the landscape of the first part of the journey was of no interest to me. I wrenched myself out of my somnolent state only after we passed Thornhill, the point from which I began impatiently to count the passing minutes until we arrived at St Aldate's bus stop, in the heart of Oxford. I sat down on a bench, in a state of total numbness, and waited for the bus to Kirkwell. Despite the years I had spent in the university city, I felt not the slightest wish to revisit once familiar haunts. I watched the passers-by apathetically, realizing that I was irrevocably cut off from my own past. Any trace of somnolence disappeared, giving way to a state almost of enthusiasm, when it dawned on me that my sense of detachment from the ideal of an academic career might indicate that I lacked the necessary vocation. This small detail, for someone who for years had prepared himself to become a professor of classics, was more significant than it might appear at first sight. It took only a single question to scatter the wanton mists of optimism: but in that case . . . what was I? Back came the interrogation to which, for years, I had been unable to find an answer. Only the arrival of the bus saved me from further sterile cogitations. I watched as the hills and fields passed by at high speed. The rows of houses with fences of brown-painted wood, surrounded by bushes and trees, delighted my eyes with the freshness of the spectacle they offered. Here, in contrast to the tiring urban landscape, dominated by cement, iron, and glass, nature itself constituted the omnipresent décor. We passed through small towns such as Yarnton, Enstone, and Southcombe, places where traditional English houses, with their pale yellow architecture, touched by nuances approaching beige, alternated with such architectural monuments as St Kenelm's church, whose origins went back to the Norman period. The dominant green was broken, from time to time, by the lighter colors of farm buildings and the white of sheep grazing here and there, in this region that you might have thought had seen no significant change over the last millennium. In just one place, some strident electoral posters, bright orange, clashed with what was otherwise a discrete and harmonious palette. As I got nearer to my destination, the tension of waiting grew. Hesitantly, I got off at the stop closest to the hamlet of Fordsall. Consisting of a cluster of houses without any distinctive feature, the place's sole landmark was a telephone box that gave the impression of an object lost in the midst of a surface covered, intermittently, with grass. At the bus stop across the road, a few people were chatting as they waited for the bus going back to Oxford.

With my rucksack on my back, I set out along the road that cut through between the nearby houses. I expected it would be easy to find the landmark that my future hosts had named in our telephone conversation: the Black Horse inn. I stopped to look—as I had done many times over the years, on the country roads of Scotland and England—at the little shelter provided for those waiting for the infrequent local buses. Although I had never seen anyone sitting on the wooden bench inside, the stubby little structure with its black roof was there. Cautiously, I entered, and sat down on the little-used bench. After a few minutes of stillness, I began to make out the characteristic rhythms shared by villages everywhere I had been. Even the farm smell seemed just the same as that which I had known in places thousands of miles apart. In Umbria in Italy, in the Scottish Highlands, in the little French country town of Creutzwald, the atemporality of the rural world was the same. The absence of the most irritating feature of the city—the ceaseless rumble of traffic—was the first thing that transformed the whole space around me into an oasis of unaccustomed sounds. The neighing of horses, the chirping of little birds, the honking of geese, the bleating of sheep, all were woven together into the background soundtrack common to any rural landscape. Suddenly, the noise of footsteps interrupted my peaceful reverie. I stood up, left the shelter, and, without a backward look, set out in the opposite direction to that of the footsteps. As was predictable in a tiny place crossed by three streets at the most, there was only a single corner between me and my destination. Hanging from a wooden beam protruding from under the roof of the house, a clumsily painted tin panel displayed a sturdy black horse with white muzzle and fetlocks. Outsize gold letters put into words what the picture already stated clearly enough. I continued on my way. The footsteps were following me, not far behind. From the description I had been given over the phone, I knew that my hosts' house was the first one after the inn. A tall, luxuriant hedge surrounded the low, white, two-story house. The large gate, also white, was waiting wide open. I stopped for a few moments to look for the door, and my eyes fell on the car in the yard, which must have been at least thirty years old. I was just starting to cross the road when a woman's voice rendered superfluous the series of conversational routines that I was inwardly preparing with a view to the imminent meeting with my hosts.

"Hello! Are you coming to us? I suspected you were Alexander from the moment I saw you. Although I can't imagine what you were doing waiting there in the shelter for a bus . . ."

I blinked awkwardly in the lady's direction, unable to tell whether the look in her brown eyes was one of questioning or of slight amusement. She was clad in a long dress of dark red velvet, partially hidden under a light grey overcoat. The tunic collar of the dress, over which poured black hair flecked with silver, gave her a distinguished air, like that with which our Paltini relatives looked out at us from the old black-and-white pictures in my mother's salon.

"Erm, yes," I stammered, before I could regain my normal tone. "No, I wasn't waiting for a bus, just resting a little after the journey. Pleased to meet you. I imagine you must be Mrs. Ascombe. Hello."

"Marie Ascombe. It's me you talked to on the phone. How else could I have known your name?! We were expecting you. Your room's ready.

My husband will be really delighted to meet you. He doesn't often get the chance of a conversation to his taste, so all he can do is read and reread the books in the library that he's been collecting all his life."

With precise movements, she quickly opened the white door, the upper part of which was occupied by a matt black window. I followed her, inwardly pleased that my search had come to such a speedy conclusion. The hall was no more than seven feet long but almost equally wide. In addition to the entrance, there was a white door on each of its other three sides. Its furniture consisted of a table covered with newspapers and keys and a coat rack supporting two light coats and several umbrellas.

"If you like, you can leave your coat here, but there's a coat rack in your room too. You've got the upstairs floor all to yourself. The guest room is up there, and the bathroom. There's no separate door to the outside, but the stair to your floor is right here in the hall, so you don't have to go through any of the downstairs rooms."

With a demonstrative gesture, she opened the door facing the entrance and invited me with a turn of her head to come after her. I hung my coat on the rack and followed where my guide trod. A switch at the foot of the stairs, right beside the bannisters, and another upstairs unleashed a warm yellow light whose glow revealed the blue of the wallpaper. The upstairs hall was as short as its counterpart at the entrance and somewhat narrower. It presented two doors at the top of the stairs, at no great distance one from the other. Through the door on the right, we entered a spacious whitewashed room, furnished with a wide bed, two wooden chairs, and an armchair upholstered in brown velvet placed beside a coffee table next to the window that opened onto the yard behind the house. A built-in wardrobe completed the minimalist inventory of the room. Everything emanated an air of perfect cleanliness. My eye was caught by some books on a small shelf at the head of the bed. A well-cared-for old edition of the famous and rare *Almanach de Gotha* rested its substantial bulk on a number of historical works, among which Edward Gibbon's *History of the Decline and Fall of the Roman Empire* and Paul Hazard's masterpiece *La Crise de la conscience européenne* were easily identifiable. Surprised, I hurriedly turned toward my hostess to thank her in as convincing a tone as possible. I was utterly enchanted by the peace of this place, and wanted with all my heart to say something friendly, something that would be a fitting response to my hosts' kindness: "I feel as if I'm in my parents' house. I've seldom encountered a place, I mean a house, so pleasant and peaceful." Then, lowering my voice and trying to accentuate my sincere appreciation for my temporary accommodation, I added, "Here I shall have the perfect rest before my meeting tomorrow with His Grace, the Duke." Completely unperturbed, Mrs. Ascombe looked at me for a few moments with what seemed to me to be a new light in her eyes, a light whose significance escaped me.

Immediately, she hurried to complete the presentation, in few words but with maximum clarity: "Next door you have the bathroom. As I told you on the phone, everything on this floor is for the use of guests. No one else comes up here. As for breakfast, lunch, or dinner, my husband would be delighted to have your company in the morning, up until nine o'clock, and in the afternoon between one and two. Here's the key. We never lock the door during the day. When you feel like meeting my husband, just come down. Try the door to the left of the stair. That's his sitting room and reading room."

Having communicated this information, Marie Ascombe withdrew without another word. I felt a total peace enveloping me. Only the sound of a door briefly interrupted the silence of my contemplation. Sitting in the armchair at the window, I studied minutely every detail of the place. The midday sun was scattering its light over the surrounding trees and fields through the lens of an atmosphere of perfect clarity. It seemed to me that I could see dozens of miles away. Around the houses nearby or along the lanes, streets, and highways within view, there was no movement to betray any human presence. A solitary wooden bench, placed in the middle of the strip of grass between two paths with a few houses on either side, invited one to contemplate the little stone church whose spire stood guard over the surrounding countryside. Lost in the rural world of eternal England. I could recognize perfectly, without being able to give it a name, that *something* specific to English landscapes that gives them a charm all their own. From a corner of my mind, however, the need to introduce myself to the man of the house imposed itself insistently. After an invigorating shower, I put on my walking clothes and went downstairs. It was lunchtime. I turned to the door on the left, knocked, and waited. My knock was met with a prompt invitation, spoken by a rather quiet voice but in an eager tone: "Come in!" I opened the door wide, and stepped into a living room whose walls were lined with tall bookcases, their shelves groaning under countless volumes. Making no secret of my surprise, I stepped toward the figure of about my own height that had risen out of one of the two armchairs.

"Alexander! Very pleased to meet you. Mortimer, Mortimer Ascombe."

With a smile backed up by an encouraging look directed at me by his blue eyes, my interlocutor, whose combed-back grey hair adorned a somewhat severe-looking face, extended a bony hand with long pianist's fingers. His rounded forehead was striking. Dressed as he was in a grey suit, with a black waistcoat and a dark green bow tie around his immaculately white collar, my new acquaintance would have been ideal for a role in one of those movies set in the period between the world wars.

"I really must thank you, Mortimer, for your hospitality. It's the perfect place for me."

"It's a pleasure having you here. A real honor. Would you care to join us for dinner?"

I was quick to accept this ingenuous kindness, although I was slightly intrigued at the over-ceremonious greeting. "Of course. But there is another thing . . . Would you mind if I have a look at your library?"

"Of course not. I invite you right now to explore it at will. It'll be a few minutes before my good lady has everything ready. What better way to spend them? Be my guest!"

Without any gesture, with his hands by his sides and his head slightly tilted, Mortimer Ascombe strode toward the shelves that lined the right-hand wall. I followed him. As I approached them, my astonishment grew at the sight of some of the volumes they bore. All the ancient and medieval chroniclers and historians from Herodotus onward were there, together with numerous historical works by such authors as Christopher Dawson, Vasile Pârvan, and Régine Pernoud. There could be no doubt that I was in the company of someone with a passion for history from all periods of human existence. He waited by my side with his hands behind his back, silent, not interrupting the meticulous examination by which I was able to appreciate the value of his library. I shuffled gradually toward the left, slowly and succinctly taking stock of the riches of his historical collections. Not one of the Oxford or Cambridge series was absent, nor were the volumes of the Dumbarton Oaks Medieval Library and other similar collections. Finally, highly impressed by what I had seen, I sat down.

As soon as we were face to face over the dinner table, whose three places were already set with silver cutlery, my host asked me, "Are you interested in history, Alexander?" Although I was expecting some such question, I would have been glad to avoid any discussion that might touch the sensitive points in my tortuous past. In as neutral a tone as possible, I answered by giving all the details that I considered inevitable: "Not so much at present. However, at one time I was directly engaged in historical study. I worked in research for a few years. I focused particularly on the history of ancient Greece, but also on the Western Middle Ages. Now, though, I work in a completely different field . . ." Here my voice failed me. Whenever the subject of my past came up, I felt sad, lost, betrayed. Life. Life itself had betrayed me. Snatches of the discussions that had led to my withdrawal from academia immediately came back to mind.

To add a further surprise to those I had already received, Mortimer Ascombe proved to be perfectly aware of all the unease I had experienced. "Your decision doesn't seem unusual to me," he said consolingly. "It's difficult, if indeed it is possible, to survive nowadays in the academic world. Although all my life I have been no more than a simple country schoolteacher, I have known plenty of scholars who have left academia. And it wasn't necessarily financial concerns that pushed them toward other fields." At this point, he stopped, and, to my relief, took the first opportunity to change the direction of the conversation: "Here comes our lunch!"

Glad to have got past the moment of painful recollections, I smiled at Mrs. Ascombe, who, with the help of a pair of coffee-colored oven gloves, was bringing in a tray from which some turkey thighs emanated an enticing odor. There followed a lunch served with simplicity and good taste, washed down with the local Hook Norton ale. The aroma of black coffee, not too strong, was wafting through the room when I explained to my hosts that I would soon have to go on a little excursion in the direction of the Newman family residence. The Ascombes exchanged looks laden with indecipherable messages. Quietly clearing his throat, Mr. Ascombe immediately continued, "Regarding that matter, you know . . . we have something important to say to you. Important and unavoidable." The pause that followed thoroughly disconcerted me. I could not imagine what two complete strangers could have to communicate to me on an issue that concerned me alone. Mortimer took a sip of coffee and continued, "My wife has told me the purpose of your visit to these parts. A matter that, when we communicated by telephone, you had absolutely no reason to reveal to us. However, this very detail is what has completely changed the situation. You see, if we had known the reason for your journey, we would not have let the room to you. . . . In fact, we could not have let it to you."

Seriously nonplussed by what I was hearing, I looked from one to the other, unable to improvise any reply. At first my lips moved indecisively, as no sound could emerge from my throat for a few seconds until my mind was able to send a message. Finally, I managed to stammer, barely audibly, "Am I to understand that I must leave?"

Frowning, Mortimer continued, somewhat louder, "Not at all, Mr. Wills, not at all! Just that, you see, all these lands once belonged, by royal privilege, to the dukes of Kirkwell. My ancestors had the honor of serving the family for generations. In those days, any guest of the Newman family was treated with proper hospitality. And it should be no different today, even if times have changed. Mr. Alexander Jacob Wills, this is what we have to tell you: we cannot *let* the room to you. For to offer hospitality to a guest of His Grace is, for my wife and myself, a great privilege. And a sacred obligation. You understand? A debt of honor! There is not much we can offer you, but please, accept this modest gift on the part of our family."

This explanation, provided in an alert and firm manner, could truly be compared to the June sunlight falling on the Oxfordshire fields. I could scarcely recover from the emotions unleashed by Mortimer's words. With my face burning and red as a lobster, I felt a knot in my chest that blocked the words I would have liked to utter. I lifted my cup, blinked rapidly, and swallowed the rest of the coffee in one gulp. I do not know if it was the liquid that spread a pleasant cooling sensation through my veins. What is certain is that all shadows dispersed before the generosity of the Ascombes. Without a further word, I looked at them calmly and then, closing my eyes, said simply, "Thank you."

The contentment in their faces was the sign that we understood one another. Somewhat breathlessly, as though she had been waiting for this moment for a long time, Marie Ascombe raised her index finger in my direction and added with a smile, "And when you have the chance, please pass on our family's greetings to His Grace. This is all we ask of you in exchange!"

"Of course, Mrs. Ascombe."

Without any further ceremony apart from a handshake, I stepped out into the warm afternoon sun and set off on my little journey of reconnaissance. I felt like a newborn child, freed of all residue of the storms through which I had passed over the last few years. I checked the map from time to time as I advanced along the edge of the A44 until I reached the point where I knew I had to turn off toward the Duke of Kirkwell's residence. According to my estimates, I ought to be able to get there in half an hour at the most. The road wound between two wide fields, lined by carefully trimmed hedges. Here and there, stubby sycamores and oaks provided shade to paths giving access to plots where various crops were growing. Among them, I could even see an area planted with neat lines of silver fir trees in preparation for Christmas. While contemplating the landscape, I still could not stop myself from thinking about my hosts. Every time I recalled the Ascombes and their unexpected gift, I sighed in gratitude. In the face of this generosity of a kind one rarely encounters, I felt truly indebted.

Talking to myself and gesticulating as I walked, I left behind the hedges and little copses on either side of the road, and arrived at a crossroads surrounded by massive sycamores, where a white sign bore in black letters the name of the Newman family residence. I continued my exploration for a further ten minutes. I observed that I had now entered an area where the road was separated from the property on either side by a low wall of carefully laid stones. In the middle of a grove of trees, the wall spread into a semicircle, about thirty feet across and broken by a tall gateway whose posts bore, engraved on metal plates, the same name that I had seen at the crossroads: Kirkwell House. There was no sign of any doorbell or video camera, but the gate stood slightly open. Because of the abundant vegetation and the trees, none of the buildings that must be no more than a few hundred yards away could be seen. I looked at my watch and quickly turned back, anxious lest someone might catch me here before the day and hour at which I had been invited.

I was more and more affected by the thought that just one night separated me from my meeting the following day. Unsettled by the prospect, I walked on, no longer noticing the surrounding green, broken only by the rectangular fields of various crops that I crossed on my way. For a few minutes, my attention was captured by a huge eagle that seemed to be resting, in solitude, on the upper branches of a half-withered tree. I stopped to watch the bird, which, in that hieratic posture, seemed alienated from its airy element and from the most characteristic action of its species, flight. The image of the magnificent creature looking so surprisingly helpless, remained with me the rest of the way.

By the time I arrived back at the Ascombes' house, I was quite tired from my little excursion, and let them know that I would not be coming down for dinner. The Ascombes accepted this and did not trouble me with any questions. There followed an unsettled sleep, with frequent interruptions and confused dreams.

✳ ✳ ✳

I woke in the morning to the sound of raindrops. The clear blue sky had given way to a cloudy grey that made it impossible to guess the time. In fact it was almost nine, but I would have guessed that the day was barely dawning. Rain was gently falling. The view from my window told me all I needed to know. Only one forecast was possible: the rain was unlikely to let up any time soon. Not that day, in any case. The usual silence of the house was disturbed, at intervals, by the crystalline tinkle of a teapot and cups being carried somewhere on the ground floor. Considering the circumstances, I knew that I had to leave at ten at the latest if I was to reach the Duke's residence without getting too splashed on the way. Fortunately, being used to such changes of weather, I had brought suitable clothes. It was only at the moment when I finished my preparation for setting out that I realized, not for the first time, that faced with the prospect of the approaching interview, I felt intimidated and inadequate. And yet, beyond these surface emotions, I could sense the vibrations of my impatience to meet the mysterious bibliophile governor of the distant island.

Likewise visibly agitated, the Ascombes were waiting for me when I came down for breakfast. We greeted each other simply and respectfully, putting all the warmth at our disposal into this little ritual of meeting. While Marie poured the coffee, Mortimer examined me from under his glasses with a slight smile. The experience of his respectable age proved its value in his ability to judge correctly my state of mind. He avoided opening any possible discussion and allowed me a more than necessary pause. I took full advantage of my hosts' elegant behaviour and ate in complete silence. As I was stirring my coffee and waiting for the dissolution of the single sugar cube, whose sinking into the brown liquid I followed with a certain curiosity, I asked in a tone that managed to surprise even myself, "Tell me, what is the Duke like?" My question was absolutely spontaneous, and I was intrigued by its direct character.

The Ascombes looked at one another briefly, with a serious look on their faces. Then, still with a thoughtful expression, Mortimer rested the palm of the hand in which he held the jam spoon on the edge of the table, breathed in deeply, breathed out, and, raising his eyebrows, offered me an unconventional lesson in scholastic terminology: "I don't think I can give you a satisfactory answer. I have enjoyed the privilege of meeting His Grace a number of times. As a young history graduate, temporarily employed to enrich the Newman family library with new acquisitions, I also met the late duke, his father Thomas Newman. But far from me to boast . . . I really don't think I am capable of offering a correct description, Alexander . . . and I imagine that most of those who know him would say the same. I can suggest only a single word that I believe fits, just one term, and a very rare one, with which to characterize him: '*aseity.*' It might at a push be paraphrased as 'dignity' or perhaps 'uprightness.' For years I searched for the right word. There is no better one, believe me. I propose it with firm conviction. After your meeting today, you will have food for thought, I assure you."

I repeated the word with a barely audible voice: "*aseity.*" It was a term I knew from medieval treatises of theology and metaphysics, but I was quite unable to conceive how such a notion could be applied to a human being. The aura surrounding the man I was to meet was taking on stranger and stranger nuances. Of one thing I was sure, however: I was going to find myself face to face with a personality out of the ordinary. No, not with a romantic. Resigned, I raised my eyebrows, nodded in a way that expressed wonder, but not comprehension, and continued to sip the last of my coffee. In the meantime, Mortimer lit a cigar and puffed on it idly, resting his eyes on the shiny surface of the little silver sugar bowl. Time passed imperceptibly. In the last minutes before ten o'clock, my inner double, anguished and doubtful, launched a new attack. The same question flew at me with tenfold violence: "What am I doing here?" Worried, I looked around the room, which suddenly seemed to have lost any familiarity. Fearful lest any gesture on my part might offend against the politeness and generosity of the Ascombes, I avoided letting my eyes rest on them while my mind was assaulted by the thought that told me insistently that they were just strangers to whom I owed nothing. The same thought continued its attack, suggesting that I could just leave the previously agreed sum of money on the table and set off immediately for the station. In a few hours, I would be enjoying the privacy of my own apartment. I wanted to flee.

Then, as if she understood what was troubling me, Mrs Ascombe lifted the index finger of her right hand: "Please don't forget to pass on our greetings to the duke."

Having been raised in a military home, the lessons my father had taught me regarding fulfillment of duty were profoundly imprinted on my inner being. It took just this one sentence to activate all my devotion to this out-of-date principle, diminishing the centrifugal effects arising from the thought that I might abandon my journey. I stood up and saluted, but not before asking her if I might borrow one of the umbrellas hanging on the coat rack in the hall.

Under the light but dense rain, I perceived everything around me with enhanced acuity. The Gregorian *Credo* resounded within me more clearly than ever. Not listening to the insidious whispers of doubt, I set off, leaping over the puddles, none of them very big, that were starting to form. I followed the same route as I had taken the previous day. The fields were covered with a thin mist, just enough to reduce appreciably my clarity of perception. Soon the trunks of the trees by the roadside were barely visible at all. Only their abundantly weeping branches shone silvery in the grey morning light. A penetrating wind coming from the front blew cold thin stripes onto my face, as the dense curtain of raindrops swayed before its oscillating blasts. I held the umbrella before me like a shield. Bending forward, I continued along the road, nourishing within myself the awareness that I was on my way to an exceptional meeting. When I got to the crossroads, the white sign was barely visible. I stopped and took a long look at it. It now seemed to be truly a symbol of my own personal crossroads. All my life was concentrated in that one point, from which only one road went in the right direction.

When I set off again, toward the right, in the direction of the New-man family residence, I was far from convinced that this was really the path I should follow. All the same, I continued until I found myself at the semicircle with the large iron gate that I had seen the day before. The path continued, without much winding, between trees that rose over a tall and recently trimmed hedge. After another hundred yards, I found myself under the vault of a majestic oak, beyond which I discovered a park occupying the space in front of a large two-story house. Nine white-framed windows could be seen on the upper floor, while the ground floor was similarly adorned with eight, the central place being reserved for a tall but not very wide door, crowned by a yellow-painted pediment. The walls were built of the same blocks of Cotswold stone as most of the houses in the area, and surmounted by a gently sloping slate roof, blackened by the passage of the years. The ground floor was almost entirely covered by climbing plants, whose green color was brightened by the raindrops falling from the eaves. Invaded as it was by vegetation, the whole building had the air of a camouflaged Amazonian temple in a landscape that might have seemed luxuriant had it not been skillfully managed by the able hands of those responsible for maintaining the lawn and the hedges.

I took a hasty look at my watch. I was sure of my punctuality. I had arrived just three minutes before eleven o'clock. The rain continued to wash the gravel of the path as I proceeded along it to the door. The same bushes, carefully trimmed, flanked the entrance. I climbed the steps and pressed the bronze button of the doorbell, which was set in a wooden frame in a niche in the wall. After a few minutes, the silence was broken by the sound of footsteps descending unseen stairs. Finally, the solid wooden door, painted brown and carved with simple geometric forms, squares and rhombuses, was opened by an elderly man with short hair, grey at the temples and combed to one side, whose face—which bore discreet signs of his age—seemed immobile. His thin lips were overshadowed by a wide grey moustache flecked with white. From under his bushy eyebrows, two dark eyes looked at me in a direct, manly manner, but without piercing the invisible frontier of my own interiority. It was an observant gaze, but not an inquisitive one. Rather it seemed to be that of someone without any sophisticated thoughts, someone worthy, perhaps even good-natured, like a colonel accustomed to taking delight in inspecting a regiment parading in good order. Indeed there was something distinctive about his whole appearance—perfectly illustrated by his black suit, slightly worn but endowed with all the possible accessories, including a fully buttoned waistcoat and a blue tie visible under the winged collar of his white shirt—which seemed that of a man of clear and unequivocal habits and gestures.

In a voice slightly touched by the tumult of my emotions, I introduced myself: "Good morning, I'm Alexander Jacob Wills. I'm here at the invitation of His Grace the Duke."

My interlocutor's eyes fixed on me with warm cordiality, the mark of a goodness hostile to caprice and irrational actions. In a manner that was ceremonious but at the same time relaxed, almost familiar, yet not without a touch of solemnity, he answered, "Hello, Alexander! We meet at last. I'm Gilbert Newman. Come in!" With a gracious movement, surprisingly firm for such a simple gesture, the latest in the line of the Dukes of Kirkwell, standing straight as a Teutonic sword, took a single step back, rotating to the left as he did so in order to make way for me. I shook the raindrops off my umbrella and stepped across the threshold of Kirkwell House. Without warning, I found myself leaving the world of the twenty-first century and entering an interior in which at every step I was reminded of the spirit of times long past.

Houses are impregnated with the warmth, with the spirit of their present occupants. Among the feelings that we experience whenever we enter the dwellings of close friends or slight acquaintances, we may distinguish, alongside so many other specific emotions, some that are true bridges connecting all the members of a culture. It's like when you meet an Australian or a New Zealander: the English they speak may have its particularities, but we easily recognize the common ground that immediately lets us say, "home." I have made this short digression in order to underline, by contrast, the fact that in the Duke's manor house I found myself unable to discover the common spirit that would have enabled me to establish any kind of connection with the setting through which I was passing. The profound spiritual energies that flowed through the vast rooms sprang from a language that was ancient and quite other. What language it was, however, I could not say. I had landed in a different world.

In the spacious hall, as indeed throughout the house, wood enjoyed a privileged position. Here, floors of varnished boards, light in color, met walls covered to half their height in dark brown walnut paneling, carved with an artistry that recalled the decorative works of Augustus Welby Northmore Pugin. Above it, beige wallpaper decorated with baroque motifs in pale green rose to the ceiling. Four suits of armor, whose luster could not hide the signs of considerable age, stood watch, their massive iron gauntlets resting on great swords, designed for mounted combat and almost a man's height in length. These immobile carapaces guarded two wide double doors, carved in the same wood as the paneling. In place of handles, they were provided with undulating gilt bars, each some two feet in length. Another six doors, smaller in size and also closed, were set at equal distances along the wall facing the entrance. The spaces between them were decorated with large paintings, from which past dukes of the Newman family, in military garb and bearing all the insignia of their rank, eyed me with a gravity reminiscent of the generals of ancient Rome. The paintings on the ceiling displayed scenes and heroes from Greek and Roman mythology. Herakles and Aeneas dominated the rest of the pantheon. The countless lights of the central candelabrum and the lamps fixed to the walls cast mysterious shadows over the scattering of secondary figures admiring the deeds of the legendary protagonists, forever bound in the grip of grotesque dances, along with beasts and monsters frozen in various martial postures. I took all this in rapidly, as I followed the tall figure of the Duke, who led me first of all to the coat rack, where I left my coat and umbrella. Freed of these accessories intended to protect me from the rain, I took advantage of the occasion to accomplish my mission: "The Ascombes asked me to convey their greetings, Your Grace."

"Thank you. But how do you know them? You're not staying with them, are you?"

"Actually I am, sir. I couldn't find anywhere else. All the rooms in the Black Horse were booked for the harvest festival."

"Indeed. In a rural area like ours, events like that are much awaited and long prepared. And the available rooms, like the pews in the parish church, have their regular occupants. As for Mortimer and Marie Ascombe, please tell them that I am waiting for a suitable occasion for a visit."

The attentive manner in which he had pronounced the couple's names, uttering them with a slight slowing of his voice, was the first example of pedagogy that I encountered in the old aristocratic world that I was visiting for the first time.

"I shall most certainly give them the message, sir." After this first polite exchange, I inwardly thanked my father, Ailbeart Wills, who had taught me the appropriate forms of address for various military and noble ranks. The sound of the echoes produced by my footsteps on the wooden floor drew my attention to the complete quiet that reigned within me. From the moment our voices fell silent, no sound, no music, no noise troubled the inner projections of all that I had avidly taken in through all my senses. It was as though I was living in a perfect equilibrium, such as would normally be impossible to achieve, on that surface, as wide as the thickness of a hair, lying at the border between the outer world and my own deepest being. My whole epidermis seemed to have become one huge receptor, just like my eyes and my ears.

Visited by such thoughts, I made my way toward the door on the right. Through the corner of my eye, I observed the sculptural profile of my noble host. I had noticed his interiorized gaze, and the barely sketched smile that imperceptibly lifted the corners of his mouth. With no apparent effort, he pushed the door, which opened silently, rotating on the axis of its hinges. We entered another hall, adorned with three windows so wide that, even in the pallid light of a rainy Oxfordshire day, any other source of illumination was rendered superfluous. A black wooden desk, whose age was given away by the wear that showed in places on its edges, covered with piles of books and numerous files, stood opposite the door, under the principal window, which reached almost to the ceiling. In the absence of curtains, the expanse of glass allowed the pale glow of the day to enter the room unimpeded. In the considerable space behind the desk, I could see the leather-covered back of an austere-looking armchair. In front of the desk, two old armchairs, also leather-covered, were placed on either side of a sturdy mahogany coffee table, on which lay trays bearing coffee, sweets, a sugar bowl, and all the required accessories. In the middle of the table, on a disc of white marble crossed by brown veins, stood a Sheffield samovar of finely polished silver, whose tap was opened by means of a little handle in the form of a shell containing a pearl.

With a slight nod of his head, the Duke invited me to sit down in the right-hand armchair. Scarcely had I done so, when an irresistible impulse made me rise to my feet and stand upright, with all my senses tensed, like a soldier on guard duty who hears the commandant coming at the dead of night with the relief patrol. With a look expressive of profound understanding, but also a wave of sadness, my host finally broke his silence:

"I perfectly understand your reaction. The portrait is so well done that I too am sometimes startled when I see it."

To show solidarity with the combined sense of amazement and veneration that overcame me, the elderly duke fell silent. Incapable of articulating a response, I nodded my head slightly while I gazed on the life-size image of Dr. Paolo Paltini. Against the background of the beige wallpaper with a pale green pattern that rose above the brown paneling, a wide gilded frame, finely modelled, surrounded the figure of my grandfather, who looked out at us from under snow-white eyebrows, raised in wonder. Or in hope. In the lower part of his face, which was as yellow as the wax in the church of his native Ussita, his mouth could just be made out under the moustache that covered his upper lip, similarly white but scattered with a few greyish or yellowish hairs, as was the short beard that hid the oval of his chin. On his forehead could be seen the three deep creases that I knew had always been there. His grey hair was carelessly combed back. He wore a grey suit, with a brick-red tie visible under the collar of his white shirt, and on his lap he held a book, the customary prolongation of his refined fingers.

It was only after I had let my gaze wander at will over the face of my old mentor that I sat down. "What a surprise! I had never heard that such a portrait existed. Here, right beside us . . ."

My host's eyes and the movements of the lines on his face accompanied the explanations that he offered as though conversing with an old acquaintance: "It was painted in Rome, in 1993, a crucial year for the start of our research. It will come as no surprise if I tell you that the painter is a determined opponent of contemporary art. He strives after the perfection of Velázquez and misses no opportunity to paint portraits of unforgettable faces. I believe this is one of his best. So, you see that we are under the most benevolent protection we could possibly have. I have invited you here—not without some hesitation, I confess—as a consequence of my discussions over the years with your grandfather. He always considered you to be his only successor."

The implicit, but inevitable, evocation of the reason for the cooling of our relations was hard to bear. Wishing to avoid such a tender point in my wounded memory, I tried to find a way out: "His successor, sir? I left the world of academia years ago . . . What sort of successor could I be?"

At these words, Gilbert Newman became meditative. He looked at me with his dark eyes, as if carefully weighing up my response. The sound of the raindrops that were forming streaks down the windows was audible but could not disturb the quiet that reigned everywhere. I was learning as I went along that in the case of an interlocutor who knew all his ancestors over a period of more than seven hundred years, even silence had considerable eloquence.

"Indeed, Dr. Paltini too had left the world of academia many years before. But this did not prevent him from continuing his research. On the contrary. However, I have the impression that your motives are different, as is the manner of your departure."

The silence that fell was just another elegant way of allowing me not to answer. Like the perfect gentleman and accomplished swordsman that he was, the Duke was moving gracefully around me, a poor amateur, in order to be able to strike at the weak points in my rudimentary defenses. He had marked out a space in which I could move without fearing any intrusion on his part. He was thus allowing me to decide for myself on the best strategy. Somewhat weary of my own ennui, I made my choice. Probably on account of his association with my grandfather, I considered that he was the only person to whom I could reveal what was troubling me. I began to speak rapidly and precisely, without a pause. I told him in detail of the episodes in my alienation from the world of classical studies, including my efforts to destroy any connection to the past by selling my books. I touched only in passing on my torment regarding my inability to establish my own vocation. I was trying to avoid that question to which, I considered, no one could give me an answer. I closed my confession convinced of one thing: I had been listened to. Listened to in the most profound, most authentic sense. Listened to as one heart listens to another.

Sadly, I sank into the armchair. For the first time, I placed both my hands on its massive armrests. I felt exhausted. The question that followed came like a shower of invigorating rain, though no less severe for that: "Alexander, what are you? An archaeologist, a historian, a philosopher, a software tester? It seems to me that this is the question that you have to answer. Do not hurry . . ." At once, I perceived the currents of a state of lucidity, of clarity that I had only occasionally felt on cold, bright winter days. I looked at the right hand of my interlocutor: his fingers were slightly raised in a sign that urged patience. Then, raising his voice somewhat, Gilbert Newman recited, without intonation but with a sense of profundity, the description of humanity made by one of the few, the very few of whom we can truly say that they understood:

—*"Tídé tis? Tíd'oú tis? Skiâs ónar ánthrōpos"*[†]

His pronunciation won my admiration. I know of only a few classicists, for example Prof. Jean Parescó, who could read texts in Ancient Greek with such a natural manner. Keeping my eyes on the Duke, I managed with great difficulty to refrain from any exaggerated display of my boundless astonishment. I would have liked to have turned the question back on him, driven by a compelling desire to get a complete answer: "Your Grace, who are you?" The light that Pindar's words shone on my mind made the grey shadows of the day fade away. Our discussion was taking on an aura of mystery that increased my confusion.

His next words only served to deepen it: "A dream of a shadow. That is what we all are when we are born into this world. We live wrapped in a strange illusion that somewhat moderates our suffering, but it calls for a great effort to know the truth. How paradoxical! This illusion protects us by putting at risk our capacity for knowledge. For *self*-knowledge. For understanding what we are meant to be. We play a part on the vast stage of life without first establishing what that part really is. This is what some call failure! And, believe me, nothing displeases me more deeply than a poor-quality play. But enough of that. The truth is that few realize the source of their unhappiness. And equally few have the courage to accept the given of their being. Those who manage to find their place are so rare. . . . Their place, Alexander, their place, your place. Only when

---

[†] Pindar, *Pythian Odes*, 8: "τί δέ τις; τί δ' ού τις; σκιᾶς ὄναρ ἄνθρωπος." ("What is someone? What is no one? A dream of a shadow is man.")

someone correctly answers the question 'What am I?' can he say that he has found his place. And it is only from that point, when he situates himself in his own state, that he can start on the road out of illusion, out of the self-deception that adds to the shadows of this fallen world. Forgive me if I have spoken too much. Permit me to hope that you will not consider me a romantic."

The Duke paused in the middle of his metaphysical exposition and took a measured sip of the coffee that he had poured into a cup decorated with silver hieroglyphs. His manner suggested to me the attitude of a commander in the interval between two battles. At the same time, my mind was going over all the arguments, all the inner debates that I had held over the years in the hope of discovering my "vocation." One detail that would have enabled me to identify it kept coming back to my mind: the ease with which I picked up and practiced certain abilities. It seemed to me natural that a man with a clear vocation as a warrior should, at all times and regardless of the circumstances, have a certain daring, indeed even a taste for fighting, even at the risk of his own life. On the battlefield, he who can maintain his self-control in the face of death, among shells and bullets, while he seeks the enemy's weak points in order to strike back effectively, is, most likely, a born soldier. The farmer has a special interest in all that concerns working the land, just as the doctor dedicates thousands of hours to the study of cases and solutions, medications and prescriptions, enhancing his ability to relieve the suffering of his patients. And when those who have a certain vocation manage to occupy the place predestined for them, they take up their occupation with a natural ease. "The right person in the right place" goes the saying.

I can state that I learned the classical languages with a certain ease. My constant, never completely abandoned attraction to the study and interpretation of ancient texts seemed to be a conclusive enough sign. However, reality did not confirm my gift. Though often appreciated for the studies I published, I was kept on the margins of vague research programs, never being given the chance to put myself forward for a tenured teaching post. That was all. What remained? My passion for reading ancient authors. I considered myself a fully-fledged citizen of the world of the old masters, from Thales and Pindar to Isidore of Seville and Thomas Aquinas. As for my own vocation, however, nothing had permitted me to consider myself more than a mere reader. With these thoughts in my mind, I uttered, without emotion, the only answer that I could conceive at the time: "What am I? A reader, sir. A passionate reader, nothing more."

The Duke looked at me for a few moments without a word. Then he put his coffee cup down on the table. With his hands on his knees, the embodiment of calm wisdom, he presented to me with disarming modesty his own way of interpreting such an answer: "Of course. I'm a reader too, you know! How could I not be? Dr. Paolo Paltini often told me about the extent of your reading. History, philosophy, literature, mythology, theology . . . From the Presocratics to Patañjali, from Proclus and Dionysius the Areopagite to the chronicles of Álvar Núñez Cabeza de Vaca and Francisco de Orellana, from Ambrose and Augustine to Isaac Luria and Athanasius Kircher. Nothing significant is missing from your personal catalogue. All the same, you well know that reading is not an end in itself. It is always directed to an end, to an ideal." I listened. It seemed to me that he was narrowing his eyes a little to stare at me with maximum intensity. I studied his harmonious face as I gradually realized the complete stability of his inner being. Gilbert Newman was perfectly settled in the place that befitted him, as a conclusive illustration of the old saying: he was the right person in a place that was completely right for him.

Sometimes I imagined vocation to be like a ray of light that had the power to transfigure our capacities of knowledge and understanding. Composed of an imponderable luminous substance, set in the volume occupied by an invisible space, it only demonstrated its capacity when, like a mountaineer arriving at the summit after a difficult ascent, a person approached the light that was destined for his transfiguration. Only then, when the right person, unique and unrepeatable, succeeded in discovering the identity of the force propelling him was it immediately activated, sustaining that person on the heights of intellectual excellence and moral perfection. The struggle of life consists precisely in the discovery and occupation of this archetypal frame destined for one's own self. Gilbert Newman was perfectly positioned in the invisible, brilliant, ethereal field appointed to him. Like a flash, I recalled the word that Mortimer Ascombe had proposed in answer to my question about the Duke's way of being: *aseity*. I was beginning to get his meaning. Aseity is the characteristic of the person whose center of gravity lies within the perimeter of his own gifts. Otherwise, like an unstable geometrical figure, the self inevitably collapses when it seeks to occupy places, ethereal cells, that do not belong to it. I was convinced that this meeting with a man in his place was my only chance to rediscover myself.

In full consonance with my inner discourse, my host's voice laid the most improbable proposal before me: "A passionate reader, you say. And why not? Even if you are not perfectly clear about everything, it seems to me that you are amply qualified to continue your grandfather's work." And then, with a quieter tone, he continued: "Alexander, what would you say to a post of librarian? Of my family's collection, of course. In this way, you would be able to put your passion to use by continuing the work of Dr. Paolo Paltini. I hasten to remind you of the only unusual, indeed somewhat exotic, aspect of the matter: the library is situated on an island in the Atlantic where, initially, you will have to spend about three weeks alone. A little patch of land that might conceal exactly what you are looking for."

His proposal was so unusual that I could not take it seriously. I had never thought of moving to an island. On top of that, such a move would mean resuming my research work. I felt exhausted, lacking the necessary disposition to further pursue the discussion of the problem of vocation. At the end of the day, it might very well be an illusion, a chimera, the dream of a young man sorely tried by the frantic rhythm of our times. How else could it be that I had never heard any discussion on such a theme among my colleagues?

I decided to close the issue, and answered strategically, in the hope that I could bring the conversation quickly to an end and leave. "Your Grace, I am not ready to give you an answer. I must give it some thought. There is too much to consider." With my eyes fixed on my grandfather's portrait, I hesitated, as if expecting advice, some suggestion, some message from that face that seemed so much alive. So much alive and yet veiled in impenetrable silence. Resigned, I stood up. "It's time I was going. I can only thank you for the proposal. I shall give it some thought and send you my answer."

"And I thank you for coming, Alexander. Let me show you out."

Without any further word, the Duke accompanied me to the entrance. After I had put my raincoat on again, he shook my hand twice, at the same time fixing his eyes on me with a gaze whose light was trying, I think, to awaken latent energies in my heart. For a moment, I felt like an officer encouraged by the general before a decisive battle. When I left Kirkwell House, I felt defeated. No one and nothing in the world could have convinced me at that moment that the battle was not already lost. I parted from the Ascombes in a straightforward and cordial manner, after being inwardly delighted at being able to bring them a reply from Gilbert Newman. The visit of such a distinguished person was a sign of special appreciation. Despite all my efforts, I could not persuade them to accept even a fraction of the price we had initially agreed on by telephone for one night's accommodation.

Keeping perfect time, the Oxford Bus Company coach picked me up from the same spot where I had got off just a day and an experience before. In heavy rain, I went through all the stages of returning home as if I were in a transparent tunnel, completely cut off from everything around me, from the moving phantasms that hastily slipped past me, a mere background to the dream of a shadow. I looked at the lights in the windows of houses whose outlines were lost in the night. The darkness deepened. I wondered what sort of life could be led in such places. Dependent as I was on the urban economy, it was beyond my power to imagine the existence of people who lived outside the big cities. All these flashes of thought were interrupted at intervals by the austere and dignified face of Gilbert Newman, who seemed to stand beside my grandfather just as he was painted in the portrait above the desk in Kirkwell House. The proposal that I might become the new librarian of collections deposited on an island lost somewhere in the immensity of the Atlantic Ocean troubled me to the core of my being, the inner forum of decisions and moral choices. Everything within me was shaking under a weight far too heavy for someone who did not know his place. Why should it be in a library, on an island?

I ate, I slept, I read, I looked out of the window as I registered the passage of those few free days, at the end of which I was to return to my inglorious and pointless work. Time passed. My inability to make a decision made it impossible to give any answer. Only the Tridentine liturgy, which I attended on Sunday in the church in Wandsworth, interrupted, for almost two hours, the ennui to which I had fallen prey. The freshness of the immortal Latin language and the discreet sounds of the Gregorian chant managed to revive my soul, wearied as it was from so much fruitless turmoil. All the same, I did not dare believe that my prayers might be answered. A new Monday found me, to my despair, in the same state of indecision. Before leaving for work, I looked at the piece of paper on which I had set down in two parallel columns the arguments for and against accepting the Duke's proposal. I was scared by the uncertainty that resulted from my inability to find an answer to the question of my calling in a confused world.

I followed my accustomed route more slowly than usual, almost completely convinced that I had no business remaining in a field that was not my place. In the Russell Square park, I sat down on a bench and watched the pigeons playing in the little fountain at the point where all the paths intersected. The sight of this place helped me to realize that I was at a crossroads, just like the one I had encountered on the road to Gilbert Newman's residence. All that was missing was the guidance offered by a signpost. Moreover, my attachment to the comfort of an IT employee's life, free of cares and responsibilities, was not an easy burden to cast off. At such turning points, one becomes aware of the network of all the bonds, habits, and comforts that make up the gilded cage in which so often we do not realize that we are held captive. Arriving in the room where I worked together with about twenty coworkers, I greeted the others without enthusiasm and dragged myself to my own desk. In the middle of the imitation walnut surface, right in front of my computer keyboard, a yellowish envelope was waiting for me: "Mr. Alexander Jacob Wills." I sat down incredulously on the edge of my chair. I took the paper rectangle and turned it over to convince myself that the sender was indeed none other than the Duke of Kirkwell. With trembling hands, I opened the envelope and read the most unexpected message I had ever received:

Dear Mr. Wills,

I am pleased to accept your application for the post of librarian of the Newman family collections. Please find your contract enclosed. You will be able to embark on the cargo ship SS Waratah in Portsmouth on Monday, 4 August, starting from 5 a.m. The ship's boat will transport you to your final destination. As a preparatory measure, you will find overleaf a list of the items that should be included in your luggage.

Yours sincerely,

Gilbert Kirkwell

These words were for me like the wind that unexpectedly fills the sails of a becalmed vessel. I knew for sure that I had not sent any answer, let alone an application. Too naïve to grasp the fact that I had already give the Duke my answer during our meeting, I could not understand the true significance of his message. I just accepted it as an act of Providence to guide my hesitant footsteps.

I had to recognize that I was enthusiastic at this twist of destiny. When I handed in my resignation, I smiled inwardly as I answered the inevitable questions about my professional future: "Ah, no, not in another IT company. I've got a job as a librarian. Yes, that's right! A librarian." The looks on my colleagues' faces transmitted varying signals, from admiration on the part of a few, who would probably have liked a change of career too, to the sarcastic irony of the majority, who thought I was crazy anyway. Although I had spent almost seven years in the company, it took me no more than a quarter of an hour to gather my few belongings and hand in my computer. This was thanks to the foresight that I had shown when I first started work there: I had asked for a single additional contractual clause in my favor, namely the right to resign and leave without notice. Thus it was that, on the afternoon of Monday, July 21, 2003, I left a world for an island. I had entered the eye of the vortex.

Chapter 4

Navigator without a Compass

I looked but did not see, listened but did not hear. Although I was studying with eager curiosity the island whose silhouette was growing larger on the horizon, my soul-searching of the last few weeks prevented me from being fully present in the midst of the reality through which I was sailing toward an improbable destination. I felt as though I had lost something—I knew not what, I knew not when, I knew not where. Despite the utter absurdity of the situation, finding that "something" had become an absolute imperative. The feeling of alienation with which I had set out on my journey turned everything around me into a landscape without substance. The ocean, the light of the sun as twilight approached, the sound of the heavy boat cutting through the waves, the broken hum of the engine . . . none of these seemed real. Perhaps that something that I had lost was actually myself. Watching the sure gestures with which Noam, the Albanian seaman, handled the wheel as he took me toward the pontoon pier that was the destination of my Atlantic peregrination, I became conscious, by comparison, of my own lack of firmness in guiding my own life, the inner turmoil that gave me not a moment's peace. How could it be otherwise?

Thousands of unseen threads bound me to the office, to my apartment, to my colleagues, to the world that, physically speaking, I had left behind, but in which my soul remained captive. That world was where I really still was. I understood all too well that what I was now experiencing,

57

with an acuity amplified by the unusual context, was of the same nature as the embarrassment I used to feel in occasional moments when I was pulled suddenly by an office colleague out of the foggy reveries in which the only clear glow of light was the impetuous urge to free myself from the straightjacket of a career with which I felt very little connection. When the voices of those around me became audible, reintroducing me into the circuit of daily work, I became, at least partially, present again. I did my best to listen patiently and to answer as expected. Reluctant to make any effort to adapt, I was always one step behind the course of the reality in which I found myself without my full consent. I heard the voices of those around me, I watched their faces, took part in discussions, nodded approvingly, responded to requirements. All the same, I could not say that I was truly there. Every day, I understood that I was not able to live, simply and calmly, in the midst of this world on whose shore I had been shipwrecked. In time, I managed to accept with resignation that my negligent disconnection from my own life—the thread along which I was sliding, sliding, sliding, like a mountaineer suspended over the abyss—could not be resolved by any of the means to hand.

Once I had understood that my inadaptability was the result of a profound solidarity with the inner world of ideas that I had conquered through my advanced studies in the field of ancient history, the only action that I had attempted, with a tenacity worthy of a better cause, consisted in freeing myself from what seemed at the time to be a ballast that was turning me into a prisoner of the life I had led before my new career. So much so that, with a cruelty that chills me even today, I began to dispose of the library I had built up with much effort over more than ten years. I was behaving like the ancient mariners who, threatened by a terrible storm coming down upon their fragile vessel, would throw all their cargo overboard in the hope of increasing their chances of survival.

After less than a month spent visiting the various second-hand bookshops scattered through the labyrinthine network of streets between Piccadilly and Marymoore Clerkwell, I met by chance Rachel la Breche, a thin, freckled woman with prominent cheekbones whose small head was adorned with orange hair, cut short, that contrasted with her pale green eyes. In a faint, almost imperceptible voice, she was asking the bookseller in whose shop I happened to be if he had any complete series of authors' works, especially in the field of the history of religions and ancient culture. She represented the library of a small institute of ethnology and anthropology, which had entrusted her with the mission of acquiring, as cheaply as possible, all the available works by the leading figures in these exotic domains. So it was that the works of the theoreticians whose books I had amassed in the course of years of searching, from Louis Gernet, Franz Cumont, and Wilhelm Schmidt, to Moses Gaster, Max Müller, Mircea Eliade, and Ioan Petru Culianu, found their way to the institute that Rachel served with the patient assiduity of a private detective. In less than two months, my library shrank appreciably. For the first time, the remaining books could be arranged in a single row, on the bookcases lined up along the walls of my living room. I might have continued this sacrificial act, had I not discovered, one sleepless night, after hunting everywhere in search of the treatise *On the Nature of Man* by Nemesius of Emesa, that the much-sought volume had vanished. The bitterness I felt at that moment determined me, without more ado, to stop disposing of the treasury of my scholarly memory.

I acquired, however, at this terrible price, a certain detachment in relation to my own past, a detachment that led to the diminution of my inadaptability to the condition of a tiny cogwheel of a digital content factory. After seven years of work in the IT field, I had managed to attain a placidity that, with a certain success for those on the outside but none at all in relation to my own self, simulated complete detachment from a past to which, institutionally speaking, I no longer belonged. I stress the words "institutionally speaking," to make it clear that mentally and affectively I was still wholly dedicated to it. I remained a lover of the wisdom of the ancient world exiled in an ambiguous present. Giving up my former systematic reading and research led to a certain alienation with regard to the preoccupations of my soul. Nevertheless, I still did not hesitate, especially on Sundays, to read the studies and papers of the erudite Egyptologist John Gwyn Griffiths of Swansea University or the polyglot Dan Sluşanschi. In other words, neither victory nor checkmate, but endless check: that might be the best way to describe the outcome of my attempt to cut the threads that bound me to my academic past. Deprived of any visible advantage, I repeated the same succession of moves in the hope of at least snatching a draw—without any guarantee regarding the honorability of the enterprise. And yet life had decided otherwise. . . .

Now after a three-day ocean voyage on an enormous cargo ship named *Waratah*—whose outline could now be seen some miles behind us—, I was completing the final portion of my journey into the unknown in a transfer vessel. Once again, I realized how vain were my determined efforts to break all connection with what I had been before. I was approaching the island where in the coming weeks I would face my own solitude for the sake of the mission entrusted to me by the Duke: the continuation of the librarian-archivist's work begun by my grandfather Paolo Paltini.

Unusually for an ocean-crossing sailor, even if it might perhaps be less surprising in a beginner, Noam knew hardly any English. However, that did not prevent him from looking at me calmly, full of understanding. To the rare sentences that I murmured, he always answered with a slight tilt of his head. Once or twice, he surprised me by addressing me in his own incomprehensible mixture of Albanian and French, just as naturally as if we were communicating perfectly. Just as he had for the few days we had been travelling on board the *Waratah*, Noam wore exactly the same clothes: black oilskin trousers, faded yellow shirt, partially covered by a jacket whose blue was only a little lighter than the color of his trousers. A stiff-brimmed cap of grey oilskin protected his large head, which was covered with curly black hair. A pair of rough boots, which had most likely never known the touch of shoe cream, completed the outfit. Day and night, on watch or in the engine room, whether the weather was cold or warm, Noam wore the same shapeless costume. Indeed, his clothes seemed to be the mirror of his peaceful, sallow, unshaven face, with brown eyes that regarded you calmly and smilingly from under black eyebrows. Concentrating on the wheel, which he handled with slow movements, the pilot displayed a calm in flagrant contrast to my own unsettled state.

I turned my eyes toward the island. A mere point on the horizon when we set out from the ship, in the meantime it had grown appreciably. It was now possible to make out a long beach, near which a veritable forest made up of palm trees mixed with small bushes and countless flowering shrubs occupied the foreground. To the right, a wall of rock vanished into the shadows of the island's north end. The luxuriant vegetation had extended its rule even over that gigantic mass of stone, which was pigmented all over with the green of plants that had put down their roots in cracks invisible from a distance. Further away, toward the south end, my eyes rested on a small mountain, perhaps 2,000 feet high, whose slopes were covered with the green of all-conquering scrub. "No less than two and half miles, but no more than four," I stated aloud. Noam indicated his agreement with a slight tilt of his head, and transferred the wheel to his left hand. With the index finger of his right, he pointed out to me a wooden construction that could be seen toward the middle of the beach. The pontoon was growing rapidly as the distance shortened. It was now no more than two or, at the most, three hundred yards to the shore of my island refuge. The piercing cries of seagulls broke out as they abruptly took to the air in a flock, frightened by the noise of our boat's engine. Tirelessly they rose and descended in a zig-zag motion. They seemed to be diving to attack the glittering ocean waves. Through the light blue of the water close to the shore, I could make out the round outline of a turtle. It was floating just a short distance below the surface. I could see surprisingly clearly how the huge amphibian's light grey flippers propelled it forward with a pulsating movement. Like the sand on the shore, the sea bed was covered with shells of all shapes and sizes, and red starfish could be seen in the shadow of the fish that glided through the crystal-clear ocean water.

A change in the beat of the engine and a change in the direction of the boat caught my attention. Raising my head toward the point on which Noam's smiling eyes were fixed intently, I saw that the pontoon was no more than a few yards ahead of us. My throat was dry and my eyes moist. Blinking repeatedly, I stood up, supporting myself with my bulging rucksack, which was stuffed with personal belongings and provisions. The hum of the propellor was now almost inaudible. It was the mere inertia of the boat that carried us toward the rusty iron ladder that descended from the wooden edge of the pontoon into the water. Two massive rubber tires absorbed the shock of contact with the lower part of the ladder. Leaning with both hands on the wheel, Noam waited. After a brief hesitation, I remembered: only I was getting off. With my right arm straining under the weight of my rucksack, I clung to the ladder with my left hand. With a vigorous motion, I swung my luggage a few times and then flung it recklessly straight onto the pontoon, which was at the level of my shoulders. Then I hurriedly climbed a few iron steps, breaking off my last connection with the world I was leaving behind me. When I stepped onto the wooden jetty, I took a deep breath. Driven with the same assurance as hitherto, the boat had already begun to move away. Noam looked up at me with a smile. He said something short and incomprehensible to me in his own language, and then raised three fingers to the peak of his cap in a salute. Struggling to appear unperturbed, I returned his salute. The little vessel headed off back to the mother ship, which I could see lying motionless on the invisible line between the sky and the ocean. I watched the boat anxiously until the figure of the boatman could no longer be distinguished.

For the first time, I could feel the full power of the breeze, which dried the sweat that was running down my forehead. The same turtle that I had seen earlier caught my attention again, this time in the immediate proximity of the pontoon, round which it was swimming in a wide circle. My unusual situation began to sink in. Alone on an unknown island. A latter-day Crusoe. Without laptop, without camera, without phone. I sat down on my rucksack and tried to collect my thoughts. The sun had crossed the heights and was now descending toward the other side of the island. The water, which only a short time before had been shiny and transparent, was turning darker in color, sprinkled with the white of the albatrosses or the grey of the petrels that floated on the waves in search of prey. I stood up, hoisted my rucksack onto my left shoulder, and set off toward the building at the end of the pontoon. The wooden boards creaked rhythmically under the weight of my footsteps. There was no other sound to be heard in the vicinity. Not entirely placidly, indeed perhaps somewhat irritatedly, I examined the whole structure.

Set on tall posts, partially visible, partially submerged, the building was a parallelepipedal construction, as simple as could be imagined, of dark-colored logs, with its windows protected by metal netting—a precaution against storm debris—and an almost horizontal roof of wooden planks reinforced with black metal sheeting riveted in place. The raised footway, which continued in the form of a little veranda shaded by a brown tarpaulin, went round the left side of the structure. Here, centrally placed, was the iron door, from which, approximately three yards away, a few wooden steps descended to the sandy beach. As I walked along the footway, I hesitated, just as when, in the yard of a strange house, you expect one of the inhabitants to come out to meet you. But no one appeared.

As I turned my head around, I caught sight of a sign whose presence could not be a matter of chance. A bronze-colored metal mailbox, fixed to the upper part of a post set right by the steps and with a strip of white cloth carefully tied round it. I put down my rucksack, leaned it against the door, and approached the mysterious box. I opened the lid. Without moving, I probed with my eyes the semi-darkness of its metallic interior. Inside was a yellowish envelope, with no stamp or postmark, in the middle of which a single line was written in the same elegant hand I had noticed on the first letter I had received from the Duke of Kirkwell. As on that occasion, the line identified me as the recipient: "Mr. Alexander Jacob Wills." I turned round at once, as though expecting to see the sender somewhere in the vicinity, but I quickly dispelled such an absurd thought.

Sitting down on the steps, I opened the envelope and drew out a single page covered on both sides with writing that looked contorted but was unexpectedly legible—just like the modulated, yet so clear, voice of the island's owner. I took advantage of the fading light of the evening to start reading, slightly distracted by the monotonous sound of the ocean:

Dear Alexander,

If I should become somewhat voluble in these letters, please do not consider this groundless. The last thing I wish is to waste our time in vain! Having expressed the wish to follow in the footsteps of your admirable forebear, Dr. Paolo Paltini, you are now on the island that is home to the library that he cared for in the last years of his

*life. And I owe it to you to provide such explanations as may contribute to the fulfil-
ment of your mission.*

*I confess that I do not know how to communicate to you certain matters that are
somewhat out of the ordinary, without appearing to be contaminated with superficiality
or a thirst for the sensational—the distinguishing marks of our ignoble times. I have
decided to express myself directly, clearly, and simply. I hope you will not be tempted to
form a hasty opinion of my character in the present moment, but will defer judgement
until the time when we shall be able to say that we truly know one another.*

*So, Dr. Paltini was seeking Atlantis. Although he had made significant progress
toward discovering the lost continent, he did not manage to bring to a conclusion the
project that united our destinies in a way that neither of us would ever have expected. It
all began with a discussion about a short passage from the treatise on the history of the
New World written by the secretary of the famous conquistador Hernán Cortés, Father
Francisco López de Gómara. Allow me to remind you of this text:*

"The Philosopher Plato writeth in his Dialogues of Timaeus *and* Critias, *that in
the old time there was in the sea Atlantic over against Africa, an Island called Atlantis
[. . .] But that in a certain great earthquake and tempest of rain, this Island sank and
the people were drowned: also that there remained so much mud of the drowning or
sinking of that Island, that that sea Atlantic could not be sailed. Some take this for
a fable: and many for a true history [. . .] But there is now no cause why we should
any longer doubt or dispute of the Island Atlantis, forasmuch as the discovering and
conquest of the west Indies do plainly declare what Plato hath written of the said lands.
In Mexico also at this day they call that water Atl [. . .] as by a word remaining of
the name of the Island that is not. We may likewise say that the Indies are either the
Island and firm land of Plato or the remnant of the same."*

*It was the conviction that the remains of the lost continent might be found in certain
Atlantic islands that led me to purchase this property. You will ask, "Why this one in
particular?" The answer is simple. While he was following the thread of Father Francisco
López de Gómara's enquiries, Dr. Paolo Paltini, your grandfather, discovered what actually
appeared to be the grave of the bold Spaniard. It was this supposition that led to my crazy
gesture. The haste with which I sold almost a quarter of my family's art collection to buy
a remote piece of the Atlantic seemed an incomprehensible whim to everyone. However, I
assure you, the action was not gratuitous. After searching for years for the possible site of
the grave of Cortés's secretary, we discovered on this island a mysterious chapel, at least*

three hundred years old, which housed a sarcophagus on which was carved the conquistador's coat of arms. Nearby ruins, as yet impossible to categorize, may indicate the reason for which the cleric might have chosen to continue his research here. This, in short, is the real purpose for which, under the cover of my apparently extravagant wish to move my library to an island in the Atlantic, your grandfather immersed himself in unravelling this enigma. It is not impossible that you are treading at this very moment on the site of the remains of the civilization described by Plato in his Critias. *Unfortunately, however, I cannot guarantee it. Dr. Paltini's research, as you know, came to an end unexpectedly. Whether you wish to continue it or not depends entirely on you.*

Alexander Jacob Wills, please consider yourself fully a part of the research that has gone on over the last fifteen years. Your grandfather often spoke to me about the qualities that you demonstrated in your childhood. You learned Greek and Latin thoroughly, a necessary requirement for a true researcher of the ancient world. Moreover, he was convinced that you are a "key-bearer," as he called those few who are capable of acquiring the art of interpreting the old texts written by enlightened pagans, like Plato, Philo, and Proclus, or by holy scholars like Ambrose of Milan and the Venerable Bede. When he was sure that illness would prevent him from reaching the end of his earthly road, he begged me to do all I could to persuade you to continue his work. In order to succeed where we have failed, you will follow the whole trail from the beginning. Dr. Paolo Paltini's work was, however, so precious that it is with no regrets that I am subjecting you to this retracing of the thread of his research. I must reiterate what I said at our first meeting: I am doing you no favor. If you accept, you assume full responsibility for all that is implied in the continuation of an important mission. And I, in my turn, assure you that I shall do my duty. I shall begin right now by explaining certain particularities of the context in which you now find yourself.

The building that you see cannot offer you very much. I recommend that you look for the map of the island and the old oil lamp. Although it is rather vague, the map will help you to localize the important points in this little world. There can be no better starting point than the modest cabin in which your grandfather lived for thirteen years. It will take you no more than half an hour to get there. Walk along the shore toward the little mountain in the distance—a long extinct volcano. You will come to the river which Dr. Paltini named, meaningfully, Atl. Advancing along it into the heart of the island, you will have no difficulty in finding Dr. Paltini's hermitage. In the deepest darkness, light will shine.

The Island without Seasons

You have no Rubicon before you, but I hope you will take the same decision that was described by Julius Caesar with a certain exaltation: Alea iacta est. *Only thus will these words become, for you, for me, for us, doubly precious.*
Yours,

> *Gilbert Kirkwell*

I read and reread the letter till the light had faded so much that reading became impossible. Atlantis . . . Francisco López de Gómara . . . the two names refused to disappear from the whirlpool set in motion in my imagination by the extract from the *Historia General de Las Indias*. Having initially been convinced that I was simply going to work as a librarian, I now found myself obliged to admit, with a certain suspicion, that I was sliding abruptly into an adventure the nature of which I did not understand. Still chewing over the words of the letter, I realized, as evening fell, that I could not simply remain where I was. I had to find the cabin. But not before collecting the map and the lamp that I was to find in the building at the end of the pontoon.

Inside, the corners of the dusty room were enveloped in shadows. Once my eyes grew accustomed to the darkness, I was able to distinguish some cupboards, between which a few well-made racks held various items of fishing equipment. Two long tables were placed under the windows through which a last faint glimmer of light entered the room. On one of these, I could make out the shape of a lamp, its glass protected by thin metal bars. Beside it was a metal cigarette lighter, which did its job as though it had only just been filled. Once lit, the lamp spread a warm, enveloping orange light around. A thin wisp of smoke emerged from the top of the glass that protected the flame from the whim of invisible drafts. I opened the drawers of the tables, where I was surprised to find a number of volumes of the works of Jules Verne and G.K. Chesterton, together with assorted small items, including the inevitable fishing accessories. In one of the drawers, a small leather satchel, long and thin, caught my attention. It was a map case, and in it I found, neatly folded, the map of the whole island. The thick paper, cloth-backed and covered with protective film, was the right thing for an environment in which water could at any moment become a threat. Thus equipped, I closed the door, ready to set out for the cabin. With my rucksack on my back, I took a last look at the grey silhouette of the building, and made my way along the beach, toward the mountain whose dark form dominated the far end of the island.

To my left was the ocean, whose threatening murmur never ceased. To my right, the compact mass of vegetation, which began no more than ten or fifteen yards away, seemed like the reclining body of a sleeping giant, the sound of whose breathing was clearly audible. Rustling, cracking, short cries, sometimes intense eruptions of sound that died away as rapidly as they had started, all demonstrated that the vegetable kingdom was accompanied by the presence of birds and beasts that found shelter everywhere. All these sounds induced more wonder in me than fear. As I walked, I contemplated the sky, which was gradually and majestically adorning itself with a multitude of stars, their brilliance unimpeded by the light pollution of the city. The magic of the nocturnal landscape was dizzying. I walked as if through a dream whose palpable realism turned it into the ecstatic opposite of the darkest nightmares. Being more sensitive to the grim bites of evil, it seems that people have not invented a fitting name for such rare experiences. Exhausted as I was, I continued on my way, eagerly peering at everything that the luminous night so generously unveiled. Only when I lifted my eyes did I stop short, transfixed, almost breathless. A white bridge of light, composed of a myriad of stars and distant galaxies, traversed the indigo sky, to the amazement of the minuscule dot of humanity lost in the middle of the ocean. It was the Milky Way. Its light lent a bluish tint to the trees, the vegetation, the water, which had hitherto been in darkness. A silvery sparkle lined the waves, from which a few distant islands emerged like silent, motionless cut-outs caressed by the rays of starlight. The moon had not yet risen. The heavenly light was strong enough to turn the deepest night into an otherworldly display. I had never felt so small as I did in those moments; I had never had a grander perception of creation as on that first night on the library island. Charmed by all that I saw, I continued on my way until I could make out what could only be the sound of the River Atl flowing gently out into the waters of the ocean.

Indeed, it was not long before I spied the glitter of a watercourse no more than a few yards wide winding delicately across the sand of the beach to disappear into the blue immensity beyond. If I climbed toward the middle of the island along the line of the river, I would have to go through the thin forest that stood guard on either side of its course. Inwardly thanking my foresightful guide, I lit the lamp and climbed a small slope right before the beginning of the woodland. After passing by clusters of palm trees in the first ranks, I came to a mass of shrubbery, of moderate height, interspersed with thick bushes with fleshy oval leaves. The light of the lamp fell on various nocturnal creatures. The most visible were a sort of ground squirrels, which would stop still for a few seconds with their ears pricked and then dash off at an incredible speed into the darkness. My reference point was the river bank, and I made sure never to stray more than two or three yards away from it. I walked carefully, treading on fallen branches and, in places, even on seashells cast up here by the ocean at high tide. Soon I had left the cover of the palm trees almost completely behind me, and could see once more, suspended in space high above the river, the stellar display that evoked thoughts of the immutability of eternity.

After walking for another ten minutes, I noticed that the bushes were getting thinner, until finally I found myself on the edge of a wide clearing, in the middle of which, raised on stout posts to about the height of a man above the ground, was the cabin. As far as I could see, it was of relatively modest dimensions. Being situated just a short distance from the river, it had been built to withstand possible floods, and indeed the remains of water weeds, branches, and shrubs that I could make out by the pale light of the lamp bore witness to the occurrence of such events. A solidly built ladder led up to a wide veranda, also made of wood, which occupied half the width of the whole structure. I tried each rung with the tip of my boot before stepping on it, not wanting to risk any unpleasant surprises resulting from the age of the wood. When I reached the veranda, I shuddered involuntarily. An iguana colored in various shades of green, with brick-red eyes that reflected the brilliance of the lamp flame, was looking at me, motionless. The tremor of its scaly throat was the only sign that this primeval creature was alive. After we had both paused to inspect one another, it laboriously started to move its feet with their long fingers like horny twigs, and made for the back edge of the veranda. From time to time it would stop, turn its head with sudden movements, examine me attentively, and then resume its tactical retreat.

I laid down my rucksack beside one of the benches on the veranda. From there, the sky could be seen in all its plenitude, the more so as the awning provided for rainy periods was rolled up and strapped to the edge of the roof. Built, like the pontoon, from beams of dark wood, the cabin had walls with large windows protected by green-painted iron grilles. Beside the door, which was also painted green, a metal shelf sheltered some boots and rubber capes. I approached the entrance. Was I really prepared to meet once again the world of the man who had enriched my childhood with so many unforgettable tales? I turned the handle and slowly but firmly pushed the door open.

Nothing has ever seemed to me more mysterious than the rectangular opening that allows access to an unknown interior. What could give a better insight into the souls of persons, their vision, their aspirations, their personal achievements, than the unique space of what we call "home"? I could spend hours going over my memories of expeditions to the abandoned dwellings that Lorenzo, my Umbrian friend, explored during long Italian vacations. We found next to nothing. Only vast empty rooms, full of dust and cobwebs, where, sometimes, moldy books and newspapers lay beside peeling walls. And yet, the moment when we opened a door—no matter how many of them there might be—was lived with the most intense concentration. On just one occasion, our emotions reached the point of incandescence. On the top shelf of an otherwise empty library, we saw what seemed to be a wooden box. I clambered, clumsily, onto some chairs stacked by Lorenzo, until I managed to reach the unusual artefact. Then we both sat, not daring to make an sound, and looked for a long time at the box, which was about the size of a paperback book. With a gesture of my head, I invited my friend to open it. "You saw it first," he replied with a solemn look in his face. I took hold of the lid and slowly lifted it. Inside, under a piece of velvet, eaten away in places, there were just some photographs of pilgrimage centers—Orvieto Cathedral, the Benedictine monastery of Norcia—and resting beside them, forgotten there by who knows whom, two silver devotional rings, on whose minuscule metallic beads, precisely ten in number, it was possible to count the succession of *Ave Marias* and *Pater Nosters* that made up the prayer of the Rosary. Nothing more than that. Although it was not exactly a treasure, the box was the greatest discovery of our unforgettable vacations. I still have one of the two rings in a drawer somewhere.

When I began to open the door of the cabin in which my grandfather had spent his last years as a researcher and historian of ancient worlds, I was convinced that I would be entering a space laden with mysteries. After the first couple of inches, the door stuck, blocked by the uneven floor. Only by carefully lifting it by the handle was I finally able to push it back against the wall. I was now looking into a room that might be as much as 30 feet long and slightly less wide, of whose austere furniture I could make out a bed, a broad table, a cupboard, and a few bookshelves fixed to the walls. At the entrance, to the right of the door, a little table bore a gas lamp and various kitchen utensils. Above it hung a barometer whose needle indicated that the weather was "fair." On the other side, on a wrought-iron coat rack, hung a black duck cape, together with a few jackets and walking sticks. The wooden floorboards were covered there by a thick tarpaulin; otherwise they were bare throughout the building.

Seeing a light bulb hanging from the ceiling, I instinctively looked for the switch. I found it right beside the door. A colorless light, not very bright, flooded the whole room. I extinguished my lamp. On the broad table at the far end, I noticed a large green torch, whose glass fixed with massive screws showed that it was an instrument designed for underwater illumination. A rectangular battery and its charger lay beside it. To the left of the table, against the wall, stood the bed, covered with a thin blanket whose faded blue betrayed its age: no doubt it would be as hard as my grandfather's bed in our Italian house, where I had spent so many afternoons leafing through his atlases of archaeology and antiquities. Dr. Paolo Paltini had become accustomed during his military service to sleeping in precarious conditions, on a piece of wood covered with a thin woolen rug.

The only element of comfort in the whole room, whose rigorous order nonetheless dispelled any impression of squalor, was a wooden rocking chair. Careful inspection confirmed beyond any shadow of doubt that it was *the* rocking chair that I had known since my childhood. And, just as in my childhood, I immediately felt an irresistible impulse to rock myself on this unique item of furniture.

For a few minutes, I relaxed, listening to the rhythmic creaking of the wooden chair. The day's tiredness was tempered, like agitated grains of sand settling again on the sea floor as the water clears. I let my head rest against the back of the chair, which was covered with a piece of soft felt. I saw how the light melted among the rafters that supported the steeply pitched roof. A few lizards darted like lightning along the thick beams, making graceful geometrical figures. The fact that they made no attempt to hide in the shadowy regions of the roof was a clear sign that they had been accustomed to the occupant of the cabin. Lacking a ceiling, the room seemed like a cross between a Benedictine monastic cell, a fishermen's shelter, and the reading room of a small provincial library. Calmly, I listened to the sounds of the night coming through the open door. Then I fell asleep.

Rapid snatches of dream, in which childhood memories were mixed with the faces of old schoolmates whose names I had long forgotten, and, occasionally, even the silent face of Paolo Paltini, flashed across the intimate screen of my heart, to the background music of the tireless rumbling of the waves. Out of the blue, that house appeared where, with Lorenzo, I had found the box containing the two rosary rings. I was walking on tiptoe from room to room, carefully opening doors and searching every corner, every shelf, every cupboard, every possible hiding place. What was I looking for? What . . .? Unable to answer, I felt that all the tension of the endless investigation was constantly building up. More and more distressed after each failure, I would probably have burst into tears if I had not awoken, in an agitated state, out of this strange oneiric pilgrimage.

Only after looking around me in confusion for a few seconds was I able to recall where I was. I got up stiffly to switch off the light. Contrary to expectations, this action did not result in the spread of darkness, but merely produced a modification in the intensity and color of the light that flooded the interior of the cabin. An ethereal blue glow, of uncertain origin, stood in the way of the full triumph of night. Only when I looked out of the window was the mystery solved: the moon, almost full, was floating low over the western end of the forest. It was almost 3 a.m. I collected my rucksack and returned to the room, shutting the door behind me. I undressed in slow motion and hung my clothes on the coat rack at the entrance. I lay down on the hard bed, and looked at the table and at the window above it. Then I got up again. The moonlight revealed a landscape in which the River Atl was lost behind banks thick with trees, and numerous bushes and shrubs. The closeness of the wild made me smile.

I was ready to return to my resting place, when, on the wall to the left of the table, I noticed some slightly phosphorescent signs, barely visible, scratched on the dark wood. Eagerly, I lit the lamp. The signs disappeared. After extinguishing and relighting the lamp several times, I grasped the reason for the mystery: it was the moonlight that made the marks visible, lending them a bluish tinge. I peered closely at the place where the phosphorescent letters could be seen and managed to decipher the following words: "*sin otra luz y guía, sino la que en el corazón ardía.*"[†] Led by the irrepressible inner drive unleashed by these words, I began frantically to fumble with my fingers along the lunar text. I grasped the end of this portion of the beam with my wide open hand, and pulled. It came away like a lid, revealing a hollow space behind it. Only then did I realize the meaning of an apparently pointless sentence in the letter that Gilbert Newman had left for me at the pontoon: *In the deepest darkness, light will shine.* Without further thought, I relit the lamp and looked into the niche in the wall. Its interior concealed another message, written, this time, on a single sheet of watermarked card, which had been laid on top of a thick notebook, protected by a leather cover with pockets. They shared the hiding place with an old gold-nibbed pen, whose state of wear showed that it had seen long use.

[†]   ". . .without any other light and guide than that which burns in the heart" (Saint John of the Cross, *The Dark Night of the Soul*).

On the first page of the notebook, in the lower right-hand corner, I was able to read with a choked voice: "Daily notes. Paolo Paltini." Without opening it further, I placed it on the table, next to the message. For a few minutes, I was content to examine the pen. It was black, shiny, with a cap that could be screwed on and off and a reservoir in which some traces of ink could be seen, and it had a gilded, diamond-shaped nib. The worn condition of the little bump at its tip gave silent testimony to the countless pages that had been written with its aid. Ever the conscientious scholar, I filled it with ink from the pot that sat at one corner of the table. With such a routine action, I sought to temper the restless curiosity that impelled me both to read the message and to explore the journal. Then I took a deep breath and picked up the little watermarked card that was covered on both sides with the Duke's message. Motionless as a statue, I ran my eyes over the words that explained the presence of the journal in its hiding place.

Dear Alexander,

Perhaps you did not expect a literal confirmation of my words in my last letter: "In the deepest darkness, light will shine." I assure you, nothing is by chance. For your grandfather, the key to the research he carried out was always closely bound to the wisdom of his favorite author, the saintly mystic poet John of the Cross. We travel through darkness. Only those who know the way toward the light can help us in our investigations.

Your reading of the journal will reveal the trail of a knowledge to which I have invited you to make your own contribution. Here you will find his final conclusions regarding the sarcophagus, the investigation of which, in the next few days, will heighten your astonishment. Or your confusion. At first, it appeared to be the last resting place of Father Francisco López de Gómara. However it now seems that it is not. The bones of its occupant have never been found. This remains one among many mysteries that you are called to unravel: for whom was the cenotaph in the chapel constructed? What connection can there be between such a construction and the mystery of Atlantis? To exercise your sharpness of mind in finding answers, I have spared neither effort nor means. I invite you to visit the main building on the island, the place where your grandfather carried out his research in his last years: the library. There, I assure you, you will come up against an enigma greater than what you have here. But . . . let me not race ahead. All this has been conceived with the sole aim of placing you in the one context that can make visible the solution to our search.

How do you reach the library? The River Atl will again be your guiding thread. Follow it to its source! From there, you will easily identify the destination of your whole journey.

At my age, nothing can please me more than the thought that you will have the chance to explore the place where your grandfather spent the last years of his life. No, Paradise is not a library, but here, in exile, such a place may be considered a veritable prelude to that knowledge that is accessible only in Paradise.

With confidence,

Gilbert Kirkwell

At once, I felt the accumulated tiredness of the previous days pressing down like a terrible weight on my head, my shoulders, my chest, my whole body. I stroked the leather covers of the journal, and then I went over to the bed and lay down, sighing. With my eyes shut, I could make out the rustle of the leaves and the occasional—but all the more penetrating for that—cries of the birds that had their nests in the rich foliage of the surrounding vegetation. The image of the Milky Way, which I had contemplated all along my way here, kept returning to my imagination, which was full of so many phantasms. More than once it was blended with snatches of dream in which I was exploring the countless rooms of a house in search of that unknown something that I knew I had lost many years before. Although I was almost asleep, on the borderline between reality and reverie, I observed that the distant roar of the waves never ceased. Was there anywhere on the island where the their sound could not be heard? This was the last question that came into my head before I sank into a sleep as deep as the unfathomable aquatic abyss surrounding the nameless island.

* * *

When midday was long past, I was awakened by a faint sound. Anywhere else it would have seemed perfectly normal, if not indeed banal: a knocking at the door. Coming quickly to my senses, I jumped to my feet with the same rapidity with which I realized that in the midst of my solitude, such a sound was in fact the strangest thing imaginable. Tensed, motionless, I listened attentively to the improbable tapping. I grasped how anomalous the sound was, which suggested that it must have a different source: the tapping, light, and at longer intervals than if it had been made by a human finger, never stopped. I approached the door on tiptoe, and opened it carefully. No one was knocking on its wood. The sound, which could now be heard more clearly, was coming from somewhere in the region of the veranda. I bent down and looked in the direction from which it seemed to be coming. The elucidation of the mystery brought a wide smile and a sigh of relief: the iguana was ambling along a wooden board, which its horny fingers kept striking rhythmically. I was truly happy to emerge onto the platform, easing my stiff bones and looking with great interest around me. I trod in the footsteps of the iguana, which stood motionless for a few moments, fixing its beady eyes on me, and then disappeared over the edge of the veranda. For the first time I examined the landscape behind the cabin.

My eye was caught by a small wooden construction with a massive cylinder on top of it. I put my shoes on and went downstairs to inspect it close up. It proved to be a rather rudimentary, but functional, shower, complete with cupboards containing all the necessary accessories. The cylinder was simply the voluminous tank in which rainwater was collected for the use of the occupant of the cabin. Refreshed with a shower, I ate hurriedly a meal from my sack and sat down in the rocking chair with Paolo Paltini's journal on my knee. I stroked the cover again before immersing myself in reading that was only interrupted by the fall of evening, when the semi-darkness forced me to switch on the light. Although there were no more than fifty pages covered with my grandfather's tiny hand, my reading, in which I returned to certain passages numerous times, continued until after midnight. In spite of the efforts I made to penetrate deeper into the content of the notes, I realized that the whole mystery of the quest undertaken by the Duke, supported by his librarian, was in no way diminished. On the contrary.

The Island without Seasons

From all that I read, it emerged that certain discoveries had been made in the last three years. I was especially intrigued by the repeated mentions of a volcanic cave containing the wreck of a seventeenth-century brigantine. In it had been found a book which the journal referred to as "Stephanus's opuscule." Although no detail pointed to this conclusion, I thought of Henricus Stephanus, the Renaissance editor of Plato's dialogues. The empty sarcophagus discovered in the chapel situated somewhere in the northern part of the island, on a plateau named "The Mandible," was mentioned most frequently. From studying the detailed notes describing this cenotaph, I found out all the questions that had been nagging my grandfather in the last years of his life. What was the purpose of the chapel? Why an empty sarcophagus? But above all, what could be the explanation for the sculpture on one of its side walls: the coat of arms of Hernán Cortés? Could it have been someone from his circle of close acquaintances? The name of Francisco López de Gómara was also frequently mentioned. On the other hand, the discovery of the brigantine seemed to have finally excluded that possibility: there were conclusive indications that the vessel could not be older than the seventeenth century, while Father Gómara had lived and died in the sixteenth.

Through the details mentioned in the journal, I was at last getting an almost complete picture of the work of Dr. Paltini and his distinguished friend. In the midst of a veritable avalanche of hypotheses and theories, the only constant, unifying reference point was the name of Atlantis. Being disciplined by nature, I decided to put some order into the mass of ideas by recapitulating as faithfully as possible all that we knew so far.

My grandfather's passion for the world of ancient Greece had meant, as for many other scholars, a lifelong interest in Plato's dialogues. In particular, the old Athenian philosopher's myths had left their mark on his youth and added to his writings a monumental dissertation on the subject when he was just twenty-one. Inevitably, but fruitfully, he had thereafter constantly confronted one of the most controversial issues to be found at the heart of the Platonic dialogues. How many historians, classical scholars, and adventurers have not wondered whether the account of Atlantis is history or myth?

The story of Atlantis fired his imagination and became his favorite theme. Over the years, his files on the subject continued to grow as he added more and more new interpretations of Plato's *Timaeus* and *Critias*. Among the opinions he diligently recorded was the mysterious passage from Father Francisco López de Gómara's *Historia General de Las Indias*. The Spanish cleric's conclusion—"*We may likewise say that the Indies are either the Island and firm land of Plato or the remnant of the same*"—pushed my grandfather to widen the scope of his historical, archaeological, and philological investigations, which had hitherto been clearly circumscribed: reflecting the extent of knowledge in the age of Columbus, the "Indies" was the name given to the lands of the New World prior to the work of the cartographer Martin Waldseemüller.

This might all have remained at the stage of a mere academic investigation if, in the 1980s, Paolo Paltini had not had an opportunity to explore the archives of the Royal Chancellery in Valladolid, the city where Francisco López de Gómara was presumed to have died sometime between 1557 and 1570. Long walks through the town's historic quarters coupled with hours of contemplation in the shadows of the Church of San Pablo or the Basilica of Santa Maria la Antigua strengthened his desire to pay his respects to the earthly remains of the author who had advanced one of the most interesting hypotheses regarding the survival of the remains of Atlantis.

We may imagine his surprise when he was informed that the burial place of Father Francisco López is unknown. Nonplussed by such a biographical lacuna, he spent several weeks in the small town of Gómara in Old Castille, the starting point of his first investigations aimed at establishing the site of the tomb.

The results of his endeavors may be summed up in three words: failure after failure. Each defeat, each false trail became a new dam capable of raising the level of the flow of a well-tempered enthusiasm. Nothing could stop him in his research. He included in his list of hypotheses the possibility that Father Gómara might have left not just Valladolid but Spain itself for a destination in that world that he believed concealed the remains of Atlantis. Gifted with the tenacity of a treasure-hunter, Dr. Paltini began to read all the catalogues and maritime journals of the age in search of the name of the Spanish cleric. Only later, after months spent in the dust of the archives of former maritime companies, did he discover the account of the captain of a small vessel, the *San Esteban*, which returned from Barbados around the year 1625. This captain referred in his log book, without mentioning any name, to a small island where he had stopped for two days to take on drinking water.

Something of an improvised explorer, the captain of the *San Esteban* apparently saw there a gothic chapel and the remains of ancient constructions. It might all have been forgotten again, if his account had not contained one astonishing detail. On the sarcophagus inside the chapel was carved a coat of arms remarkably similar to that of the famous Hernán Cortés. According to the practice of the time, only a member of the conquistador's family or a very close protégé of his would have had his burial place decorated in this way. Mobilized by this detail, my grandfather put together a list of all the islands that might be the location of the mysterious cenotaph. His tireless research led him even to the Vatican archives. It was there that he first met Gilbert Newman.

A discussion started in the halls of the library was sufficient to make my grandfather aware of the Duke's interest, free of any facile enthusiasm, in dangerous historical subjects. After explaining to him the consequences of the impossibility of establishing the location of the tomb of Father Francisco López de Gómara, Dr. Paltini found in the latest of the Dukes of Kirkwell the ideal backer, eager to support him in his efforts to identify the island. It was not long before their collaboration began to bear fruit. Together they managed to establish the precise location of that tiny point lost in the ocean. After a few months of discussions and explorations, the Duke decided to buy the island, in order to facilitate the continuation of their investigations in optimal conditions. Thus appeared the cabin where I am at this moment, and, a little later, the library where the scholarly treasures of the Newman family were to find their oceanic home. The last years of my grandfather's life were marked by the feverish exploration of ruins whose classification remained debatable, along with the ceaseless search for the remains of the person for whom the sarcophagus had been intended. In spite of a number of discoveries, sufficient to justify the purchase of the island, not even one of these investigations had been brought to a conclusion. It was clear to me why Gilbert Newman had drawn me into this unusual adventure.

Each page of the journal awoke in my soul a state of joy that I had considered utterly lost and most likely inaccessible for all the rest of my days. In just a few hours, I had revisited the reading of my childhood and adolescence, together with fragments of the studies of my early youth, which had touched on exciting subjects like the existence of Atlantis, the theories of the Jesuit monk Athanasius Kircher, or the possible connections between the ancient culture of Egypt and the sunken island. But, above all, I could perceive the discreet scent of revealed beauty in the last sentence of the journal: *Nella lontana isola dove regna una sola stagione . . .*

I fell asleep resolved the next day to make my way, without further delay, to the focal point of the island: the fabulous library of the Duke of Kirkwell.

Chapter 5

The Trial of the Labyrinth

I stopped and looked carefully around, trying to detach myself from the world of inner storms and to let myself be flooded by all that surrounded me. Not long after resuming my journey, I was sliding inevitably down the steep slope of unanswerable questions. With my rucksack on my back, I leaned heavily on the silver-headed walking stick that I had taken from the rack in the cabin. I advanced along the riverbank, all the time turning around in my mind Gilbert Newman's words and the notes in my grandfather's journal. Veiled in the aura of its tragic tale, the island of Atlantis floated like a gigantic star over all my shadowy imaginings. Out of the handful of threads supplied by my grandfather's notes and the guiding letters, I was weaving the tapestry of a story whose content was no less strange than the unicorns I had contemplated in the Cloisters Museum in New York. The name of Father Francisco López de Gómara, interwoven with that of Hernán Cortés, would not give me peace. His biographers maintained that he had died sometime between 1557 and 1570—no one knew precisely when or where. That was all. The unease that accompanied all my attempts to come up with a plausible scenario was partially tempered whenever I reminded myself that I was on my way to the library where I was to continue the research work to which one of the most knowledgeable scholars of these "exotic" subjects had devoted the last fifteen years.

Guided by the contorted line of the River Atl, whose meanders led me through the undergrowth of the forest that, at a certain distance, guarded its banks, I proceeded toward my destination. Here and there, the odd solitary palm tree rose sloping, but no less majestic, over the water. An insistent chirping could be heard coming from the roots of the twisted shrubs that filled the spaces between the trees. A few strange birds dived into the water and began to swim energetically. Their grey plumage was almost black in the region of the head, and their eyes—little orange beads—glinted over their milk-white beaks. The passing noises helped me to realize the silence that surrounded me. In contrast to the night, whose intense whispers I had heard two days before, the day seemed much calmer, and the multitude of sounds produced by the birdlife could be taken as mere background noise, rich and extensive but far away. Though I had no knowledge about the flora and fauna of the island, I guessed that during the day the vast majority of the birds regrouped in the area of the shore or on the small islands offshore. Only there could they scour the ocean at will, seeking the fish on which their survival depended.

I stopped by a fallen tree whose crown was immersed in the water of the river. I had seen several such sights along the bank and had even noticed a few uprooted palm trees whose leaves were already desiccated. Having no experience of the furious storms that haunt this part of the Atlantic, I failed to decode the warning message of these remains. After almost half an hour of walking at a relaxed, and more often than not hesitant, pace, I noticed that to the right, there were no longer large bushes and trees, but only low scrub, though the vegetation was no less dense than before. On the other side of the river, the vegetation had changed in a similar way. Ahead of me, the disappearance of the trees revealed to view a cluster of granite crags resembling a crouching giant with his forehead pressed against his knees. Large rocks flanked the banks of the river, forcing me into a labyrinthine slalom. In just a few minutes, I arrived beside the granite giant, who was grey in places and yellowish white in others. Once past the rocks that, in my imagination, formed his legs, I now saw a different landscape, dominated by the continual noise coming from a little waterfall. Its stream fell onto a wheel fixed to a massive metal axle that protruded through the wall of a cubic structure on the other side of the river. The cables hanging from posts left no room for doubt: this must be the island's generator. The noise of the waterfall was like the sound of water constantly pouring out of a jug. I noticed how the liquid mass that flowed onto the wheel was thrown up rhythmically by its blades. For a few minutes, I watched the fascinating spectacle, a perfect metaphor for the flow of the years in my own life, for time lost beyond recovery.

Between the scattered bushes to the right of the building, the line of a grass-covered path wound its way up to the level from which the water was pouring. I could see another post up there, carrying cables to a destination as yet invisible. Leaving the bank of the river behind me, I began to climb, stepping as carefully and firmly as before. I was increasingly impatient to get a wider view of the island. Once I reached the plateau, I could see among the bushes part of the lake shown on the map. Its still waters, on which the gentle wind raised only small waves that washed its banks, suggested the name written over the coordinates of its location: Mirror Lake. It was over a three quarters of a mile wide. When I came closer to it, I found that its shore was sandy in places, but otherwise stony, covered with gravel and remains of plants. The bushes that surrounded its shiny waters thinned out toward the right. By the side of the lake nearer the ocean stood an impressive construction. Light grey in color, it had been built on a Victorian model, enriched with pointed windows in the purest Gothic style. Surrounded by a wall, and adorned with stained-glass windows whose colors could barely be distinguished through the storm-protection nets, it seemed transplanted from Gilbert Newman's homeland. Grandiose without being overpowering, with a ground floor more than 100 yards long, the library was dominated by a square tower whose windows and narrow crenellations suggested a medieval castle. To an informed eye, it evoked the upright, harmonious figure of the Duke of Kirkwell himself.

Before setting out again, I stopped for a few minutes to examine the landscape in the opposite direction to the lake. There, at the north-eastern end of the island, among the trees at the edge of the forest that seemed to rise and fall like waves, the glint of sunlight on a reflective surface caught my eye. At that distance, it was impossible to tell what its source might be. I turned back toward the lake, and looked at the stream of water tirelessly falling and keeping in motion the wheel of the generator. Then I wiped my brow and set off toward the building inside which I hoped to find satisfactory answers to all my questions of the last few days.

There was no longer the slightest breeze. The dark surface of the water was completely still. All that could be heard was the endless murmur of the ocean, covered from time to time by the cries of gulls and other birds. The rustling in the shadowy areas of the scrub briefly stopped when I relieved my loneliness by letting out a loud whistle. Splashes on the surface of the water signaled the presence of fish catching little floating insects. However, nothing of all this could distract my attention from what lay ahead of me. At the sight of the library, I could barely refrain from breaking into a run toward the focal point of my entire journey. The tower seemed to grow taller as I approached. Soon the flight of steps in front of the imposing entrance came into view. When I reached my destination, I was not at all surprised to discover a mail box similar to that which had been waiting for me on the pontoon.

The inevitable watermarked envelope was there, printed with the name of the Duke of Kirkwell in the distinctive Roman type. I quickly put it in my breast pocket and began to climb the steps. My heart was leaping with enthusiasm. The prospect of exploring a library always made me feel like Brother Bede, the Venerable Bede as we know him, in the days when he walked the corridors of the monastery of Monkwearmouth–Jarrow, murmuring his prayers.

A rhythmic noise of uncertain origin tempered my haste. I trod more and more lightly. Then I stopped and bent my head down. I listened intently in the hope of being able to establish the direction and the nature of the indecipherable sound. It was coming from somewhere to the left of the entrance door, on the stone platform to which the steps led. Only the post supporting the porch roof hid the source of its regular beat from my sight. It turned out to be an iguana just like the one that had greeted me on the veranda of the cabin. It withdrew grudgingly to the end of the stone platform.

With that puzzlement solved, I approached the tall doors. Right in front of my eyes, the wrought-iron handles, with their silvery matte surface, seemed immovable. Like an embodiment of the timeless nature of the knowledge contained in the volumes within the library, the door marked the undoubtedly difficult passage between the visible, palpable world of evanescence and the unseen, intelligible world of universals. Determinedly, I pressed the rounded tops of the two handles. A dry click announced the unlocking of the doors, and I pushed with all my might, expecting that their full weight would oppose the opening movement. I found myself facing a rectangle the width of the two doors together, a dark section that absorbed the light of the day but allowed not a single photon to make its way back to my curious eyes. It took me a few minutes before I dared to take the first step. I heard the creak of the wooden floor as clearly as I could hear the rhythm of my own breathing. I had reached the zero point of my journey. I was in the labyrinth.

Gradually, my eyes grew used to the semi-darkness of the interior, and I began to make out the shadowy forms of columns and of further doors just as imposing as those through which I had entered. With the help of the rays of light coming timidly through the wide open doors, I found a gilt light switch to the right of the entrance. I pressed the little black button at its center with the same urgency with which, as a child scared of the dark, I used to switch on the lights in the attic of the house in Umbria. The thousands of beams scattered by two huge candelabra made me blink. A little further on, in a tall, slender glass case, the light flashed from a suit of black armor finely ornamented with gold filigree. The skill with which the rivets were applied that fixed the shoulder pieces to the breastplate, the precision of the joints, the elegance of the helmet, whose crest began from the metal peak over the visor, all pointed to the high rank of the man who had worn it. My enthusiasm faded before a wave of skepticism when, on the little bronze plaque on the glass case, I found the following explanation, which, incredulously, I read aloud to myself several times: "The armor of Hernán Cortés." It was hard for me to understand, to accept, to admit the possibility that a private collector might own paintings and antiques such as normally one encounters only in the great museums.

Once I had pulled myself away from the conquistador's warlike carapace to explore the interior, my eye was caught by an armillary sphere that dominated the center of the whole space. Almost ten feet tall, this extraordinary representation of the universe, whose origins are lost in the dawn of the school of Pythagoras and the gardens of Plato's academy, displayed, in great detail, the circles of the seven planetary heavens, together with the sphere of the stars, which was surrounded, in its turn, by the threshold of the ineffable *Primum Mobile*. Here was the whole world in the hall of the library.

I immersed myself in contemplation of the quintessence of ancient and medieval culture, this three-dimensional astrolabe, whose theoretical substratum, opaque to the uninitiated eyes of neophytes, offered the most complete, subtle, and profound interpretation of creation and its countless hierarchies. The scene of the tumultuous history unfolding after the Fall, the earth, a blue sphere marked with clearly defined areas, orange in color, that indicated the continents, was at the heart of the whole system. It was the site of paradise lost and sought tirelessly by mystics and adventurers in all ages and cultures. Embraced by the two tropics and cut across obliquely by a wide band to indicate the course of the sun, the planetary spheres surrounded the world of people. Above the eight concentric layers, the presence of the unmoved mover of all things placed the cosmic and stellar hierarchies in the vicinity of the spiritual hierarchies of the metaphysical world. As I carefully examined the gilded structure, the whole visible world of the stars and other heavenly bodies took on in my mind the form of a magnificently crafted hieroglyph of the unseen world. The ambience of Gilbert Newman's library was awakening unsuspected intuitions within me.

I had spent a good few years surrounded by the writings of the ancients, and yet I had never before understood so precisely the cardinal value of the notion of symbol. At first merely an extravagant object, a faithful replica of the famous astronomical model made by Antonio Santucci on the orders of Duke Ferdinando I de' Medici, the sphere illustrated in the fullest manner the analogy of being, that mysterious correspondence between the material realities "below" and the essences of the "supralunary" world. Only thus was it possible to explain the marriage of the physical cosmos with the sphere of pure intelligences, represented by the stars, beyond which lay the ultimate, apotheotic level of the heaven of eternal bliss described by Dante. But the miniature world in the hall of the library did not speak only of God and the cosmos created by Him. I realized that the huge cosmological artefact, in its supreme theoretical obsolescence, was the perfect image of the Duke of Kirkwell and his faithful collaborator, Dr. Paolo Paltini.

Around about, a number of wooden chairs and armchairs occupied the space of the hall, looking embarrassed by the splendor of the unparalleled astronomical object. Brown doors, of normal dimensions, each decorated in the center with the silver "N" of the Newmans, were placed symmetrically along all the walls of the ground floor. Members of successive generations of the family over at least seven centuries looked down at me, distant and distinguished, from portraits that adorned the walls. Above them, a balcony rimmed by a dark brown wooden balustrade surrounded the entire hall, delimiting the ground floor from the single upper story of the building. On a suspended bridge that crossed the middle of the empty space, connecting the opposite sides of the balcony, I could see bookcases with laden shelves placed face to face. On either side of the entrance doors, two spiral staircases gave access to the upper level.

Overwhelmed, I sat down on one of the armchairs placed around the cosmic sphere. For a while, I examined the endless multitude of details enciphered in the structure of the metallic globe. Then I stood up and proceeded to explore the rest of the ground floor. I wandered through tall rooms, mostly unfurnished, that might have been built to recall the words of the Sicilian prince who could not conceive of a respectable castle in which all the chambers were known to its august owner. Apart from the creaking, always unexpected, of the floorboards, it all breathed an air of restful timelessness. The absence of dust increased the sensation that this was a space in which the natural flow of time was suspended. The light of noon, filtered through the multicolored windows, spread through the rooms without bringing with it the stinging heat of the ocean sun. Dry, though not cool, the air inside was unexpectedly fresh for a place that no one had entered for a long time. While the majority of the rooms had doors allowing passage from one to the next, one alone, occupying a quarter of the left-hand side of the ground floor, broke the chain. The double door of this privileged room opened into the hall, directly facing the armillary sphere. Intimidated by all I had seen so far, I entered it and found the same austere ambience of the salon where I had first met Gilbert Newman. The only notable difference consisted in the much greater number of books that lined the walls, filling the shelves up to the ceiling.

Two massive desks, placed by the huge window through whose stained glass the light cascaded into the room, were almost completely covered by an impressive number of books and scholarly journals. The space between them, seven feet at the most, was occupied by a baroque terrestrial globe, held in a mount whose gold color recalled that of the armillary sphere. The carpet, in which shades of brown and green were woven into a combination that was sober and discreet, but no less reassuring for that, partially covered the wooden floor. To either side of the desks, a small table supporting a bronze lamp with a moveable arm was flanked by a leather armchair that invited one to reading and reflection. In contrast to the portraits in the hall, here all the free spaces between the bookcases were occupied by insect cabinets.

Dozens, or rather hundreds of species of butterflies, beetles, and dragonflies proved beyond doubt that in your heart there is always a nascent entomologist ready to launch into the study of these extraordinary creatures. What I found almost frightening was the apparent state of expectation of the coleoptera in the collection. They looked as though they might be capable, at the signal of some queen of the world's bugs, to take flight. The impression resulted from the art with which the insects were fixed in their places, where they seemed to be resting as though struck by a strange somnolence. I spent some time examining the tiny creatures.

Together with maps, paper knives, weights, magnifying glasses for reading, and bulletins of learned societies of literature and history, I noticed, on one of the two desks, in a frame leaning against a little pile of books, a photograph that I immediately recognized. It was the same family portrait that had always graced the middle shelf of my parents' bookcase in Cambuskenneth. Taken when I was five years old at the most, the photograph immortalized me in the arms of my father, Ailbeart Wills, colonel in the

Royal Scots, beside my mother, Francesca Paltini Wills, who was smiling happily. The presence of such a precious family memento left no room for doubt: it was the desk of my grandfather, Dr. Paolo Paltini.

I sat down on the plain round-backed wooden chair, rested my forearms on its arms, and sat motionless. I listened to the silence, against the background of which the roar of the distant waves could barely be distinguished. At the same time, I ran my eyes around the room to familiarize myself with the place. It was here that I was to carry out my work as archivist of the Duke of Kirkwell's bibliophile collections. Through the wide open door, I could see the armillary sphere. Every time I tried to gauge the distance with my eyes, I became conscious of the huge dimensions of the library building, dimensions to which, as a habitual inhabitant of cramped urban spaces, I was unaccustomed. Eventually, I found the courage to open the two side compartments of the desk. There I discovered the card index scrupulously maintained by my grandfather and the voluminous catalogues in which all the volumes were listed alphabetically in his orderly hand. Leafing through them, I had an advance taste of the treasures amassed on the shelves of the upstairs rooms, where the library collection itself was located. My study of the catalogues was accompanied, however, by a discomfort that, although initially barely perceptible, ended up demanding my full attention.

The movement of my left arm met a certain resistance coming from somewhere in the region of my heart, as when you wear a starched shirt whose rigidity impedes your joints. It was only when I felt my breast pocked that I found the source of the problem: Gilbert Newman's latest letter. Unlike the earlier messages, this time the envelope was much thicker and not in the least flexible. Inside, as well as the usual yellowish page, there was a rectangle of thick paper, a sort of nondescript pale brown in color, folded fourfold. I opened it. I was looking for the first time at the plan of the whole library, drawn in thin lines of black ink. Evidently its contents were arranged in chronological order, as was clearly indicated by letters and figures in the corners of some of the rooms.

Of the twelve rooms arranged in a rectangle, four occupied the corners of the building, while of the remaining eight, six were positioned on the two long sides, three on each side. Each of the short sides was home to a single room, above which nothing was written. If the plan was positioned with the entrance at the bottom, as the orientation of the letters suggested, then writings of the sixth to fourth centuries BC were to be found in the first room on the left side of the upper floor. The room opposite, in the lower right-hand corner, appeared to close the chronology, covering the period from the seventeenth to the twentieth century AD, while nothing was written about the room above the entrance. The position of the shelves, indicated by thin lines, was represented faithfully.

Thus edified, I began to read the letter that accompanied the plan.

Dear Alexander,

Although the world of thoughts is independent, free, and absolutely superior in rela-tion to the world of our poor writings, we need these withered autumn leaves in order to decipher guiding signs in the filigree of their veins. As far as Atlantis is concerned, we come up against at least two distinct levels of reality, alongside which may be mentioned a third, far from improbable, but whose existence remains to be demonstrated. The first is the text of Plato's dialogue Critias *itself. Indeed it is one of those "leaves" that may serve as a starting point for any present or future investigation. A second level of reality, represented by the thoughts of Plato and those who, in the shade of the Akademos, knew the interpretation that the Athenian master gave to the story of Atlantis, is accessible only to exegetes gifted with the right keys to the doors of his mind. You yourself are a bearer of keys, are you not? The sunken island may itself, of course, be a third reality, empirical, palpable, concrete, although we cannot exclude the possibility of its non-existence. Whatever may be, it is certain that we would never have embarked on such an adventure—whose almost frivolous air sends us to the edge of the precipice of the ridiculous—if we had not started from the traces contained in that text in which the tragic history of Atlantis is revealed.*

You will understand, I am sure, what I am suggesting: to continue the research, it is necessary to identify this reference point, the text of the Platonic dialogue, concealed somewhere in the orderly labyrinth of my library. In place of Ariadne's thread, I propose a guide who holds the key to Plato's thoughts: Emperor Tiberius's old friend, the Alex-andrine Thrasyllus. Follow him! In his company, you will cover the most important part of the journey that we ourselves have covered. I have sent you a plan of the library only to invite you to note the clues offered by the famous scholar. Although at first sight, any journey through a labyrinth may seem superficial, if not indeed trivial, a game hardly suitable for adults, nevertheless, the fruits that may be collected at the end of the road might surprise even a world-weary spirit. About this, the Venetian Bartolomeo, whose work you may contemplate on the upper floor, and his mysterious friend in that painting are the most conclusive testimony to the secret learning. I hope with all my heart that you will enjoy my bibliophile collection.

    Yours sincerely,

    Gilbert Kirkwell

I put the letter down on the table. Perturbed by all these enigmas, like mirrors hanging at a slant along a path whose end I could not even glimpse, I felt the need to rest my forehead on my open palms. No matter how much I might have wished to maintain the enthusiasm of the last few days, I was forced to admit that, insidious as a little snake, stridently colored, slender, and poisonous, doubt had slipped into my heart. I do not know how it was that this epistle, unlike those before it, cast over my whole being a shadow under which the criticisms and reproaches of my colleagues in the academic world came to life. If the mere mention of the name of Atlantis was enough to unleash the most acid remarks, hypotheses concerning the question of the historical existence of the sunken island had always aroused a storm of reactions of a violence beyond all imagining. Otherwise peaceable and courteous people, scholars preferred to block all avenues of research that were considered laughable, superficial, ridiculous, in a word—and what a terrible word!—"*unscholarly.*" All this rhetoric, most of the time a mere camouflage for their own obtuseness, had left deep marks in my heart, which had been repeatedly wounded by the sarcasm that had greeted my timid attempts to demonstrate that some "alternative histories" might contain more truth than the theories accepted by the scholarly community. The only real satisfaction I had experienced when I left the academic world had been the freedom I had won by breaking away from all this senseless, endless, and above all fruitless hostility. And yet now, here in the Duke of Kirkwell's library, doubt had given me a blow under whose unexpected shock I was reeling in confusion.

I stood up in a state of extreme agitation, went out into the hall, and started to walk through the empty rooms that I had already visited. The question that cast doubt on all the Duke's messages concerned their very meaning: what was the point of all these charades? In fact, the situation was much more serious.

After several circuits of the ground-floor rooms, the true question, which I had so far rigorously avoided, burst from my lips like the helpless cry of a mountaineer suspended over the abyss and unable to find any handhold: "What am I doing here?" Surprised by the cracked sound of my own voice, I looked around with helpless urgency. I would have been delighted to get an answer from one of the Newman ancestors, but they were content to look out thoughtfully at me through the frames of their portraits.

Exhausted and unable to find peace, I stopped in front of one of the two spiral staircases that led to the upper floor. At the end of the day, I had nothing better to do. I began to climb, carefully holding onto the balustrade. I shuddered every time the wooden steps gave a sharp creak. Upstairs, the walls were covered with the same wooden paneling as on the ground floor. Above the entrance to the building hung a moderately sized painting, an exceptionally well-made copy of the famous portrait of a gentleman by the Italian master Bartolomeo Veneto.

Illuminated by a lamp that threw a sharp-edged beam of light onto the dark ground of the paneled wall, the painting showed an elegantly dressed man with calm, balanced features, suggestive of complete self-mastery. His long face was framed by carefully combed chestnut hair. Slender, delicately arched brows framed eyelids raised to show penetrating brown eyes. His straight nose, whose fine, clearly drawn nostrils added to the sense of balance that characterized his whole face, cast a pale shadow that slightly darkened the left end of his thin, beautifully defined lips. The man, thirty years old at the most, was directing a clear look toward me, though whether it was one of worry or merely of questioning, I could not say. His black coat, trimmed with panther fur, was decorated with a gold motif consisting of two chain links intersecting to form a cross. His white shirt was only partly visible, just enough to show the pattern of yellow and blue thread embroidered below the gold hem around his throat. The front of his jacked was occupied by an astonishing piece of embroidery: a detailed depiction of a labyrinth such as can still be seen on the floors of the cathedrals of Chartres and Lucca.

As I looked at the face of the anonymous Venetian, a new and, I dare to say, encouraging feeling began to dispel the shadows that had assaulted me earlier: I was not alone. Although the invisible barrier of time separated me from him, I could see in the gentleman painted by Master Bartolomeo a veritable guide on my journey through the Atlantean labyrinth. Emboldened by the presence of such a distinguished companion, I was, however, still far from understanding the true nature of the twisted volutes of the search I had scarcely begun.

I decided to follow the plan of the library. I entered the first room, situated in the left-hand corner of the upper floor. According to the Roman numerals carved above the doors, here I would find all the authors of the first centuries of Greco-Latin culture. Windows of blue stained glass ornamented with the coat of arms of the Newman family allowed the daylight to flood the whole space with a delicate glow. Intimidated by the abundance of precious volumes, in the midst of which I found myself at once overwhelmed and excited, I took stock of the contents of the room.

Eight units of shelving, grouped in pairs, rose from the floor to the ceiling in the central area of the space, while another twelve units, some single, some double, were supported, slightly inclined, against the walls. All could be explored by means of two mobile ladders, like platforms on wheels, which rolled easily over the parquet flooring in spite of their impressive size.

In the free space between the shelving units, a round table, with a few chairs placed around it, was covered with dictionaries and lexicons of the classical languages: Liddell and Scott, Lampe, Baily, and Chantraine were there, plus the inexhaustible *Thesaurus Linguae Latinae*. Close by, much older works, carefully placed in line, awaited readers—for example, a *Lexicon Graecum* published in 1539 by a certain Johann Walder. All of them, instruments much desired by the archaeologists of ancient texts, illustrated imperfectly, but no less eloquently, the preeminent value of the word, that controversial visible vehicle of the invisible senses that alone are able to give humankind the measure of its reason. Humankind, or rather rational humankind, I should say.

Driven by that odor specific to collections of old books, I began my ascent with the aid of one of the two ladders. Rewarded with indescribable emotions, I read, I leafed through, I handled volumes whose content mirrored the world of the thoughts of the most brilliant minds of antiquity.

My exploration grew more extensive. My enthusiasm too was growing, continually enhanced by the most impressive private library I had ever seen. I was inclined to believe that not even the classical studies collections of the universities of Oxford and Cambridge could be compared with the bibliophile treasury amassed by the Duke of Kirkwell. The classical authors were present in all the fundamental editions, starting with those of the original texts. Any scholar could test his mastery here on the Greek texts of the *Iliad* and the *Odyssey*, then on their Latin translations, followed, of course, by numerous renderings into modern languages. English, French, and German were often represented by two, three, or even more versions of the writings of a Greek or Latin writer, shelved alongside translations into Italian, Spanish, or Portuguese.

The texts themselves were accompanied by numerous monographs and studies, old and new, published in the main languages of international circulation. Among them I noticed the works of some of my favorite scholars: Franz Cumont, Louis Gernet, and André-Jean Festugière. The collection of philosophers prior to Socrates occupied whole shelves, not to mention the works of the ancient and medieval commentators who had discussed the ideas of Thales, Heraclitus, and Parmenides. The corpus of medical texts from the school of Hippocrates, the poems of Pindar, the histories of Thucydides, Herodotus, and Pliny were present in staggering numbers of editions, their volumes filling numerous shelves. My bibliophile initiation was characterized at first by veneration, and then underwent a gradual metamorphosis, which led me to a state of mind close to frenzy. Surrounded as I was by monuments to the thinking of so many authors in whose illustrious family I would, at one time, have wished to be a member, the Atlantean library took on in my mind the form of an atheneum, like the multi-level auditorium of the theatre in Aquila.

I do not know if the right words exist to say what that theatre meant for me. It was there that in my adolescence, I had sat transfixed and motionless as a rock amid the storm of unleashed emotions, with my eyes fixed on the angels gravitating around the blinding sun painted in the middle of the ceiling—the eternal God of Father Antonio Vivaldi—as I listened to such rousing compositions as "Cessate, omai cessate," "Lauda Jerusalem," and "Credo." How could I describe the world to which I was transported by these jewels of sound? All I can say for sure is that in the midst of that ocean of invisible vibrations, the mind tended to settle in its natural place, the heart, through whose window it could observe in peace the storm of the world immortalized by the composer in his acoustic sculptures.

It was in such a state of mind that I now found myself. The "Credo" and other pieces by Vivaldi resounded in the ears of my soul with complete clarity. With dazzling speed, my imagination was modelled by all these silent sounds. The library shelves became the theatre boxes—white and gold, upholstered with red velvet—while their occupants were none other than the authors, who simultaneously, as if at a signal, taking each of their works from a shelf, leaned toward me and looked at me thoughtfully, or perhaps nonplussed by their own presence in such a pantheon, into which they found themselves invoked out of their untouchable immortality.

The hours passed unnoticed. Even here, in the empyrean of pure intelligences, the light began to fade. The shadows thickened, and the distance at which I could make out the titles and authors on the spines of the books shortened. A sharp sensation of hunger reminded me of the inexorable flow of time, which, always and everywhere, remains the strict censor of the excesses of our uncontrolled enthusiasm. I went downstairs and sat down on an armchair, where I ate a light meal, consisting of canned food and dried bread. These were ingredients that I would have to content myself with for the next few weeks, but as I had always preferred frugality to culinary sumptuousness, this did not bother me.

When I stood up, I was enveloped in semi-darkness. However, the light from the huge candelabra allowed me to navigate without difficulty between the pieces of furniture in the office. I crossed the hall and opened the door, to the left of which the faint glint of the gilt ornament on Cortés's armor could be seen.

Once outside, I breathed in deeply the moist evening air. Leaning back my head, I watched the birds flying over the volcano in great circles before heading for their nests. Tinted by the last rays of the sun, sent from beyond the horizon, the light color of the sky was giving way, toward the east, to the inky violet of night. In the same direction, I could make out the twinkle of a star, which made me smile as though I were renewing the acquaintance of an old friend. The lake, whose waters could be clearly seen across a large area without vegetation, looked like a dark, motionless mass of some unidentifiable material. Reduced now in intensity, the ocean breeze gently rustled the leaves of the palms and other trees that I could see in the direction of the cabin. I walked the length of the stone terrace in the form of a gigantic letter U that embraced the front and the wings of the building. Behind the library, a thick wall of vegetation blocked my view of the ocean, though its overwhelming presence was apparent from the sound of the waves endlessly washing the shores of the nameless island. Now and then, the rustle of some unseen creature caught my attention briefly, especially when the movement of the bushes was accompanied by the sounds of fierce struggles. As suddenly as they had broken out, so they died down without showing themselves to my curious eyes.

The first stars were already appearing in the sky when I withdrew behind the massive entrance doors and closed them slowly. Determined, first of all, to establish the place where I was to spend my first night of rest in the library, I took the torch from my rucksack to help me find the light switches in the unknown rooms.

I climbed to the upper floor and continued my exploration, in no hurry. I went from one room to the next using their intermediary doors. In this way, I covered the length of one side. For the time being, I refrained from examining the contents of the shelves, which were bent under the weight of thousands of volumes. The room in the middle, opposite the huge entrance hall, was square and free of shelves or objects. It contained the first surface of completely transparent glass that I had seen so far.

To the right and left of the window, at a distance of a few paces, two sloping ladders provided access to the last level of the library. Before climbing, I cast my eye through the huge window. Somewhere, far off, beyond the crowns of the trees, which followed a descending line, I could see some dark forms partially sunk in the ocean, whose waves intermittently reflected the luminous images of the stars. Having resolved to make an excursion to that shore, I started to climb. There was not a creak from the wooden ladders. The wear on their edges indicated how often they had been used. As can happen to anyone confronted for the first time with the unknown, I discovered that the slow pace at which I was moving indicated the tension that smoldered in my restless soul.

From the very beginning, I had let myself be enticed by the idea of adventure. A superficial, modern, frivolous thought. That was why even now I was waiting—as tensed as I was ignorant—for something to happen, anything, some incident, some event that might be termed an extraordinary occurrence. But nothing happened. Only much later was I to understand that the "extraordinary" lies not outside us but, on the contrary, hidden deep in the secret places of the heart.

I followed the beam of light projected by the torch until I reached the attic of the building, where, without unnecessary haste, I pressed a button the same shape as those on the ground floor. A calming yellow light poured down from the arms of the lamps set along the sloping walls immediately under the roof. A capacious room, furnished with a single stack for books, ended in a wall covered with the same paneling with which I was already familiar. In the center of the wall, a double door was flanked by two side doors; all were closed. I went up to the left-hand door and tried the handle. It opened into a long evenly lit corridor, bordered on one side by the sloping wall and interrupted half way along by a double window. I walked along to the only door on the left-hand wall, close to the end. Behind it was a room of some size, clean and austere, containing, among a few other pieces of furniture, a narrow bed covered with a blue woolen blanket.

Nothing extraordinary, just a very welcome bedroom with a single window, which opened onto the lake. I checked the door in the other wall. To my surprise and delight, I found a small bathroom. After a few moments waiting, the cavernous rumbling of the faucet came to an end and a jet of cloudy and rather cold water burst forth.

Once I had brought up my rucksack and arranged my things in the sole wardrobe in the bedroom, which was empty, I spent some beneficial minutes under the shower, which helped me to forget, at least for the moment, all the shocks and discoveries of the day that was now ending. Emerging refreshed, I realized that I would be unable to sleep in the midst of so many unexplored spaces.

I went back along the corridor to the hall with the three doors. For no particular reason, I opened the one on the right. It gave onto a space very similar to the first, but with no other means of access and full of dozens of carefully stacked boxes. It obviously served as a storage space. I came out again and tried the middle door. When I opened it, I was astounded. It gave access to a chapel, consisting of a single long room, sumptuously paneled, with a high ceiling, supported on solid wooden beams, in the center of which a mosaic of colored glass allowed the daylight to flood in.

On either side, the walls were covered with small portraits, mounted in thick gilded frames, of the famous Catholic kings and nobles. Fascinated, as always, by any time machine that enabled me to evoke vanished worlds and personalities, I walked through the gallery, carefully reading the names of those represented.

They were all there, from the saintly Alfred the Great of Wessex to Saint Louis IX of France, Saint Thomas More, and Blessed Karl of Austria. Their luminous but sober, sometimes severe faces made one step timidly on the thick carpet, in which silver, blue, and beige threads were woven into elaborate patterns.

In the center of the wall opposite the double door, a medieval triptych, dominated by the scene of the Crucifixion of the Savior Jesus Christ, was placed over a small altar of white marble adorned with three large candlesticks, in which candles shone like polished ivory. A short distance to the right of the altar, there was a beautifully crafted prie-dieu, whose red velvet cushion bore the signs of long use. To the left stood a single bookcase, reaching only to my shoulders. It was laden with various editions of the Septuagint and the Sixto-Clementine Vulgate, together with editions of the Roman Missal and the Breviary. There were only two chairs in the chapel, standing against the left-hand wall. On one of them I sat down.

I saw all these things as the remains of a past from which our world had long broken away. Who gives a thought today to the crowned heads and their subjects who had ended their lives, like Charles V, amidst the austerities of an anonymous monastery? What seemed truly strange to me was a hidden thought—cleverly camouflaged in the mass of contradictory and confused sentiments—that had imposed itself on my whole being with regal firmness: no, we did not belong to that world, yet all the same . . . all the same . . . I would have liked to belong to it.

I said "hidden thought." This was my most secret thought, the thought that even today never ceases to amaze me. Mere icons, or shadows, if you prefer, of historical personalities, the paintings in the chapel of Gilbert Newman's library had the power to speak to you, without words, about a life based on the excellence of virtues. A life that thrilled you. And now I am talking about something that has nothing to do with the spontaneous reactions, fleeting as the flakes of ash produced by a volcanic eruption, that are aroused by this or that stimulus as superficial as a piece of pop or rock music. What I mean is something that touches our deepest core—that incandescent point at the heart of a person who, no matter how anchored in the world he may be, constantly aspires to the ethereal heights of the Good. Although I am afraid to admit it, although I am afraid to testify openly to something so intimate, I have to say it: I am speaking about the virtuous life. I mean, about the life based on the secret measure of the hidden reasons behind our actions. It was such an aspiration that the icons in the chapel awakened in me. It was a good few minutes before I understood the unique chance I had before me: the chance to do something worthy of such an idea.

I left the chapel determined more than ever to carry forward my grandfather's research to its conclusion. Worn out after the experiences of the day, I fell asleep fully dressed, enveloped in the darkness of the bedroom and lulled to sleep by the ceaseless murmur of the waves.

*　*　*

The brilliant light of the Atlantic sun, filtered through the matte white of the window, warmed the room in which I had been asleep for more than twelve hours. The distance sound of the ocean was replaced, in the inner ear of my heart, by the angelical notes of the Gregorian *Credo*. Already accustomed to such auditory interludes, I got up eager to continue my research.

The secret idea: yes, this was what from now on would guide my steps. Once I had finished with the hygienic prelude to a new day, I ate in haste, and then, impelled by an inexplicable feeling of nostalgia, I made my way back to the chapel.

I opened the doors as though afraid that the magnificent place might somehow have disappeared. But no, it was still there. However, the difference between the artificial illumination at night and the colorful brilliance of the stained glass on the ceiling in the daytime was astounding. The blue of the carpet took on oceanic depths, while the gilt flashes of the patterns in the velvet could easily suggest the play of light on the gold of a submarine treasure. The play of green, red, and yellow beams seemed to bring the triptych and the altar to life. In spite of the cruel torments to which Christ, the King, was subjected, the beauty of the horizon of another world burst through the sordid appearances of His sufferings, as brilliant embers smolder under the shadowy mass of ashes. Who would have believed that in the midst of the greatest darkness so much light might lie concealed? Master Hieronymus knew all too well. It was only now that I realized that all those royal and aristocratic faces watching the sufferings of the divine Savior were not simply deep in thought, but overcome by a strange thirst for humility, for self-effacement, for submersion in His Passion. Behold, I said to myself, the secret of the illustrious inhabitants of the chapel. In the face of such a discovery, I withdrew, still with my face toward the altar, not forgetting carefully to close the doors.

I returned to the first room of the library. Sitting at the table that offered that substantial feast of lexicography, I re-read the Duke's last letter. It was all abundantly clear now: I had as my first point of reference the name of Thrasyllus of Alexandria. The period in which he lived, at the turn of the first centuries BC and AD, directed me immediately to the third room. Thrasyllus, who provably died sometime after the fourth decade of the Christian era, organized the thirty-six works of Plato—thirty-five dialogues plus the entire corpus of letters—into nine tetralogies of four writings each. These would provide me with the necessary clues. They were Ariadne's thread to lead me out of the labyrinth.

It took me more than five hours searching among the forest of works sheltered in one of the stacks dedicated to the Alexandrian authors to find what I was looking for. A slim volume, taller than most of the others, bound in light-colored leather, with no title, no name, simply marked on the spine with the Greek letters τ (tau) and α (alpha). When I opened it, all my doubts were scattered like smoke in the wind: I held in my hand the dialogues of the first tetralogy of Plato in the famous edition published in Venice in 1578 by the scholar Henri Éstienne. While the original edition contained all the writings of the Athenian philosopher, organized in three massive tomes, here I had just four dialogues from the first volume—*Euthyphro*, *The Apology of Socrates*, *Crito*, and *Phaedo*—bound in a single fascicle. As I leafed through it, a little rectangle slipped from between the pages. It was a visiting card with the Newman family watermark. On the back, it was carefully inscribed with a Greek title, Ἔργα καὶ Ἡμέραι (*Erga kai Hēmerai*), a clear reference to the *Works and Days* written by Hesiod sometime in the kingly period of Greek culture in the eighth and seventh centuries BC, a text in which the ages of history—the ages of gold, silver, bronze, of the heroes, and of iron—are presented allegorically to indicate involution, the degeneration of history.

I returned to the first room of the library, and quickly managed to identify the stack dedicated to the earliest Greek texts. Squeezed in next to a black-covered volume with the title of Hesiod's work imprinted on its spine in capital letters, there was a second fascicle, whose light brown binding, identical to that of the first one, was marked with the letters τ (tau) and β (beta). The second tetralogy of Plato's works contained, in this order, the dialogues *Cratylus*, *Theaetetus*, *The Sophist*, and *The Statesman*.

Knowing now what to look for, I extracted the little card from between the pages at the end of the volume. This time it mentioned a Latin title:

De ortu et tempore Antichristi, the famous treatise on the Antichrist by Abbot Adso of Montier-en-Der. Now all was clear. As he put my erudition to the test, Gilbert Kirkwell was using the titles written on his visiting cards to offer me clues as to the stacks where the successive volumes of the nine tetralogies of Plato's works were to be found. But where were all these tests of scholarship leading?

Lacking vision and weary of prolonged waiting, I allowed my doubts to cast their shadow again over a mind incapable of anticipating the conclusion of such a trial. The labyrinth constructed out of books seemed disappointing. I was using up precious time to no purpose. Precious time? What was I expecting? Or what was I losing if instead of a few hours in the office I spent days, weeks, even months just searching, reading, thinking? What was the value of time in the midst of a life in which the daily routine, anchored in needs such as paying insurance premiums or car running expenses, meant no more than the exercise of my capacity for self-deception? Yes indeed! That had been my principal specialty for the last ten years of my life! I had invented a career, a set of stupid and pointless habits, and now, when I had the chance to step off the absurd carousel in which I was spun around by a world without pity, without a horizon, without a heaven, I was complaining about lack of time. Involuntarily, I grimaced bitterly.

From the world beyond, my grandfather had offered me a friend whose qualities were far in excess of all I could have wished for. I blushed at the thought of how solemnly, how evocatively my father—Ailbeart Wills— would have looked at me if he had lived to learn that I had made the acquaintance of such an admirable person. The mere recollection of my father was enough to influence my attitude. His bearing as an officer in the Royal Scots was, as usual, enough to determine me to correct my behavior. Sometimes I had been surprised by the image of his firm and imposing face even in the middle of tedious daily meetings at work, when I allowed my mind to wander. Such a recollection was sufficient to put me on the right track at once. I would straighten my back and place my hands on my knees. It was the same now: I straightened my back and strode on at a steady pace. Inwardly, I invoked the spirit of *gravitas*, the fundamental virtue of the great Roman military commanders that were

Colonel Ailbeart Wills's favorite subject. In such a state of mind, I continued my exploration of the library until, in the second-to-last room on the left-hand side, I discovered, next to an elegant edition of the work by Adso of Montier-en-Der, the third Platonic tetralogy, bound, like the others, in one volume. All the four dialogues were there: *Parmenides, Philebus, Symposium, Phaedrus.* And tucked inside the cover, the expected visiting card bearing un unforgettable title: *Scivias.*

I recalled perfectly the Latin edition that was always on my grandfather's desk in our Umbrian house. Until then, nothing had fascinated me more than the mysterious engravings that presented the cosmos in the form of a yellow egg, inside which could be distinguished the starry sky, the winds (represented as gigantic faces whose breath could launch hurricanes), and at the center, the earth, like a tiny walnut watched over by the sun and the moon. I had learned the title of Hildegard of Bingen's book together with the alphabet, and repeated it aloud, letter by letter. As I set out again on my exploration, I came up against a new problem: although Hildegard was the author of a body of work consisting of many volumes, I could not identify a single one of her writings on the shelves in the rooms dedicated to the eleventh and twelfth centuries.

Frustrated after hours of searching, I ate without enthusiasm and made my way up to the bedroom in the attic. In the hall with the three doors, I switched on the light. As if out of nowhere, the single book stack appeared before my eyes, standing awkwardly there as though it had wandered in for some purpose or other. Incredulously, I stopped in my tracks. Suddenly everything seemed much easier. Although I had no reason to reject such a possibility, I remained reserved until I began to read the titles on the spines of the books. I felt a satisfaction as profound as that which I used to experience as a teenager whenever I managed to decipher Latin texts at first sight, without a dictionary: the shelves before my eyes were exclusively dedicated to the works of the famous medieval saint of Bingen.

Among the editions of her principal prophetic writing, *Scivias,* I discovered a fascicle containing the fourth tetralogy, the one comprising *First* and *Second Alcibiades,* together with *Hipparchus* and *Amatores,* shelved next to the massive Volume 197 of the *Patrologia Latina,* edited by Jacques Paul

Migne in the mid-nineteenth century. The little rectangular card was inscribed with the title of a book so fascinating that it would be worth learning Latin just to be able to read it: *Enarrationes in Apocalypsim Sancti Ioannis*. Only one author has left us a commentary on the prophecies of Saint John the Evangelist under this title: Albertus Magnus.

Just as there occasionally appear in history individuals capable of pushing the arts of war and conquest beyond all limits, so there are sometimes born giants of knowledge whose level of culture exceeds all that we can normally imagine. Saint Albert, known not without good cause as "the Great," is one such conqueror of territories of the mind that few have dared to approach. An experienced commentator on the most important authors, pagan and Christian alike, he had no hesitation in writing about all that we can imagine: from the wondrous secret tears of the earth, the minerals and crystals hidden in its entrails, to treatises on metaphysics, theology, and natural magic. So much so that it comes as no surprise to learn that the *doctor universalis* was credited (albeit by less than reliable sources) with having constructed an automaton that could, on command, perform the most laborious chores in the Dominican monastery where he lived. The commentary that he devoted to the mysterious Book of Revelation written by the "eagle of Patmos," Saint John the Divine, was one of the medieval texts that could be interpreted correctly by very few scholars.

I carefully marked the position of the newly found volume on the plan of the library. Then I put it back on the shelf, and spent a good few minutes examining the massive tome containing the writings of Saint Hildegard. I have never managed fully to understand who that majestic woman was whose head touched the sky, as described by her in a letter of 1170 addressed to Werner of Kirchheim. Later, well after midnight, with my memory refreshed by a leisurely perusal of the texts, I fell asleep fully dressed, still pondering on the questions raised by the fascinating visions of the German prophetess.

* * *

It was not yet full light when I was gradually wakened by what sounded like the noise of running water. With my eyes still shut, I listened intently. It was not water, but the rustling of all the trees and bushes in the vicinity of the library. I raced down the stairs, crossed the hall, and opened the entrance doors. A powerful wind was battering the vegetation. The surface of the lake was striated by small waves, closely packed and clearly defined. The sky was clear, changing its color in the east. Only a few stars were still visible, twinkling ever more faintly before melting into the blue of the dawn.

I headed in the direction of the lake, feeling the caress of the swirling gusts of wind that circled the island, ruffling the surface of the ocean like invisible fingers, withdrawing and then throwing themselves back, wild and cold, against the lone outpost of land. Having no experience of Atlantic storms, I did not grasp the warning that I had just received. In my excusable but fatal innocence, I continued my investigations in Gilbert Newman's labyrinth of books quite unconcerned.

Encouraged by my discoveries, I knew exactly where to renew my search: in the thirteenth-century room, where I should find the writings of the great Albert of Cologne. In my impatience, I took no breakfast. I walked to the upper floor of the library, and headed for the right-hand side. Here were to be found the rooms housing the bibliophile treasury of the second Christian millennium.

The stacks dedicated to the thirteenth century bore the weight of the twenty-one volumes of the 1651 Jammy edition and the eighteen thick tomes edited by the brothers Borgnet—tomes containing the complete works of the *doctor universalis*, Albertus Magnus.

Sumptuously bound in dark brown leather, with the titles of the works they contained glittering in gold letters on their spines, two of the volumes of the Jammy edition, the eleventh and twelfth, held between them a volume whose spine bore the letters τ (tau) and ε (epsilon). The fifth Platonic tetralogy. I would have liked to have stopped to refresh my memory by reading again one of the dialogues it contained, *Theages*, *Charmides*, *Laches*, or *Lysis*, but my desire to continue along the last corridors of the labyrinth made my impatience more and more acute.

With the help of the clues provided by the titles written on the inevitable visiting cards, I soon found another two tetralogies, the sixth and the seventh, shelved beside the works of authors of the sixteenth and the nineteenth centuries: Roberto Bellarmino and Vladimir Soloviev.

While the treatise *De Controversiis* of the Italian cardinal who engaged in subtle discussions with the proud Galileo belonged within the same family of writings of great erudition that included also the commentary of Albertus Magnus, Soloviev's unclassifiable book *Three Dialogues on War, Progress, and the End of History* was a bizarre work of fiction. So far, I had naively considered that the titles that the Duke had used to guide me to the Platonic tetralogies were mere pointers, with no further significance. The Russian philosopher's little book, however, offered an incontestable, if completely opaque argument for there being some meaning—as profound as it was obscure—to this string of apparently unconnected authors and works.

The card that I extracted from the volume bore just two words: *Vulgata Clementina.* Coordinated by Pope Clement VIII and published in 1592, the edition in question was nowhere to be found in the room dedicated to that period. Nonplussed, I looked once again at the card on which the two words were written. Only then did I notice a clearly marked dot right in the center of the capital C. With the help of one of the magnifying glasses kept in the ground-floor office, I was able to make out the little depression that had been produced by firm pressure on the pen and then filled with ink. So this was the microscopic insect in the middle of the letter C. Disheartened at the mere possibility of a failure that would make a mockery of my entire search, and of the efforts of my predecessors, I wandered through the hall and the ground-floor rooms.

Again and again, I puzzled over that almost imperceptible black dot. The only idea it seemed to suggest was that of centrality: the hand that had put it there had targeted precisely the heart of the letter C. Only that, and nothing more, presented itself as inescapable evidence to my mind. No conclusion could be drawn from this observation, which might ultimately result from no more than a chance accident of calligraphy. After wrestling with the problem for several hours, I sat down in frustration on one of the armchairs, and threw my head back.

I let my eyes wander vaguely over everything that came in view from that angle: the massive crystal candelabrum, a good part of the armillary sphere, the suspended bridge linking the two sides of the upper floor, the book stacks, a few of the ancestral Newman portraits. Again and again,

I looked at the same things, the same objects. I might have dozed off, had not one small element in all of this attracted my attention by its strident visibility, though it was not in itself noticeable. It was a detail so natural, and yet so elaborate, that only someone very perspicacious could have realized at a glance that it was precisely planned: the suspended bridge. It was the only element in the whole context of which it could be said that it occupied the center of the space. The *center.*

I dashed as if shot from a bow to one of the two spiral staircases. Should I reproach myself for not thinking sooner of something so simple? As I climbed the steps, I quickly reconsidered my perspective: I had not thought of it because the simplicity was Gilbert Kirkwell's, not mine. But if . . . I forbade myself to continue the interrogation. Frightened by a new subversive question, I turned my head energetically. I concentrated so much on examining the dates on the plaques of the rooms I was passing that the question mark perished under the thoughts aroused by the chronology of the library.

I went, for the first time, to the bridge that traversed the central space of the huge hall. The shelves on it contained dozens of editions of the Holy Scriptures: Hebrew Masoretic texts of the Pentateuch, numerous editions of the Psalms of David, of the major and minor prophets, the Greek Septuagint, the New Testament writings, and many more. All were gathered here, in five stacks placed parallel on this central platform whose purpose was *not* simply to provide a shortcut between the two sides of the library. Impelled by the image of the dot at the heart of the letter C, to which I was directed by imaginary concentric circles aroused by the mere memory of it, I focused my attention on the middle stack of the five. Here, in a black binding on which the gold letters indicated only the year of printing: M ·D ·X C I I (1592), sat a plain edition of the Clementine Vulgate, and beside it another volume, much thicker than those I had found so far, containing Thrasyllus of Alexandria's eighth tetralogy of the Platonic texts.

Anxiously, I took out the massive opuscule that should contain the dialogues *Clitophon, Politeia, Timaeus,* and *Critias.* I opened it and leaved through it impatiently. I was wrong: its contents were those of the ninth volume. That explained its exceptional thickness—due to the presence of the longest of Plato's writings, the *Laws*, alongside *Minos*, *Epinomis*, and all the letters attributed to the Athenian philosopher.

While simply touching a book hundreds of years old was enough to give me lasting joy, now all this investigation was causing me a veritable inner pain. I was afraid of failure. Driven by inertia, I turned page after page. It was only when I found a yellowish envelope that I could breathe at ease. I returned the book to its shelf with my mind full of questions: why the ninth tetralogy? Why a letter? I felt overpowered. The melancholy and solitude of the library had become, without my wishing, the only possible constants for my soul.

With a fixed smile, more like an interrogatory grimace, I made my way to the office on the ground floor. Before leaving the upper level, I took a few moments to examine Bartolomeo Veneto's portrait of the gentleman. I was sure now: although there was questioning in his look, it also showed the calm of a warrior before his last battle. His hands, clasping the hilt of his sword with firm elegance, indicated a decided, engaged mind, free of the doubts and unease of the modern Alexander Jacob Wills. The battle ahead of him was nothing less than the trial of the labyrinth that he wore embroidered on his chest. Here I found myself. In my own labyrinth.

Sitting at one of the two work tables, I took out the plan of the library and marked on it the locations of the last books found. The absence of the eighth tetralogy, which contained Plato's Atlantis dialogues, *Timaeus* and *Critias*, coupled with the enigma of the presence of a new letter, suggested that my investigations were about to take a new turn. Reading the letter came like a shower of summer rain, short and refreshing, but insufficient to quench the thirst of a traveler lost in the middle of a torrid desert.

Motto: Et vidi aliud signum in caelo magnum et mirabile.[†]

Dear Alexander,

As you well know, for the ancient thinkers who were dedicated to contemplation, the archetypes of earthly things were to be found, without exception, above, in the intelligible

---

[†] "And I saw another sign in heaven, great and marvelous" (Revelation 15:1).

heaven. They were not mistaken. A copy or pale reflection of the world of true things above, this our provisional home does not have any of the essential reasons below, on earth. The meaning, even the concrete direction of life, depends on the interpretation of the heavenly signs. What I now propose is just such an exercise in contemplation: you will go up to the heavens. Only there will you find the certain clues that will guide you to the eighth tetralogy.

I congratulate you for all you have done so far. The mere fact that you are reading this epistle may be taken as proof of the dedication with which you have followed Ariadne's thread. I do not expect you to be without doubts. The state of mind of the gentleman painted by Bartolomeo the Venetian is an exceptionally rare one, which only the devout can attain. Perseverance is the essential ingredient that can contribute to achieving it.

What can you do to persevere? A visit to Polyphemus. There, mirabile dictu, *you will have the unusual occasion to meet Argos Panoptes. Do not worry! The terrifying mythological figures are fully pacified. They will do you no harm. On the contrary. They will offer you the occasion to examine the sky just as you dreamed in your childhood.*

Dr. Paolo Paltini told me about the passion you invested, when you were just ten years old, in designing a Newtonian telescope. Please permit me to respond to this noble aspiration of the little Alexander with a surprise dedicated to his adult double. I shall say no more. You will find the place precisely indicated on the map. If you have the curiosity to explore the tower beside the library, look toward the north-east: it is not impossible that you will be able to spot the brilliant eye of Polyphemus. However, only an excursion there will reveal to you the substratum of the mythological characters invoked and perhaps—who knows?—it will provide you with the key—not at all alchemical, but rather philosophical—to the Emerald Tablet: Quod est superius est sicut quod est inferius.[†]

With confidence,

Gilbert Kirkwell

The fascination of the library, interwoven with the labyrinthian quest, had, for the time being, extinguished any desire to explore the outdoor spaces of the island. I had been there for three days, interrupted only by a single excursion as far as the edge of the lake. It was time for a more

---

[†]   "That which is above is like unto that which is below."

extended trip through the Atlantic landscape. In anticipation of my coming peregrination, I left the library to explore the tower that stood to its right. Inside, in the little cubical room on the ground floor, a stone staircase fixed to the wall ascended to the upper levels of the building. I climbed through three stories with floors of solid unplaned wood, where, together with numerous utensils, I saw rubber capes hanging on hooks, boots of the same material, and various other accessories for protection against the caprices of the weather. The stairs stopped at an iron trap door, which with considerable effort I managed to lift.

From the platform of the tower, I could see for the first time the whole outline of the island. The sun was setting in the West, its orange color shifting toward red. In the opposite direction, the slopes of the little volcano were covered in the same garment of bushes and scrub, which shone green under the caress of the last rays of sunlight. Intensely illuminated, its grey upper slopes seemed much lighter in color, but no less impressive for the silence in which they were submerged. When we think of a volcano, it is more natural to hear its muffled roar that to see it enveloped in a total silence that seems to make it all the more threatening.

To the north-east, there was a veritable forest, edged with a scattering of palm leaves. The chapel was too far away to be seen from here. Standing still and straining my eyes to the maximum, I examined the whole north-east side of the island. After a while, toward the shore, I spotted a faint, intermittent flash, as though someone were playing with a fragment of mirror, trying to get my attention. With tears in my eyes from the effort, I consoled myself with the decision to set out first thing the next day on an expedition to the lair of Polyphemus.

I went downstairs without wondering *who* or *what* the mythological cyclops might be. The only thing I could not repress was the shadow of skepticism with which I received this unexpected invocation—a game for grown-ups—of the world of Greco-Latin antiquity. I should have recognized the reactions of a disenchanted mind—a mind for which, as in the case of most of the unhappy inhabitants of the Cartesian mathematical universe, the symbolic dimension of things was absent. It was too early for such critical discernment, that rare flower of the world of the Gothic cathedrals, but not of the monstruous megaliths of functionalist architecture. I had not yet reached the end of the initiation designed to help me to recover the symbolic, even mystical, dimension of the intellect. After each stage completed, the commanding yet gentle voice of the Duke of Kirkwell had just one message for me: "Do not stop!"

The Island of the Nameless One
Manor
Shipyard
Polyphemus
Ruins
Chapel
The Mirror
Waterfall
Dr. Paltini's Cabin
Cemetery
Volcano

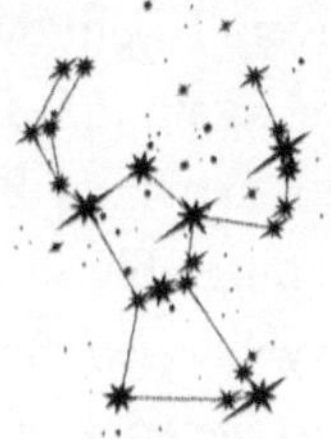

Chapter 6

The Mystery of the Constellation Orion

I woke feeling oppressed by a great sense of unease. The noise of the waves had become unbearable. I sat up and examined the vague shadows of the objects in the room. Questions kept running through my mind about the meaning of my own life and the strange, obscure, unintelligible labyrinth into which the Duke of Kirkwell had pushed me. The futility of these charades, the more or less cryptic messages, the phantasm of Atlantis, all had ceased to seem *merely* absurd: now I perceived them as a real threat to my peaceful life at home. I would have liked to have woken up in my little London apartment, with a coffee waiting for me, ready to face a new—though no less absurd—day. But no, I was alone, in the midst of this hopeless wilderness, solving the riddles set by an extravagant aristocrat. Utterly sickened by it all, I told myself that it had all gone against the fundamental decision I had taken when I had opted for an ordinary career instead of an academic one. What had led me suddenly to follow that line of my family—represented by Paolo Paltini—that could offer no guarantee of a safe, quiet life with clear prospects? What was I doing here?

Snatches of the conversations I had had in Kirkwell House, Oxfordshire, kept coming back, acutely audible to my restless soul. For sure, I had never given my consent to such a journey. All I had done had been to defer politely any discussion about my possible decision to become the new librarian of the Newman family's Atlantic summer residence. And yet the letter I received after that meeting had left me speechless: "I am pleased to accept your application. . . ." Although I had not applied for anything, it had all continued in the same tone of certainty founded on an answer that I had not given. I went over the conversation again in my head to convince myself yet again that I had never accepted Gilbert Newman's proposal, at least not explicitly. But what was the point?

Having completed my morning ablutions, I breakfasted hastily, took my rucksack, and left the library. I hoped that a long walk would improve my state of mind. I went first to the edge of the lake, whose dark waters seemed possessed of a peace that I envied. I looked at them intensely, as if hoping to absorb into myself something of their calm. I examined the surroundings, considering which way I should proceed. Although I would have given anything to have sufficient resolution to ignore the suggestions in the last letter, I could find no other possible destination. I decided to start by returning to the generator by the waterfall. I looked around me without the slightest curiosity, my hands stuffed in my trouser pockets. From time to time I kicked the pebbles with the toes of my boots. When I reached the basin where the water gathered before continuing its flow toward the ocean along the course of the River Atl, I headed in the opposite direction to my grandfather's cabin. I judged, correctly, that this way I would be able to explore the north-western shore of the island.

Sliding cautiously through the dense scrub, I managed in no more than half an hour to reach a place where grass and palm trees, still thinly scattered, almost completely replaced the varied bushes. Another fifty yards at the most, and I reached the edge of the plateau, from which the land dropped sharply toward the beach that I could see some distance away. Despite the steep gradient, the numerous flat stones formed something of a natural staircase. By dint of some leaping and some giant strides, I managed to make my way down to the shore. Now I could examine the little islands that were visible from the attic window of the library. Adorned with a scattering of vegetation and a few palm trees, their trunks bent almost horizontal, they seemed far too small to be of any interest. Nothing and no one could find shelter there. To my right, large rocks burst out of the sand and gravel in the strangest forms and positions. There was no shortage of massive boulders, taller than a person and rising out of pits where the ocean water had gathered and little captive sea creatures dashed about. Boulders further away were crowned with white flocks of sea gulls, resting in the sun before venturing out to sea again in search of their fishy prey.

Everywhere there were remains of seaweed, mostly black but some still green, surrounded by shells, whose endlessly varied forms caught my eye. Now that I was right beside the ocean, I could perceive the noise of the waves as a living voice, distinct and almost intelligible, accompanied by a never-ending breeze. A penetrating smell, in which the aroma of sea salt mingled with that of rotten seaweed, tickled my nostrils, while the sea breeze played havoc with my hair. Freed from the burden of my troubles, I felt minuscule, a mere moving dot on a tiny piece of land in the middle of the ocean. It was precisely this feeling of humility arising from the awareness of my own nothingness that caused my worries to vanish. The moments when we are granted the gift of self-knowledge, which helps us to perceive our own being at its true scale, are always reinvigorating, if not necessary pleasant.

The sun had risen on the other side of the island. The light of morning transformed the expanse of ocean into a vast sparkling surface through whose crystal could be seen the grey shapes of barely submerged rocks. Close to the shore, the emerald-tinged blue of the water was crowned with a pure white foam that dissolved into the patches of sand scattered along the stony beach. Yellow-beaked albatrosses skimmed the surface of the water, diving, with their wings forming the shape of an arrow head, on the marine prey that their sharp eyes detected without fail. I walked along, contemplating the oceanic life that manifested itself in so very many forms calculated to awaken wonder in any occasional spectator. Quite unexpectedly, I found myself in front of a low tin-walled shelter. The sliding door was open, and through it I could see three wooden boats, painted grey and blue, one of which, in addition to its motor, had a pair of oars leaning against its starboard side.

I opened my map-case, took out the map and spread it out over my knees. The location of the boathouse was marked with the sign of a ring crossed by an oar. Some distance ahead, on the edge of the plateau named

"The Mandible," a wide open eye was labeled with the name "Polyphemus." A little further on, toward the middle of the plateau, a drawing of some massive stones bore not so much a name as a simple but expressive description: "Atlantean Ruins"—though I could not fail to observe the question mark placed within parentheses at the end of this designation. I folded the map, and, leaning on the gunwale of a boat, I ate a sandwich and studied the endless panorama that unfolded before my eyes. I imagined the currents that stirred the waves from well below the surface of the water, twisting like giant sea snakes that could cross at unimaginable speed to the next shore, and then to the one after that, coiling as they traversed seas and oceans, circling the globe only to return to where they had started their journey. For a few moments, I imagined myself carried away by these currents, unable to say where they would stop.

After covering another thirty or forty yards along the shore, I spotted a slope in the form of a wide gulley, like a ditch descending straight down to the shore, by which the plateau to my right was separated from the one marked on the map as "The Mandible." I wondered if it might not be better to climb by this route toward the upper bank. I decided to continue for at least 100 yards to see if there were no other routes of access to the plateau. It was thus that I saw for the first time the structure named after the savage Polyphemus. It rose proudly over the top of the long slope covered with stones, shrubs, and a thick blanket of tall grasses. The construction resembled nothing I had ever seen before. At the center of its upper story, made from metal with a silvery shine, there was a single pane of glass that looked just like a gigantic, perfectly round eye. The analogy behind the name was obvious.

Though my curiosity was aroused by this new discovery, I preferred to return to the great gulley, whose ascent seemed more manageable than the much steeper slope here. As I climbed, I found myself in a veritable forest of trees with tall thick trunks. The assorted shrubs and bushes formed an impenetrable green net, which prevented me from turning to the left in the direction of the building. After walking for almost a quarter of an hour, the bushes began to be less dense, and the trees appreciably fewer and farther between. The curvature of the side of the gulley was gentler now, and I was able to climb it with ease. I emerged onto a plateau where I found the view blocked by solitary megaliths and gigantic fragments of masonry.

I made my way between all these relics with hesitant steps, trying to avoid the roots and boulders that were scattered all over. There was no room for doubt: these must be the Atlantean ruins. When I spotted the first bas-reliefs a short distance away, I understood why they had been given that name. In the middle of an ornamented rock, even if its edges were eroded by the countless years that had passed over these architectural remains, it was still possible to make out a disc surrounded by four concentric circles, their diameters crossed by two perpendicular axes. The design recalled the structure of the Atlantean capital described by Plato in *Critias* (115e–116a):

> *The largest of the rings, to which there was access from the sea, was three stades in breadth and the ring of land within it the same. Of the second pair the ring of water was two stades in breadth, and the ring of land again equal to it, while the ring of water running immediately round the central island was a stade across. The diameter of the island on which the palace was situated was five stades.*

Some images scratched in the rock close by bore a surprising resemblance to the faces on the bas-reliefs of the galleries of the Palenque pyramid. I eagerly explored the ruins, which were spread over an area about half the size of a regular soccer field. I discovered three places where traces of excavations could be seen, now overgrown by the luxuriant vegetation. They were clearly of a considerable age. All that could now be distinguished was the shape of the trenches, which, being almost seven feet deep, were easily visible. After a frugal lunch, I continued my exploration of all the corridors between the stone blocks and the walls, whose creators remained hidden in the thick mists of history. I moved as though I wished to blend into the traces of their spiritual bodies, which, I thought to myself, must still be there, invisible, in the vicinity of the temples they had hewn. Setting aside its impossibility, I have always found the idea of a time machine irresistible. I would have given anything to be able to go back in time, for example to the moment when these megaliths were set up on the island, to be able to watch at will the labor of those who had achieved such a cyclopean work.

Nothing would have delighted me more than to participate directly in historical moments of ancient or more recent times. I kept touching remains, feeling them, measuring them, out of the simple desire to run my hands over the most agonizing element in our ephemeral lives: time. The mere fact of being in the proximity of such artefacts, signs of the existence of human beings who lived their lives in other ages, unleashed within me a complete rupture with the everyday horizon of normal states of consciousness, yet without taking concrete form in a clearly defined land through which I might navigate with certitude. On the contrary, everything became mysterious and inaccessible, and I found myself in a state of perplexity that was scarcely bearable. On top of that, the lack of any clear, unequivocal clues gave rise to more and more doubts and unanswered questions. The only thing I recalled precisely was the explanation provided by the Duke of Kirkwell in one of his letters: the discovery of these vestiges had attracted to the island, well over four centuries ago, someone who is presumed to have been none other than Father Francisco López de Gómara, the secretary and confidant of Hernán Cortés.

The sun had already begun to descend toward the line of the horizon when I abandoned the ruins and went to my meeting with Polyphemus. After sizing up the wall of vegetation that hid from sight the edifice on the lip of the plateau, I decided first to go to the north-west, judging that this way I would get a suitable angle from which it would be possible to identify my target. I advanced through the thick grass, from which rose the occasional tall bush adorned with little blue or yellow flowers. I was getting close to the edge of the plateau when I finally spotted the construction whose round window sparkled in the rays of the gentle afternoon sun. Immediately I changed my direction. I climbed up and down slopes, sometimes turning to the side to get round some large boulder, without for a moment losing sight of the curious building, which appeared larger and larger as I approached it. When I was no more than 100 yards away from it, I discovered, in a hollow shaped like a wide dish that looked as though it would allow access to the beach, a flight of metal steps that climbed up toward the door of the silvery-domed construction, in a contorted line that followed the bumps in the ground below them. Although badly rusted, they seemed firm. Relieved of the burden of extra care with which, until now, I had had to check the ground, I began to climb the steps without taking my eyes off the observatory. It was not far now to the entrance. My attention was attracted by the magnificent landscape: the ocean, the birds, the little islands, all the elements that seemed to have been taken out of one of Claude-Joseph Vernet's marine paintings. I stopped. I nourished the feeling, as vivid as it was rare, of an unimaginable achievement. Captivated by the charm of the entire surroundings, my inner being had managed to be perfectly superposed on my exterior, corporal dimension, granting me the privilege of full presence. For the first time I was truly here.

No decentering, no desynchronizing between my deep being, hidden within, and the world outside, troubled the peace of this Atlantic afternoon. I looked around simply, naturally, as though all that surrounded me was, in some indescribable way, part of my own person. Normally, we say that we have come home when we are overwhelmed by that strengthening feeling of safety, of peace, that comes from arriving at a certain place. What I felt was different, however: it seemed that everything around me had at last found its place within me, in a space that had expanded as far as my eyes could see. I was at home, even though there was no familiar place there that I could have called "home." But it was not on a resting place of that sort that my state depended, but on my positioning in the flow of the secret forces unleashed by Gilbert Kirkwell's proposal, unseen guides that had carried me till I stood before this edifice.

I entered and carefully closed the door. I was acting under the power of the emotion that you experience when you enter, late, the interior of a cathedral immersed in that silence full of whispers that follows the close of the evening service. The thin creak of the hinges, the click of the latch, the contrast between the light outside and the semi-darkness of the interior—all these were clear signs that I was crossing a new threshold, that I was at the start of a new meander of the labyrinth. I had entered the belly of the cyclops.

Enveloped in the darkness of the room, I remained for a few moments motionless. With my eyes half open, I listened to the distant rumble of the ocean. Filtered by the curtains that partially covered the windows, the golden light of the sun transformed the whole place into a hexagonal aquarium populated by floating specks of dust that my entrance had set in motion. I could have sworn that time stood still. Quite clearly, and with the images succeeding one another to a precise rhythm, there appeared on the inner screen of my memory the film of the moment when once, in Edinburgh Castle, I sat by a stained-glass window to watch the rain that was covering the courtyard of that grand building with a silvery glaze. Just like back then, I now found myself completely absorbed by a unique and unrepeatable experience, so imperfectly suggested by a word that, although I particularly treasure it, I use it very seldom: *diaphanous*. The barely perceptible sound of the waves, the crepuscular light of twilight, the objects making up an ambience created to sustain contemplation, the discreet colors of the interior, all blended together to create a diaphanous experience—the accessible, transparent part of the unseen world whose hieroglyphs I had been fumbling for as I followed the tracks left by my guides.

It all reminded me of a truth I had intuitively grasped even as a teenager. Under the visible, evanescent, ephemeral, and passing surface of things, there lies dormant, but never absent, another being, another universe, a quite different dimension of the world, of existence, of our terrestrial lives into the midst of which there sometimes burst unexpected flashes that reflect the fascinating brilliance of the unseen. Thus it is that a forgotten place like the overgrown yard of an abandoned synagogue, the street along which the shadow of a little girl driving a hoop is projected onto silent walls, the house with unoccupied rooms, the shadowy corridor of a castle whose lords died out hundreds of years ago, any of these places may constitute the window through which, for an instant, another reality presents itself to us. Never too intense, never enough to allow us to cross "over there." Our condition as prisoners of this provisional exile permits us only short intuitions of the core of the hidden world under the opaque surface of that which can be seen, heard, smelled, tasted, touched.

I explored the ground floor of the observatory with the same eagerness with which, most likely, Odysseus and his twelve companions investigated the cave of the cyclops Polyphemus. The main difference was the absence of terror: in my case, there was no reason to fear any man-eating giant. The fading light revealed before me an austere interior, similar to the countless rooms and halls of the labyrinthine library. A massive desk, whose surface, covered in rather worn green baize, was laden with the inevitable books, just as in every other building on the island, stood under the wide window that opened onto the ocean. I walked over to the armchair in front of it, slid off my rucksack, and sat down, paying no attention to the layer of dust. As when I first arrived on the island, during my first visit to my grandfather's cabin, or in the course of my minute exploration of the library, now too I felt the need to make a pause in order to be as rested as possible when I examined all the contents of the parallel world in which I was moving as slowly as an astronaut separated from the body of his ship. I continued to seek that stability that results from the acquisition of a certain comprehensive—revealing, I would say—perspective on these improbable extraterrestrial spaces. The explorer of the cosmos at least has the chance to recognize the stars and constellations that surround him, but for me everything was new, with no recognizable point of reference. The only reassuring support remained my grandfather's research. Thanks to this discreet but firm reference point, I found myself in the position of the navigator bound to his ship by the umbilical cord familiar from photographs and films of space missions. What I could not determine, at least for the time being, was the anchor that lay at the other end of this lifeline.

I began—once again—to take stock of the contents of an unfamiliar room. To my right, leaning against the wall diametrically opposite the door, a massive bookcase displayed rows of finely bound volumes, whose gilt ornament shone under the caress of the rays of the dying sun. On one side of it were tall piles of books, stacked somewhat precariously, and on the other, a basket, from which emerged the ends of some rolls of paper.

Higher up, extending beyond the level of the top shelf, Pythagoras and Solon casually addressed an invisible auditorium. Above them, colored in blue, was one of the ancient representations of the world that I had seen in the library office. The name of Nicolaus Germanus, the Benedictine geographer and cartographer of Reichenbach, could be made out near the bottom edge of the paper, together with that of the famous Alexandrian Claudius Ptolemaeus. The year of printing was also stated: 1482. Under another window, whose curtains allowed a glimpse of the twilight glow whenever the discreet drafts from the entrance moved them slightly, a huge terrestrial globe, framed by circles of varnished wood, presented one of the models used in the Baroque period. Beside it, a spiral staircase, the only stair in the building, rose through a circular hole in the ceiling and was lost in the darkness above. Close to its bottom steps hung a representation of lunar geography, around which plump cherubs scrutinized our earth's satellite through a spyglass of the sort with which naïve enthusiasts of natural magic in the seventeenth century hoped to be able to see the inhabitants of other planets. On the other side of the staircase, a huge panel displayed the extremely detailed plans of a fighting ship. All the compartments of the vessel were presented in cross-section, their use indicated in tiny letters on either side of the drawings. A red circle, hastily drawn, drew attention to the location of the captain's cabin. A few paces to the left, beside the door, stood a metal cabinet with numerous drawers, and beside it the inevitable barometer, whose wooden support contained also a thermometer and a small clock. The second hand was still, betraying the absence of a hand to wind it and set it in motion to mark the passage of the hours. I imagined my grandfather opening the clock face and turning the key with his long fingers. In the middle of the room, there was a table surrounded by six chairs, loaded with maps and books of astronomy and astrophysics. I spotted Ptolemy's famous treatise on heavenly mathematics, the *Almagest*, among many other works that invited reading. Beside them, an astronomical catalogue, in which the positions of the heavenly bodies were carefully recorded according to the time of year and the moment of observation, bore the marks of long use.

When I turned my eyes back to the massive desk beside me, the pale yellow of a letter marked with the Newman coat of arms caught my attention. Held in place by the metal base of the desk lamp, the epistle was covered with the even but asymmetrical, legible but disorderly handwriting that was already familiar to me:

Dear Alexander,

Please permit me another recommendation, an inevitable one for a host who appreciates an exceptional guest's capacity for attentive observation. This is why I invite you to interrupt your reading of this epistle to look carefully through the window facing the desk. You will see the landscape on which I rested my eyes in the periods, alas all too rare, that I spent alongside your grandfather. Here, seated at the table in the center of the room, we plunged into unforgettable conversations. What did we discuss? The secret doors in the Great Pyramid of the Pharaoh Khufu, discovered by Rudolf Gantenbrink; the significance of the bas-reliefs carved on the lid of the sarcophagus of the Mayan king Pakal I; the interpretation of the arithmetical theology practiced by the creators of the pyramids, the disciples of Pythagoras and of the Neo-Platonist Iamblichus; the arguments for the existence of God in Thomas Aquinas's Summa contra Gentiles; *and so much more . . .*

All this without ever ceasing to look on a landscape that, it seems to me, illustrates very well the nature of our quest: lacking a visible end, just like the sky and the sea that unite in an apparently inaccessible distance, beyond the terrestrial surface sprinkled with such varied forms of life.

Forgive my digression. You are here to follow the last stage of the road taken by Dr. Paolo Paltini and myself. At its end—which for you will mark the start of a new journey—something was revealed to us that, very probably, you will also have the occasion to see and to touch: the most evident clue as to the existence of that strange visitor. Right from the beginning, I have stated openly, at the risk of exposing myself to ridicule, that an impassioned unearther of the past has his little peculiarities. One such peculiarity, springing from a passion for the theory that there are correspondences between certain constellations and monuments constructed in ancient times, inspired the most eccentric decision in my whole life: to organize the tetralogies of the Platonic dialogues on the shelves of the library in the relative positions of the stars in the constellation Orion. Mircea Eliade and Robert Bauwal would have reason to be delighted! Unlike the ignorant Renatus Cartesius and his epigones, I value so highly the wisdom and ingenuity of the ancients that I followed the same principle of sacred architecture. A metaphysical theory as significant as that of the correspondence between the microcosm and the macrocosm deserves full attention on our part.

You are here to look at the stars. Only thus will you succeed in deciphering what the master Thrasyllus of Alexandria cannot show you: the place where lies the volume containing the eighth tetralogy of Plato's dialogues. This volume constitutes the point at which our research became bogged down. The Gordian knot. How many sleepless nights we wasted investigating this clue—without succeeding in deciphering it! But there is no need to pity me: I was not, am not, and will not be disappointed. Where we failed, perhaps you will succeed. Completely at peace, in the last year of his earthly life Dr. Paolo Paltini inspired in me the same confidence that he had in the gifts with which you were endowed. The jubilation I feel in moments when I consider that you will prove adequate to this mystery of my library is nothing if not real.

On the top floor of the building, you will find the most appropriate means for examining the sky. On account of its numerous "eyes"—for this wonder of optics, a high-caliber telescope, is fitted with lenses of various capacities and even a modest solar coronagraph—I thought it amusing to give such a sophisticated instrument a name borrowed from that other famous giant of old Greece, Argos Panoptes. Thus domesticated, neither he nor Polyphemus, the one-eyed, can cause harm to anyone any more. Another priceless aid is the catalogue of heavenly bodies on the table beside you. Likewise the set of eyepieces: I recommend the 2.5 mm one.

I must warn you that at this point in your search, you will come up against a subtle trap laid by the idol of technology. That wretched demon! Urged on to observe the sky with more and more effective technical means, most of our contemporaries forget—a fatal amnesia that is not at all by chance—the ancient lesson addressed by Socrates to Glaucon: "We will let be the things in the heavens, if we are to have a part in the true science of astronomy and so convert to right use from uselessness that natural indwelling intelligence of the soul." The "true science of astronomy" to which Plato's master is referring treats the sky as a mere pretext for the exercise of that part of the soul, the intellect, which alone can decipher the significance of what our bodily eyes observe without understanding. This is the test that you must pass. Follow Socrates's advice! After you have contemplated the constellation of Orion with the telescope, put aside the stars of the physical sky. Use the thinking part of your being, which alone can help you to discover the place where the last volume of Plato's tetralogies lies.

Likewise, I feel obliged to mention a certain detail that might, at the right moment, prove crucial: the solution used by Alexander the Great to undo the Gordian knot is open only to kings. Out of respect for His Majesty, you will not hastily choose the sword's cutting edge. The true lover of wisdom can use only its point.

I shall stop here to let you become familiar with all that this friendly giant—Polyphemus—whose eye unfailingly looks to the heavens, can offer.

With confidence,

    Gilbert Kirkwell

P.S. Only humility can uncover the hidden secrets of holy places.

I cannot imagine anyone who would not have found the challenges of this epistle agreeable at the very least. The manner of writing, ceremonious without becoming pedantic, amply confirmed the aphorism of Count Georges-Louis Leclerc de Buffon: *"Le style c'est l'homme même."*[†] The absence of such a guide would have turned me into an ignorant castaway. I put down the letter to rummage in my rucksack. From my notebook I took out the plan of the library, on which I had marked with a sign the places where I had found the eight volumes of Plato's dialogues edited according to Thrasyllus's classification. I drew a line connecting the locations of the tetralogies and looked at the plan again as if seeing it for the first time. I could now see that all these signs themselves made up a heavenly hieroglyph: the outline of the figure of the hunter Orion. I had to inspect the heights in order to makes sense of what was down here, on a lost island in the Atlantic. Deep in such thoughts, I raised my eyes and stared into the distance, where the ocean met the sky along an invisible line.

The orange sun was rimmed by an incandescent yellow line. Its light had lost its power. Only the blue of the sky around it was still tinged with a golden glow. Between yellow, orange, and mauve, thousands of intermediate shades recalled the tones of the lilac flowers that grew along the garden wall of our house in Umbria. The moments of childhood reverie, when I spent hours on end looking at the sky and at the sunset, came back to

---

[†]   "The style is the man himself."

my mind, arousing senses whose vibrations I had not perceived for many years. How is it possible to take such intense delight in the mere fact of being? Although quite another person now than that little boy lost in the endlessness of the sky, I could recognize, to my surprise, his superiority in comparison to what I was now. For I, the grown Alexander, had lost what that little Alexander still had: the simplicity of gaze that was not, fundamentally, different from that horizon that now held me captive, the place where the sky and the sea meet. I sat still, and let the joy of childhood flood over me.

In this state, I almost jumped when I realized the meaning of the imperceptible admonishment hidden in the Duke's words: "The solution used by Alexander the Great to undo the Gordian knot is open only to kings." It was a very real warning. When you never meet a genuine noble or a scion of royalty, you can easily lose the good sense that tempers any exaggerated perception of your own worth. I had lived for years as though I were a king, but without bearing on my shoulders the burdens of such a calling. I was proud . . . proud and empty. Simultaneous with the sense of release that came through this stern thought, a gust of the tireless ocean breeze stirred to life the leaves on the bushes and trees behind the observatory. It was time to move on. It was time to fulfill my calling.

As usual, I first chose the place where I was to sleep: between the bookcase and the huge terrestrial globe. I leaned my rucksack against the wall, unrolled my mat, and laid my sleeping bag on it. I caught myself smiling with delight at this austere accommodation, which was very much to my taste. I held on only to my small torch. Now I was ready to continue my exploration. I stepped lightly over to the door, beside which I had spotted a switch in the form of a button. I pressed it. The globe in the ceiling flickered intermittently, accompanied by a vague humming sound coming from somewhere upstairs. After a brief moment of intensification, the light stabilized, driving away the shadows of the evening, which until then had reigned over the interior.

Without further thought, I climbed the wooden steps of the spiral staircase that led to the room above. I now found myself in a windowless space, hexagonal like the floor below, in the middle of which was what seemed to be the motor of a huge installation whose axle went up through the ceiling. The room was lit by a single light bulb and was otherwise almost completely empty. A current of air entering through the fine mesh over the ventilation holes cooled my forehead. The stair continued upward, leading to a trapdoor of well-polished brown wood, which covered an opening with a black metal rim. I took the handle, also black, in my right hand and pressed my left palm against the shiny wood. Stepping slowly, I continued to climb while the trapdoor began to open. Momentarily unable to use my torch, I continued upward into the dark space of the metal dome. A few faint rays of light from below transformed the absolute darkness into a twilight zone whose contents gradually revealed themselves through the metallic glint of a huge installation. Stepping out onto the floor of the room, I left the trapdoor open and switched on the torch. It was then that I got my first sight of that other legendary colossus: Argos Panoptes.

A telescope at least three feet in diameter stood in the middle of the room. In front of it, completely covered by an iris composed of numerous silvery metal petals, fitted together with remarkable skill, I could see the huge window, the eye of Polyphemus, currently blinded. Attached to the massive metal foot anchored in a disk right in the center of the room was a chair whose right arm was equipped with numerous buttons. Even after walking several times round the magnificent object, I was still not fully convinced of the reality of what I was seeing. One of the dearest dreams of my childhood, on which I had spent dozens, even hundreds of hours, designing and improvising modest spyglasses with which I examined the sky, had become reality. This return to the horizons of the happiest period in my life could not be accidental.

I continued to move with care, afraid that I might not be able to handle such an instrument correctly. I put all my knowledge of astronomy and optics into action, and established that it was a sophisticated system, of the type named after its inventors "Maksutov-Cassegrain," provided with two auxiliary viewfinders and a solar coronagraph. On the arm of the observation chair, I discovered a button labeled "Light." I pressed it. The bulb on the ceiling came on. I sat on the chair and stroked the finely shaped wood, feasting my eyes on the tubes in which the lenses of the eyepieces glinted. Without more ado, I pressed a button that bore the label "Iris/ Window." A noise like that of a sewing machine broke the silence of the evening, drowning out the distant rumble of the waves. I stepped out of the chair to get a better view of what was going on.

A dark spot appeared in the center of the iris. Without interruption, the little orifice grew, allowing a view of the window glass, which was sliding along thin rails. When this mechanism had carried out its function, I found myself before a vast circular opening through which I could contemplate the night sky. Its dark violet color was pierced by the incandescent heads of the stellar pins fixed in its velvet surface. The lights above could be seen below too, quivering in the restless mirror of the ocean, which shone like the perfectly cut faces of a diamond whose dark color could not prevent its inner fires from breaking out.

The green of the palm trees and the bushes along the shore had a bluish tinge, which melted into the grey of the rocks scattered all around. The little islands close to the shore appeared like shadows whose shapes could be distinguished only with difficulty. Now that the window stood open, the diffuse music of the waves could be heard with exceptional clarity. The sharp cry of a belated seagull drowned out for a moment the sounds of the great aquatic symphony whose delicate harmonies seemed the pale copy of the music of the spheres described by Plato. Motionless, I let myself be caressed by the gentle breeze that blew into the observatory. As the darkness of the night claimed its due, the number of stars increased. It was time to proceed with my mission. Armed with the catalogue of heavenly bodies that I had taken from the library table, I took my place again in the telescope chair.

The buttons on the right arm were grouped simply and ergonomically in two distinct sets: the first enabled the movement of the chair simultaneously with the rotation of the instrument, while the second controlled the light, the altazimuth mount, and the opening of the "eye." The red color of the button that switched on the altazimuth mount indicated its decisive importance. I pressed it. A barely perceptible hum was the sign that it was working. I looked into the viewfinders and realized why there were two: the first, the smaller of the two, had a reticle that enabled one to localize the zone of the sky in which the object of interest was to be seen, while the second, which had much higher magnification, allowed the detection of any heavenly body with maximum precision. Fascinated as I was at the prospect of exploring the sky with such a powerful instrument, I never for a moment forgot the real reason for my being here: to study the constellation of Orion. I consulted the star catalogue and learned that in less than two hours, it would enter the telescope's field of view.

I spent the intervening time exploring the heavenly depths, submerged in the waves of the cosmos like a diver in the depths of the ocean. I used the telescope just as, when I was a child, I used a tall box, fitted with a window at one end, which I put into the water to look at the little creatures wriggling around all over the sandy bottom. Only that now the many-eyed Argos was the means that enabled me to scour the abyss of the night, the instrument that, through its lenses and mirrors, brought the light from above closer, and projected me into its remote depths.

The minutes flowed by at an astonishing rate. When I looked at my watch, Orion had already been visible for some time. With the dexterity of one already familiar with the succession of operations necessary to locate specific stars, I used the secondary eyes to direct the lenses toward the constellation of the hunter. Its eight principal stars—Betelgeuse, Meissa, Bellatrix, Mintaka, Alnilam, Alnitak, Saiph, and Rigel—stood out brilliantly like the jewels in an imperial crown. The similarity between their positions and the places where I had found the eight Platonic tetralogies, as I had marked them on the plan of the library, was clearly confirmed. My attention was drawn by a group of another three stars, much smaller, that sparkled under Orion's belt. It was only at that moment that I decided to use the main telescope for observation. Its power of magnification was beyond all my expectations. The stars of the constellation could no longer be seen together: they could only be observed one by one. It took me a good few minutes before I managed to set the position of the instrument correctly so that only Orion's sword would be visible. The three stars of the weapon—the middle one of which shone more brightly—twinkled volatilely in the draft of an unseen cosmic current.

Unaccustomed to sitting hunched up for so many hours, I got out of the chair again to stretch my whole body. I looked through the wide open window and thought about the location of the as yet undiscovered tetralogy. I was missing something. According to the plan of the library, the position of Orion's sword corresponded to the interior of the entrance hall—but in that wide space there were no books of any kind. There remained only one possibility: for the location in fact to be somewhere above. That could only mean the chapel, where I had seen just a single bookcase, whose contents were all dedicated to the Catholic faith. Nonplussed, I picked up the letter again. It was only now that I noticed a detail that, prior to the astronomical experience I had now enjoyed through the use of Argos, had not attracted my attention. The author of the epistle recommended that I use a 2.5 mm eyepiece. The one that I had been using up till now was of 12 mm.

I took from my jacket pocket the little nickel-plated tubes, three in number, that I had found in their little box on the desk. Next to the upper lens of each one, its value was written in white letters on black: 8 mm, 17 mm, 2.5 mm. I sat down again in the chair and directed the instrument toward the observation position. I looked again through the present eyepiece, taking care to keep the three stars of Orion's sword visible in the center of the field of view, and then I changed the optical system. I loosened the little lateral screw as carefully as a jeweler handling the diamond mounted in a royal ring. I took the end of the little silvery tube between my thumb and my index finger and slowly pulled it out and put it in my pocket. Then I inserted the 2.5 mm eyepiece in its place and tightened the screw with the slow movements of one who is fearfully postponing an experience with an uncertain outcome. Once the operation was complete, I breathed more easily. I switched off the light and brought my right eye to the cosmic microscope.

For a few seconds I had no idea what I was looking at: a superb snapdragon flower, colored in the most diaphanous shades of mauve, pink, scarlet, and burgundy, on whose wide-open petals sparkled dozens of trembling drops of mercury, ready at any moment to roll through the valleys of that landscape millions of miles away from Earth. The wide open mouth of the extraordinary creature was directed toward the lower part of the sword, the point of which was so far not visible. I activated the levers and directed the gentle Argos in that direction. After a few tense moments, a superbly brilliant star entered my field of view. Its incandescent white core was surrounded by blue haloes, contrasting strongly with the dark mauve background of the night sky. I interrupted my observation to wipe my brow and consult the start catalogue. The wonderful celestial flower was, in fact, the most famous stellar cluster that can be seen by lovers of astronomy: the Orion Nebula. The star to which the mouth of the apparent dragon pointed was the first of the three making up the system known as Iota Orion. The other two were, to my surprise, what astronomers call twin or double stars. Undoubtedly, I had seen all that was to be seen.

Dazzled after the hours I had spent with my head in the stars, I ended the observation session by putting out all the lights. Returned to its rest position, the false Argos seemed no more than the shadow of a mysterious artefact, illuminated by the starlight that entered the room through the open eye of the giant Polyphemus. I was thrilled and delighted, but no less confused than at the start of this new episode. The Duke's references to the sword of Alexander of Macedonia seemed connected to the stars of Orion's sword, but in a way that was as yet intangible. The image of the plan of the library and the task of locating the Platonic dialogues added to the complexity of an equation that, at least for the time being, was beyond my power of understanding.

As the night approached its end, I curled up in my sleeping bag under the watchful eyes of Pythagoras and Solon. The rhythmic rustle of the branches in the ocean breeze seemed like so many voices repeatedly whispering, in different tonalities, the unanswered questions that my astronomical observations had only served to multiply. Lying in this place that was quite new to me, I opened my eyes from time to time to look at the massive globe that stood close by or at the map that could be vaguely made out to the right of the door. Almost asleep, I took note of the fact that doubt had not made its way into the inner depths of my heart. I wondered how this was possible, especially after the experience of the latest storms provoked by all these unaccustomed tests of perspicacity. From a corner of my mind, a clear and luminous image shed its beneficent rays on my inner world: it was the idea of a secret place in the library that ought to correspond to the position of the stars in the sword of Orion. The tip of the sword, represented by the twin stars that I had seen with the aid of the magnificent instrument, probably offered a decisive clue. Encouraged by this intuition, I fell asleep when the albatrosses, awakened by the dawn of a new day, were already flying over the shores and heading out to the open sea.

*   *   *

Back in the library building, I spent almost two days in a state of lethargy. Weighed down by so many unexpected experiences, so many ideas and guiding threads, I found that I was quite unable to make any fruitful decision. Melancholically I wandered the spacious rooms. Sometimes I leafed through the odd book. I ate. I dozed. I read and read again Gilbert Newman's letters and the notes in Paolo Paltini's diary, but I could glimpse no sense in anything there. Of my astronomical observations, nothing remained but the memory of that cosmic snapdragon flower and the image of the twin stars constantly flickering.

I visited the chapel several times. I was becoming convinced that it was all no more than a joke, a caprice, the whim of an eccentric aristocrat. There was no other tetralogy to be found there. Or anywhere else. Then an absolutely unexpected desire broke the train of these thoughts: the urge to pray. Since I had moved to live alone in London, my church attendance had been limited to holy days of obligation. The spirit of the Lord's day was one of those precious things that had remained with me as a memory from my Italian vacations. I had always felt strongly the difference between what I might call the "air" of Sunday and the atmosphere of ordinary days. Sunday had remained different. Its light made beings shine differently. This acute awareness of the uniqueness of the first day of the week was all that remained of my walks to the basilica of Saint Benedict of Norcia. There I watched the Benedictine monks, adorned with their majestic beards, celebrating the Liturgy of Pope Gregory the Great. It was the only place that was able to impress me more than the boxes of the theatre in Aquila. Only that church, today reduced to ruins by a devastating earthquake, aroused in me emotions and reflections that cannot be communicated. Finding no comparable place, it was no wonder that in London I distanced myself from the heaven of my ancestors. And yet here, in the Newman family chapel, the vague but insistent urge to pray had somehow been rekindled in my soul.

Clumsily and without fervor, I knelt in the middle of the chapel and waited for some minutes in that silence broken only by the murmur of the distant ocean. When I tried to recite the Our Father, I realized that I was unable to remember more than half of the prayer. Puzzled, and perhaps even ashamed—for it is a terrible thing for someone knowledgeable in ancient languages to discover the shortness of his memory—I rummaged through the chapel's sole bookcase in search of a prayer book. I was relieved to find the Lord's Prayer in a fine Latin missal. The sonority of my own voice made me stop. I continued to read inwardly. I struggled to memorize all the words again. It was when I had already given up any such attempt in frustration that the extraordinary event occurred.

I was standing in silence, facing the massive crucifix in the center of the wall. I perceived a presence that was looking at me intensely, enveloping me. Intuition told me that, if I were to turn round, this whole out-of-the-ordinary sensation would stop abruptly. I remained still, unable to decide whether or not to risk bringing an end to an experience as strange as all that I had experienced until then. The fruit of my patience was an impulse that directed me toward the prie-dieu to the right of the altar. Previously I had not given it any attention. Standing before it, I looked around, confused, and then knelt down. Just at that moment, a sound of breaking wood, something like a bang ending suddenly in a short creak, made me shut my eyes as though I expected the whole building to fall down on me. I have no idea how long I knelt there with my eyes shut, waiting. Nothing happened. I could no longer feel any presence around me. It all dispersed like a light smoke, insubstantial, illusory. When I got up, I had to wait a few more long minutes before the numbness left my legs, unaccustomed as they were to the exercise of humility. Like a summer shower that bursts without warning when the sun is bright in the sky, a single sentence—more precisely, a *post scriptum*—in the Duke's letter sparkled like a diamond in the thickest darkness of the mine: *Only humility can uncover the hidden secrets of holy places.*

Humility . . . What else could better characterize prayer than the attitude in which, recognizing your own powerlessness, you seek help from Heaven? Humility . . . The fact of my kneeling, humbly, on that prie-dieu had instantly unleashed the noise whose source I had not identified.

With my heart pounding in my chest, I turned first to the altar, and then to the bookcase to its left. The mystery became clearer. The bookcase had shifted from its place: no more than a palm's breadth, but enough to expose an open space between its edge and the wall. A secret door. I cautiously put the fingers of my right hand into the gap and pulled slowly. The bookcase rotated on an axis that was hidden from my eyes. I continued to pull until the opening was wide enough for me to pass through. With one step, I crossed the threshold of the unknown. I found myself in a room as long as the chapel, but no more than five feet wide. A stained-glass window allowed the light to enter this tiny space, whose only ornament was a narrow carpet the color of over-ripe wild cherries. The room housed an altar and a crucifix identical to those in the chapel. After taking a careful look, I was satisfied that they were in the same position and at the same height as those on the other side of the wall. "The twin star!," I exclaimed in surprise. On the altar, there was a closed wooden box and a framed list of some thirty names, written one below the other. Next to each name, in parentheses, was an interval of years. That was all.

With the care of an archivist engrossed in the task of restoring an ancient manuscript, I lifted the lid of the box. Inside was a large-format volume, carefully protected by a black leather wrapping, and on top of it was a long envelope, bearing the Newman insignia. Without removing the book from its leather case, I immediately opened the letter. I hoped everything would now be clarified, that it would all be finished once and for all, here and now. I began to read:

Dear Alexander,

You are in a room that illustrates the history of my family. As you may have realized, it is a hiding place for Catholic priests—pursued, to be put to death, in the dark periods of English history. Since then, in memory of those saved in this way, the Dukes of Kirkwell decided that all our properties should contain such a secret place. It is with pleasure that I have used this room, otherwise of no use here, to keep, in optimal conditions, the volume of Plato edited by Stephanus that belonged, centuries ago, to the captain of the lost ship. Unfortunately, however, this remarkable discovery has offered us nothing conclusive.

That is why my epistolary trail ends here. Yes, you have understood well: you are reading my last letter to you. I hasten to console you. The fact that your grandfather and I came to a dead end does not mean that the same awaits you! For this reason, with confidence, I invite you to consider and to weigh up all the consequences of the presence of a work such as that which you have before you. Hidden for hundreds of years in the captain's cabin of a brigantine anchored in an unconventional port, it is the only connection with a mysterious seeker of Atlantis. There is nothing to suggest any connection to Father López de Gómara. And yet, this volume of the famous Stephanus edition of Plato's dialogues is a clear testimony to the real interest of someone who landed on the island more than two centuries ago. Who he was and, above all, why he remained here remain unsolved mysteries. I consider them an invitation—I hope a motivating one—to you.

What should your course of action be from now on? I do not know. For days on end I have refused to conclude this letter without suggesting a clear line of enquiry. I recommend to you the only plausible course: visit the chapel. Then, if you feel the urge to do so, explore for yourself the brigantine—the silent witness to the existence of the man who spent time on the island centuries ago. You are free to take whatever decision you consider appropriate. All that you see is at your disposal. As for myself, I await impatiently the moment when we shall meet again. If you will permit me, I would enjoy sharing with you some of my discussions with Dr. Paolo Paltini. I hope we shall have the occasion, against all possible forecasts, as soon as possible.

Yours sincerely,

Gilbert Kirkwell

A few minutes later, sitting at my grandfather's desk, I opened the leather folder to reveal the spine of a thick volume bound in reddish-brown leather, decayed in places, with nothing written on it. I pulled the book out of its protective envelope, and then, after some time spent wiping the beads of sweat from my forehead, I opened it with infinite care. In spite of my concern, however, it was in unexpectedly good condition. On the title page could be read, in perfectly legible print, the title of the massive tome:

PLATONIS,

AUGUSTISS. PHILOSOPHI,

omnium quae extant operum.

TOMUS TERTIUS.

Graece & Latine,

EX NOVA IOANNIS SERRANI

interpretatione, perpetuis eiusdem illustrata: quibus

& methodus & doctrinae summa breviter &

perspicue indicatur.

EIUSDEM Annotationes,

quibus obscuri quidam loci illustrantur.

So I was holding in my hands the third and final volume of the famous edition of Plato's dialogues published in 1578 by the French printer Henricus Stephanus. The missing tetralogy, the eighth, would be found here.

I turned a few more yellowed pages until I came to the list of the works it contained. The title of the dialogue *Critias* immediately caught my eye. I leafed through pages 105 to 121, and continued to explore the volume as far as the final index. It concluded with some blank pages, one of which had a very unconventional appearance. Its yellowish surface was covered with a chaos of signs that did not resemble any alphabet known to me. What was striking was the unitary aspect of this conglomerate of distorted graphemes which were packed tightly together to form the shape of a compact disc with a hole at its center. No matter which way I looked at it, I could make out nothing intelligible. I leafed one more time through the whole volume, and then, disappointed at the lack of any clue, I put it back in its leather case.

I flopped back in the armchair. My eyes rested on the huge armillary sphere that glittered under the light of the numerous bulbs of the candelabrum in the hall. I was free. No other thought could take priority over this conclusion that I repeated to convince myself of its complete veracity: yes, I was free. Utterly alone, but completely free to set out in any direction I wished. Apart from a vague suggestion that I might explore the chapel, nothing had the character of a constraint aimed at guiding my footsteps. Though disoriented, I felt a peculiar sense of release, which, instead of extinguishing my desire to explore the surroundings, served only to amplify it. The feeling remained with me as I took a leisurely dinner, overriding even the taste of the mackerel, which had always been one of my favorite dishes.

It was past midnight when I fell asleep listening to the waves, which, this time, gave voice to an invitation to explore, without any plan, without any target, a land that might conceal unexpected surprises. Who could imagine a better start to a new day?

Chapter 7

The Last Resting Place

In fact, the start of the new day was far from being as promising as I would have wished. I was wakened by an uncertain sound, under whose influence my imagination had concocted a terrifying nightmare. Outside my London apartment, which looked down on the urban landscape from the ninth story, I could hear the roar of diluvian torrents. I rushed to the window and discovered, to my shock, that a raging flood of blackish water had drowned the city. As far as the eye could see, starting from right under my balcony, everything was covered by an endless expanse of water. Wakened from this strange dream, I could make out an intermittent noise much louder than anything that I had heard until then. I quickly dressed and went to the ground-floor office. From the stairwell, I looked out at the trees and the beach. The noise in my dream had, most likely, been produced by the powerful blasts of wind that shook the vegetation. The first rays of the morning sun cast their yellow light on the tops of the tallest palm trees. Strings of grey-white clouds were rolling, like gigantic cylinders, across the fresh sky. Once I had established the source of the mysterious noise, I regained my calm. I told myself that it was no more than a mere manifestation of the ocean currents, albeit rather more intense than usual.

I spent the next few hours in the office, where I set down in my journal all the details of my investigations over the last few days. I dedicated a quite special space to the volume I had discovered, which contained the two dialogues, *Timaeus* and *Critias*, in which Plato speaks about Atlantis. I carefully examined all the pages of the tome, only to confirm, with some disappointment, my conclusion of the previous day: there was nothing more to be found there. Resigned, I renewed my exploration of the rooms of the library. I was trying not to waste my hard-won inner peace.

I stopped several times in front of the portrait of the gentleman painted by Bartolomeo Veneto. Intimidated by his enigmatic attitude, I ended up being troubled by a possible unexpected solution. His look suggested something more than worry: it was a discreet but insistent reproach. A reproach directed at any viewer who had not grasped the urgency that determined this anonymous Venetian to grip with such delicacy the hilt of his sword, a weapon that he would be capable of using at any time. Faced by the labyrinth whose image he wore on his chest, he had obtained the necessary peace to make great decisions wisely. And his hand resting like that on the hilt of his weapon indicated the existence of a capacity of self-control stronger than the brute force of war. As I looked tensely at the image, I spotted a tiny detail that had hitherto escaped my notice. Placed above the labyrinth, in fact right at its exit, there was something that looked like a green fir cone. Around its point, seven little pearls could be clearly seen. Never had any symbol seemed to me more transparent than those tiny jewels. There was no doubt about the perennial association of the number seven with the gift of wisdom. Certainly this was the virtue whose rigors were sought by the anonymous Venetian. But what meaning could the virtue of wisdom have any more, for a modern person? Indifferent toward my moral precarity, the tacit message was unequivocal: in the absence of the radiant virtue, nothing could light the meanders of the path out of the inner labyrinth.

Fully equipped, with my rucksack on my back, I left the library. I could not help wondering about the concrete meaning of the "changeable" weather indicated by the needle of the barometer. However, preoccupied with my route, I quickly set aside such secondary questions. I decided to explore the beach beyond the boathouse—the place where I had seen the astronomical observatory for the first time. I have never found weather with a grey tint disagreeable. On the contrary. In any case, there could be no prospect of rain, as long as the clouds were moving with considerable speed at a high altitude. Without the slightest concern, I set out decisively toward a well-known landmark, the electric generator. From here, I continued to advance in the direction of the observatory. In less than half an hour, I found the wide depression that led to the beach. I followed it down. I was more and more captivated by the clarity with which the little islands could be seen to the left. The atmosphere had become like a huge lens that enlarged and clarified details. Without the slightest effort, I could make out the few rocks that had become over the years a resting place for the myriads of seagulls and other ocean birds. Unable to take my eyes off the glittering of the agitated ocean, I admired the play of the first rays of the morning sun as they were reflected by the grey-green water mixed with the white of foam from the crests of the waves. The branches of the palm trees on the islands jerked spasmodically at irregular intervals, tugged by the invisible waves of the same currents of air that struck me too, slowing down my progress. The fresh blue of the sky, visible between the cavalcades of clouds, was reinvigorating, and helped me to hold to my decision to proceed without allowing the caprices of the weather to interrupt my journey.

On the beach, I noticed an abundance of branches, pieces of wood, coconuts, starfish, and countless shells scattered on the shore. In some places, whole clumps of seaweed were already drying and turning black. Ever more furious, the waves were reaching higher and higher, so I preferred to walk along the stony soil at the head of the beach, avoiding the constantly wet sand. I kept a respectable distance from the water, stopping from time to time only to take a short break and to examine the surroundings. I was delighted to see, through the crystal-clear air, some dolphins, their shiny backs cutting through the waves as they advanced by rhythmic leaps. I followed them with my gaze till they were lost to sight far out in the ocean.

The smell of seaweed and salt was much more intense than it had been a few days before, when I had explored these places for the first time. I continued walking till I saw, on the lip of the plateau named "The Mandible," the shape of the astronomical observatory. Its round window, the eye of the cyclops, shone in the morning light. This was the furthest I had reached on my previous expedition. Finding a flat oval rock, I rum-maged in my rucksack, where, under the tightly bound blanket, I had put the map of the island. I spread it out to examine the details. On the plateau, toward the north-east, at the highest point of "The Mandible," a single feature was marked: "Conquistador's Chapel." There followed the long strip of beach that surrounded the height. After I had folded the map, I noticed, in passing, the opaqueness of the ocean, in which it was impossible to see the bases of the rocks whose tops pierced the surface of the water here and there. To a neophyte like me, however, such details communicated nothing.

Lacking any other possible objective, I continued along the beach at a much slower pace. I hesitated. I wavered between the thought of turning and climbing along the gulley onto the plateau, where, after passing the ruins, I could visit the chapel, and the alternative that invited me to con-tinue as far as the north-eastern extremity. My hope was that perhaps there too it would be possible to ascend the slope. There was no variation at all in the landscape, apart from the presence of palm trees, more and more numerous, which had appeared at a certain point in the space between the strip of sand and the ever steeper walls of rock. After walking for a few minutes, I became aware of a slight change in direction: the shore of the island was curving toward the right. Ahead, no more than three hundred yards away, I could see a wide expanse of sand along which the number of palm trees and bushes increased considerably. From there, I looked out at the ocean, which embraced the island to the north. I noticed to my surprise, at a distance of a mile at the most, another sizable island. Its rocky base rose above the waves along what, at this distance, looked like almost two hundred yards of shoreline. Although its left half was covered with grass and scattered shrubs, to the right it was hidden under an abundance of bushes, from the midst of which rose palm trees that surrounded a stubby peak of wide slanting rock. I could find no plausible explanation for the impulse I felt at that moment: I absolutely had to visit that island.

All through my entire adolescence I was fascinated by the journeys of the first explorers of the New World. Eagerly I read and re-read the narratives of adventurers like Bernal Díaz del Castillo and Álvar Núñez

Cabeza de Vaca and the accounts of the clerics and monks who accompanied the conquistadors' expeditions. Of all these, the testimony of the Dominican friar Gaspar de Carvajal, who took part in Francisco de Orellana's 1541 expedition along the Amazon, left an impression in my imagination whose traces still seemed as vivid as twenty years before. Faced with the existence of this newly-sighted piece of land, I found myself animated by intentions similar to those that had driven the first explorers, whether they were saints or sinners, on their unprecedented journeys. As determined as I was imprudent, I took the plunge into the unknown. I turned round at once and hurried back the way I had come.

My mind was focused on how best to prepare one of the three boats in the hut on the beach in order to achieve my aim. When I saw the protective construction ahead of me, I almost ran. Over-excited by my own initiative, I checked the fuel tank of the best-looking boat. It was empty. The second, intact but battered, had not only a motor but also a pair of oars. Its fuel tank was full. I looked around the interior of the hut, and discovered, on the wall to the right of the open door, another gilded barometer identical to that in the library. This time, the needle had almost reached the zone labeled "Rain." Unconcerned, I untied the ropes that bound the boat to a sort of metal cleat shaped like a sturdy anvil. I pushed my rucksack and the oars under the two benches, and set about dragging the boat, yard by yard, down to the shore. My breath was fast and deep. As I advanced, I took care to place the three wooden cylinders that I had found in the hut one by one in front of the boat. When I got close to the water's edge, I stopped and took them back, so that the tide would not wash them out to sea. The last few yards I covered barefoot, with my trousers rolled up, pushing the boat into the ocean waves. The emotions that ruled me reached the point of incandescence. I remained barefoot, not just because I anticipated the need to make contact with the water again when I landed, but out of impatience. I did not want to miss a moment. I lowered the propellor into the water, and anxiously pulled the cable that should set the mechanism in motion. After just two attempts, I heard a dry cough, followed by the vibrant noise of the motor. We were off. Sitting on the rear bench, I handled the rudder with minimum effort but maximum stress.

Keeping parallel with the coast, I cut through quite high waves without going more than a few dozen yards from land. In a time comparable to what it had taken me overland, I arrived off the point at which the wide portion of beach began, covered with much more vegetation and numerous palm trees. From here, the offshore island could be clearly seen. After a brief moment of contemplation, I changed direction, pointing the bow of the boat toward my new target.

It was lunchtime. The sun had disappeared without trace. Grey clouds had appeared in the opposite direction to where I was going. Grouped in a compact mass, they looked like an endless line of horses, approaching menacingly, ready to crush all they met in their way. Above me, and far ahead, I could still see patches of blue sky in among the dark masses that flew with ever-greater haste. The wind was building up. Drops of water kept splashing against my face as the bow of the boat cut through the waves. I could feel the soles of my feet and my calves getting wetter and colder. In spite of the discomfort of such an unplanned journey, my enthusiasm was not in the least damped, not even by the thought that I might not have enough fuel. It was a possibility that I preferred to ignore. I told myself that in any case I had the oars that I had placed under the two benches.

After almost half an hour, my anxiety began to grow. When I got closer to the little island, I realized that there was no spot suitable for landing in the direction to which I was heading. The rock walls were not very tall, but they still stood up to ten feet above the water in places. Having established that it would not be possible to stop here, I veered to starboard to circle the island. My anxiety was dispelled when, through a gap in the rocks that might be as much as sixty feet wide, I saw sand, and beyond it a dense chaotic cover of shrubs and grass.

Landing was much trickier than I had foreseen. The oar that I used to sound the depth touched no solid support, which convinced me that I could not jump into the water and pull the boat safely to the shore. I would have to jump straight onto the beach. I took a towel from my rucksack and vigorously rubbed my legs to get the blood circulating. Then I put on my shoes. I closed my rucksack, swung it a few times, and threw it onto the sand. Stopping the motor, I rowed gently to get close to the shore again.

A clumsy acrobat, I performed a balancing act as I stepped toward the bow and took a big, risky jump onto the sand. Worn out with the stress of a good hour spent maneuvering, I landed on my hands and knees, supporting myself with the fingertips of both hands on the ground. Relieved, I tugged on the docking rope until I had lifted the bow of the boat onto the shore. With considerable effort, I managed to drag the whole vessel onto dry land. I missed the wooden rollers, which would have made the operation much easier. Dripping with sweat, I quenched my thirst from the thermos of tea that hung alongside the water cannister and enjoyed my lunch in peace.

When I had finished my little feast, I set out at a leisurely pace in the direction of the dense curtain of vegetation. Once past the portion of sand and gravel, I concluded that no one had visited the island for a very long time—if indeed anyone had ever set foot here before. The only way of access seemed to be by a thin strip of rough ground covered with stones and moss at the foot of the ten-foot high wall of rock. I made my way along it until I reached a place where the boulders, which were now barely up to my waist, allowed a view of the immensity of the Atlantic. The ocean was terrifying. In contrast with their earlier agitation, the movement of the waves was now up and down, and they were rising higher and higher, just like liquid in a basin that is swung from side to side. The water, usually green or blue, was now dark. Crisscrossed by foamy crests, the aquatic mass seemed to be approaching boiling point.

Feeling more and more uneasy, I continued to advance with difficulty. To the left, in the direction that I would have liked to have taken to reach the center of this little patch of land, the wall of vegetation proved to be impenetrable. The bushes between the shrubs and the palm trees were so thick that I could have made no progress without proper equipment. As I had no machete, I continued on my way, aware that all I was doing was walking round the island, which could be no more than five hundred yards, and a good part of which was simply rock. I was already telling myself that I had no reason to be here, when my eye was caught by an excrescence protruding from the last outcrop of rock by my side, which was taller than the height of a man. I looked carefully. After a few seconds, my puzzlement gave way to amazement: I was looking at an iron bolt covered with a thick layer of rust.

The hole into which it had been hammered seemed to be a little pit, whose invisible end was most likely a narrow shaft concealing the tip of the object. According to this evidence, someone had, at some time, been on the island. When? And more importantly, who? The advanced state of decay of the bolt suggested considerable age. My curiosity again reached the level of enthusiasm.

When I reached the point beyond which the rocky half of the island began, I noticed that the bushes, and even the smaller shrubs, were becoming thinner and thinner. Here, I changed direction, following the edge of the wood until I found a way through the trees and undergrowth. I protected myself as best I could from the branches that grew out in all directions. They poked my arms, scratched my face, and continually caught on my rucksack and clothes, but they could not completely block my tenacious progress toward the crag whose top I had spotted before entering the wood. I nourished the hope that my excursion would not be fruitless. A fragile hope, hanging on one nail—and an old and rusty one at that.

I did not feel at all like a bold conquistador. With no machete, no sword, no other means of cutting my way through the wiry scrub, I was rather a lost person desperately seeking a way out. I advanced with difficulty, stopping frequently, especially when the gusts of wind became fiercer. The branches caught my rucksack and forced me to pull with all my strength to free myself. The odd lizard, bothered by my groans and gasps, would spring out of the bushes and disappear rapidly into the grass.

I could see nothing above my head but a roof made up of the trunks and crowns of the trees and bushes. I guessed that it could not be much further to the foot of the crag. The air seemed more and more stuffy, and the humidity was rising exponentially. Completely soaked, my trousers clung to my thighs. A slightly yellowish light illuminated the dominant grey. I felt as though I were under a leaden dome whose pressure was constantly rising. With my hands and cheeks scratched, I swam with more and more difficulty through tall grass that reached up to my chest, not knowing what awaited me. Then I saw the hut.

A few yards ahead, between the tree trunks, which were less dense here, I could clearly see a greyish mass that could not be a rock. I took a few more steps and stopped. The cracks between the planks were now abundantly visible. I was standing before a human construction surrounded by wild vegetation in all directions. When I got closer to the timber wall, I saw a precarious door and a window no larger than the cover of the Stephanus edition that I was carrying in my rucksack. I put down my burden in the grass out of which I had just emerged, and walked around the construction. I trod heavily, bending, or even breaking if necessary, the thin trunks of the bushes growing immediately beside it. All in order to create around the rudimentary construction a space no wider than a few feet. In this way, I discovered that the building was in fact shaped like a stumpy letter T. The foot of the imaginary letter was fixed into a huge rock that rose out of the ground here. Someone had discovered the cavity, and had extended it by constructing the hut, which probably had several rooms. The abundance of the vegetation showed beyond doubt that no one had trodden here for a long time, indeed a very long time.

Back in front of the entrance, I made another discovery. On the door, a succession of scratches could be seen, forming a row of barely distinguishable Roman letters: MDCCXLVIII. 1748. The surprise discovery produced in me a paradoxical feeling of banality, like that of a medical specialist dispassionately identifying the deadly virus of a patient suffering in agony. Without incontrovertible proof, I refused to believe that it could signify the foundation year of this remote hermitage. With weary gestures, I tried the door, which would probably have opened if its lower edge had not been stuck in the rotten timber of the floor, where, by the sheer pressure of its weight, it had carved a hole. I struggled with all my strength to push it open while at the same time trying to lift it by its rusty handle. The result was unexpected: the piece of bent metal that served as the upper hinge broke away from the rotten wood and the door shifted about twelve inches, while at the same time falling back toward the right. Although I could not say it was truly open, the space thus created was enough for me to squeeze in without any difficulty. Once inside, I realized how hasty I had been. The light hardly entered at all through the tiny window, which was covered with leaves and dust, and the faint rays that came through the cracks were far from sufficient to light the interior. I had to go out and recover my rucksack from the clump of grass where I had left it. I extracted my torch from it and returned to the hut.

Under the beam of photons, which took the form of a truncated cone whose wide base varied in size according to how far away was the surface onto which it was projected, I could now see an interior full of dust and cobwebs. I was in a simple room, entirely built in wood, rotten in places, with the underlying soil and short grass showing through gaps in the floorboards. The empty space contained only two pieces of furniture, once brown in color but now covered with black spots: a chair and a small table.

A nail hammered into the beam above my head held a strip of torn black cloth. After a few hesitant swings of the torch, sweeping the whole space, I directed the luminous disc at the chair. On it, casually thrown, was the most unlikely object: a tricorne hat of the sort worn by French and British officers in the seventeenth and eighteenth centuries. I felt waves of heat passing through my body in an invisible, perfect correspondence with the great waves of the ocean, which sounded wilder and wilder.

The tricorne lay on the worm-eaten wood of the chair as though it had just been thrown there by an unknown visitor. Made of felt, once black but now grey, in places almost completely white because of the dust and cobwebs that covered it, the hat rested on the chair as though to defy the flow of time, to ignore the course of history. Gradually, I began to perceive in this space something that I had felt very rarely, and only in a few privileged places, like the subterranean chapel in Saint Mungo's Cathedral in Glasgow. I was crossed by two temporal horizons; I lived simultaneously in two historical moments, in a "now" of the present and a "then" of the past. A past that had taken on a palpable veracity. After contemplating my new situation, I was seized by the desire to explore this enigmatic refuge of "once upon a time."

Stepping cautiously on the creaking floorboards, I made my way to the only door, made of unplaned wooden boards fixed with iron staples, which could be seen in the wall facing the entrance. Having been protected from contact with the rain that pounded the island, this opened much more easily, with a dull metallic creak from its rusty hinges. I shone my torch into the interior and saw the little cave onto which this last room, almost twice as long as the first, had been built as a prolongation of the natural cavity. It was here that I encountered the hunched figure of the most unlikely individual it has ever been granted to me to see.

Kneeling on a prie-dieu set in front of a large crucifix carved from two grey poplar trunks with the bark still on them, the Nameless One held tightly between his fleshless fingers a rosary, whose white ivory beads hung on a golden chain that flashed like fire. Supported on the upper part of the prayer bench, his white skull was covered with grey locks of hair so dry in appearance that it looked as if they would turn to dust at the slightest touch. The anonymous man had died in his prayers. The coat he wore, on which shades of white and grey had not yet managed completely to cover the original blue of the fabric, was adorned at the collar with lace—once white, now grey. Similarly grey, his stockings hung loosely on the bones of his legs, at the end of which two black shoes lay overturned and crushed, full of dust, their silvery buckles eaten away by corrosion.

I felt an uncontrollable tremor within me that made my teeth chatter every time I tried, wearily, to hold them still by clenching my jaws. My heart ached and two trails of tears began quietly to run down my burning cheeks. Mixed in a retort containing all the affective ingredients imaginable, an exuberant enthusiasm projected into my mind, still paralyzed by the shock of discovery, a single message: very likely, this was the absent occupant of the sarcophagus in the chapel. Alone, with no help, and above all, without following any suggestion on the part of my distinguished host, I had attained the Greenwich Meridian of the Duke and my grandfather's research.

I could not say how long I lingered, examining from every angle the objects there, which were as few as in the first room. The dominant feeling that took hold of me was an immense admiration for the mysterious recluse. On the little table, whose broken leg gave it an inclination like that of the Tower of Pisa, a dust-covered volume had been left open. I hesitated for a long time before daring, with the utmost caution, to blow off the layer of dust so as to be able to make out the text. Only then was

I able to see that it was an old Spanish treatise on contemplative prayer and meditation. I would have liked to have endlessly prolonged my first moment of contact with a book some two or three centuries old. I moved my hands with the slow pace of a calligrapher. I tried to turn the pages, lightly touching their edges with the tips of my fingers. I could feel the rigidity of the leaves and feared lest the dry paper should crack and crumble. After a few moments of reflection, I decided that it would be wiser to close the book and then just lift the cover to see the first pages. Kneeling down, I held the outer edge of the pages with both my hands. I put my thumbs under the thick leather cover and slowly lifted the left-hand part of the volume until I could lay it down over the other part. Then I took a deep breath and re-opened the cover. I turned a few yellowish pages stained with black spots at the beginning, until finally I reached the title page: *LIBRO DE LA ORACION, Y MEDITACION.* The work of the Venerable Dominican friar Luis de Granada, the text bore the place and the year of its publication: Barcelona, 1708.

My tense reading was interrupted by a blast of wind so strong that every joint in the hermitage groaned. It seemed ready to collapse. I waited anxiously for the fury of the wind to die down, and then made my way to the outer door. Through the branches, I could see a dark layer of clouds filling the sky. The noise of distant thunder claps could be heard over the ever higher-pitched roar of the ocean currents. A few large drops of rain had started to fall. I quickly pulled my rucksack inside, and then, with the help of the knife I had brought with me, I began laboriously to cut some trunks of bushes. A reliable instinct told me that I would need some good props to fix the feeble door from inside. After almost an hour of struggle, I returned to the room with four quite substantial pieces of wood. I propped up the entrance door as best I could. The storm was now unleashed with unimaginable fury.

The deafening roar of the waves could be heard coming from all directions. The rain fell in torrents so dense that when I tried to look through the cracks in the walls, all I could see was one dark curtain of water. The air seemed about to liquify, and was becoming more and more unbreathable. I found it hard to believe that this little hut had not been broken to pieces from the start by the elements that assailed it from all directions. I tried to regain my courage. I took the blanket from my rucksack, crouched down, and wrapping it round me, leaning against the wall to the right of the door to the room where the remains of the unknown man lay. I preferred to keep the torch switched off, to economize on the energy stored in its batteries. I was seized by a state of somnolence, from which I was only occasionally torn by bouts of inner trembling that were amplified whenever the hurricane struck the precarious refuge harder than usual. An ice-cold chill woke me out of that state: drops of water were running down my neck from the walls, which, by the light of the torch, proved to be completely covered in a thin film of liquid. Slowly but surely, the rain was entering through every crack in the building. A fear as thick as a suffocating cloud of smoke assailed me mercilessly. For the first and last time, I regretted my reckless expedition with all my heart. I told myself that on the main island, I would have been much better protected in the solid building of the library. It was only now that I fully appreciated the role of the metal bars and grilles that I had seen at all the windows.

I was ready to venture out when, through the crack to which I had pressed my left eye in an attempt to distinguish something, anything, I saw a terrible flash of lightning striking the crown of a palm tree. The broad leaves were scattered in thousands of pieces with a bang that could be heard clearly even from where I was sitting. I consoled myself with the thought that at least in such rain no fire could last more than a few seconds—which was soon to be proved true.

For minutes on end, the image of the boat came back to me obsessively, as though an ocean voyage would be possible in such conditions. Later on, I collapsed with exhaustion, finally giving up any idea of this sort. It looked as if the denouement was inevitable. Paradoxically, I found that this conclusion no longer aroused in me the anguish that had gripped me a short time before. I realized that the very presence of the Nameless One had contributed imperceptibly to the feeling of inner peace that was taking over my troubled soul. Ultimately, the hurricane was no more than the exteriorization of my profound unease, skillfully camouflaged for years under the appearances of a settled life. The anonymous man's having met his end in that posture so alien to my rebel spirit inspired in me an unbounded trust in a life that could not be destroyed by the physical death of the body. For what else could have determined an officer of the seventeenth or eighteenth century to choose such an end, in such a place?

I fell asleep supported by my rucksack, repeating, I do not know why, just two words: "*Pater noster.*" A strange dream carried me far out in the ocean, into the captain's cabin of a French brigantine of the seventeenth century that had fallen victim to a storm identical to that in which I now found myself. Before the tragic denouement, the captain had managed, using a piece of charcoal, to write on the sole volume kept under his desk two words that I was able to read with perfect clarity: "IN MENSA." He had just finished scratching the letters when, with a terrible crash, a violent movement caused the ship to roll over, almost crushing me against the right-hand wall of the cabin. Everything was overturned. Before the light of the lamp breathed its last, a brief flicker enabled me to make out the words on the pages of the volume, as it took flight like an albatross with wings spread wide: "PLATONIS, AUGUSTISS. PHILOSOPHI . . ."

* * *

Waking from a sleep that that lasted well past midnight, I checked the volume that Gilbert Newman and my grandfather had discovered on their island. Pallid, empty of thoughts, uncomprehending, I found the two words written on the edge of the last page of the book, the page where a disc made up of senseless scribbles surrounded a yellowish point that looked like a wax button. All my questions of the last few days came back with an intensity as great as that of the storm that was continuing its infernal concert. The names of Atlantis, of Father Francisco López de Gómara and of his protector, the conquistador Hernán Cortés, mixed in my mind with the titles of the works that had served me in the library as clues pointing to the tetralogies of the Platonic dialogues established by Thrasyllus of Alexandria. The one certain thing was the identity, which, constrained by the evidence, I accepted, between the character in my dream and the old inhabitant of the hermitage. Prolonged reading in the field of the history of religions had taught me to accept as credible the possibility of extraordinary occurrences—such as the unpredictable communication in dreams between the living and the dead. Equally certain was my conviction that, whatever efforts I might make, I had no clue that might enable me to uncover the captain's name.

Just when I was telling myself that it was truly miraculous how the old shelter stood up to the hurricane, one of the boards of the roof was torn from its place. I left the outer room and retired to the hollow in the rock where the Nameless One had ended his earthly journey, and closed the door. By the gradually fading light of the torch, I began to write down the chronicle of my Atlantic adventures. I was prepared to do anything to leave Gilbert Newman a sign of the discovery I had made. When I fell asleep again I was trembling, enveloped in the darkness that was only dispersed by the lightning flashes whose incandescent brilliance was projected in parallel lines of light through the cracks in the walls. The peace I had regained granted me the most profound and restful sleep. And it was the same peace that, along with the light shining into the hermitage, woke me.

Numb, unable to feel my arms or my legs, I opened my eyes and listened tensely for a good few minutes. Only the relentless roar of the waves could be heard. The noise of the rain and the thunder had ceased. A pale, timid light entered the room in the rock. The walls were still damp, but they were no longer dripping with the streams of water that had been constantly running down them. The storm had passed. And I was alive. Alive and hungry.

When I opened the door, I found where the light was coming from: the right-hand wall had completely collapsed, pulling down with it about half the boards of the roof. There was an unobstructed view of the sky, still crossed by clouds racing before the strong wind. Sitting among the debris of the first room, I ate the few provisions that were left in my rucksack and drank the last portion of tea. I thought about the way back and kept a double portion of water in case of need. Returning for the last time to the room under the rock, I carefully wrapped the volume of meditations that lay beside the remains of the anonymous man. At the risk of destroying the tricorne, I also put it into a light waterproof bag that I was carrying on me. The rosary I did not touch. The two objects I was taking were sufficient to prove the existence of the shelter and of its occupant.

Outside, I looked with astonishment at the devastation caused by the hurricane. Battered, contorted, in many cases stripped of the green ornament of their rich foliage, those bushes that had not simply been uprooted were twisted in all directions. Some of the palm trees were almost bent down to the ground, their huge leaves hanging like inert arms. The shrubs and tall grass were also severely battered and in places broken, leaving many empty spaces among them.

My way back, in the direction toward where I believed would be found the gap between rocks in which I had abandoned the boat, took the sinuous form of a labyrinth of vegetation. I jumped over trunks and branches, made my way round shrubs and rocks, zig-zagged along a chaotic route, leaving footprints that immediately filled with water. The soil of the island was sodden. It often seemed as though I were stepping on a sponge hidden under the green-brown cover of the grass and remaining wood. After a few dozen yards, I found myself in front of an opening through which I could see the grey rocks at the edge of the island. When I reached the limestone excrescences, I saw that the stretch where I had landed began not far off. To my despair, however, the boat was nowhere to be seen. With my heart pounding in my chest, I went down to the water's side and looked in all directions. Although I could feel my legs folding under me, I refused to give up. Then a sudden impulse pushed me back, to the place where I had come up against the impenetrable curtain of vegetation. Without knowing why, I set off in the opposite direction to that which I had taken the first time. After just a few steps, a splendid sight dispelled all fear from my soul: stuck among some bushes, whose luxuriant crowns made them look like crazed theatrical characters, my boat lay overturned.

I put my rucksack down and hurried toward it. Dangling at the end of its chain, the cap of the fuel tank swung freely with each breath of wind. There was not a drop of gasoline left inside. Fortunately the oars, tied together, were lying there, half covered by the tangle of vegetation under the boat. After much effort, in which the most difficult part was extracting the boat from the grip of the bushes, I managed to lay it again on the surface of the water. With no further delay, I set off toward the library island, rowing with all my might.

Unaccustomed to the effort involved in continuously plying the oars, I had to stop frequently and rest my weary arms on my knees. However, the most frightening moment was when I felt for the first time the force of the currents driving me off the straight line along which I hoped to reach the safety of my destination as quickly as possible. After more than two hours of continuous rowing, I realized that I was not getting any closer to the island. In fact, I was veering to the left. As far as I could see, I was following the course of a current that ran almost parallel to the shore. The current was carrying me faster and faster. It took only a few strokes of the oars to keep the boat straight, but propelled solely by the movement of my arms, without the power of its motor, it could never pierce the line of force traced by the invisible flow of the subterranean waters. Resigned, I continued to row, waiting to see what was to come.

Settled into strata floating at different heights, the clouds looked as though they were grouped according their variations of grey, which ranged from almost white to black. At intervals, the wind burst out in powerful gusts, followed by moments of complete calm. The waves were quite high, but posed no real danger to the boat. The only cause for worry remained the current, from which I had no way of escaping by my own strength. Already I had passed the end of the island, and was gradually drifting further away from the coast. With my last reserves of strength, I made one last attempt to break diagonally out of the flow that was carrying me out to sea, but I was easily beaten by an adversary unconquerable in its liquid environment. I gave up looking at the island, which was steadily getting smaller. Lying back, I gazed absentmindedly at the clouds, not wishing to know what my chances of survival were, alone, out in the ocean. I was lying there drained of energy when I felt a great shudder and a sudden change of direction. Lifting myself up on my elbows, I saw a line of white foam that seemed to be separating the waters, and along which countless eddies were furiously rotating, some small, others several times larger than the length of the boat. It was one of these eddies that had caused the vessel to change direction. As far as I could see, at least two different currents had met, causing the strange aquatic phenomenon. I immediately realized what an unexpected chance I had.

I handled the oars with great care, aware that it was on these instruments that my salvation depended. To start with, I succeeded in moving parallel with the island. After a while, I could see that I had already been plucked out of the course of the current that was carrying me out to sea. With my heart in my mouth, I continued to keep watch, until I reached an area where the flow of the current slowed down, although it was still perceptible. They say that fear can give you unsuspected powers. Indeed it can. I rowed at that crucial moment with all my strength, until I managed to turn toward the island. When I had to stop, because of the numbness that had overtaken my arms, I observed that only the waves were moving the vessel. I had escaped. I was no more than two hundred yards from the place where the River Atl flowed out into the ocean.

The daylight was starting to fade when I reached the shore. I pulled the boat onto the sand and then lay down among the clumps of seaweed, branches, dead fish, and dead birds that the storm had scattered all around. The torrent of emotions of the last few days had dried up. I would never have thought myself capable of facing such an experience.

I went to the waters of the river and spent some time washing myself. Reinvigorated and at ease, I set off for my grandfather's cabin, sizing up, as I went, the extent of the damage the hurricane had left behind it. Branches, shrubs, bushes, sometimes even whole palm trees lay all around.

Largely untouched by the effects of the storm, the cabin looked just as it had when I first arrived, apart from being covered in places with branches and other material carried by the wind. The platform too was full of fragments of vegetation and the carcasses of birds cruelly brought down by the flying debris. I contented myself with clearing the space in front of the door, and then I went in. If the daily routine and our inability to keep the gift of contemplation in the midst of our useless agitation prevent us from grasping the essential, it is in such moments as this present arrival that the significance is revealed to us of that space that we call, so simply, "home." In my case, only now did I understand, at least partially, the profound reasons for which the ancient Greeks gave such importance to the hearth, the sacred fire, words that denote a single reality, that of the domestic sanctuary. I had only once visited Paolo Paltini's refuge, and

I entered again now with a joy that may be considered, without any risk of hasty exaggeration, true bliss. I was home again.

With great care, I took the tricorne out of the waterproof bag and placed it on the desk together with the battered book of the meditations of the Venerable Luis de Granada and the third volume of Plato's dialogues edited by Stephanus. Sitting on the edge of a chair, I looked at them in silence. They were the palpable signs of my journey to the island of the Nameless One, testimonies to a past that stubbornly defied the present by its very existence.

Few things would have delighted me more than this escape from under the fatal rule of the god Chronos. Lost in contemplation of artefacts from another age of history, I achieved a certain disconnection from what was going on around me, a disconnection that offered me a delicate, solemn enchantment, barely perceptible. Sometimes, such a state was crystallized into inner images. Unfortunately, despite all my efforts, these could not be fixed for more than a few seconds. But no—now it was not a matter just of mere experiences of withdrawal from the waves of present time. I suspected the presence of an unaccustomed gift: the spirit of the anonymous Venetian in Bartolomeo's painting. This sense of inner strength was the fruit of my discovery of the Nameless One's hermitage. It was I, Alexander Jacob Wills, who was to carry forward the research of the Duke of Kirkwell and his friend, Dr. Paolo Paltini. An unfailing intuition told me that this was the nature of the thoughts that animated my father, Ailbeart Wills, colonel in the Royal Scots, every time he took part in the military parades that I watched with delight as a child. If I were to try to express adequately my state in those moments, I would say something simple, so simple that it is very hard, if not completely impossible, to understand. I had found my place. Just as he who is in this moment writing the story that you are reading can say that he has found his place: his place as a writer, I should say.

The dream was over. I was absolutely present in all that I experienced in the midst of the watery desert. The world of the past, the world of my career of the last few years, the Italian world, the London world, to which I was bound by so many invisible threads, evaporated like fog dispersed by the first rays of dawn. Outside it was dark. And I was standing in the full light of the sun. My whole quest shone under the light of meaning that indicated the way that I was to take. When I went back over the stages of my investigations so far, the next stage presented itself to my mind with the freshness of the landscapes in Raphael's paintings. I had received from the Nameless One a sign that could not be more conclusive. Two Latin words. Written with charcoal on the margin of the last page of the volume containing the dialogue *Critias*, they must certainly conceal a message. A message that showed me the direction in which I must go.

I opened the book and looked, one more time, at the succinct, cryptic text: "IN MENSA"—"On the table." Just that and nothing more. I was intrigued by the fact that the only thing I had seen on the captain's desk in my dream had been precisely this volume that was now in front of me. I already knew from Dr. Paltini's journal that the volume containing the dialogue *Critias* had been found on a table in the old brigantine hidden in a cave at the heart of the volcano. I must visit the ship and try to locate the table and what else I might find there.

From the journal, I had learned that the original means of access, from the ocean by way of a natural tunnel that passed through the southern slope of the volcano, had subsided long ago. Another way must have been discovered. Although Gilbert Newman had said nothing to me about all this, he had, in his last letter, encouraged me to visit the chapel. I suspected that I would find the next clue there.

Visited by all these thoughts, I felt deeply ashamed of my moments of lack of trust in such a generous host. Like the soldier who only truly knows his severe officer when the latter saves his life under the first enemy attack, only now did I understand that the purpose of all his riddles had been to tear me away from my attachment to the life I had been living in recent years. The pedagogy he had adopted was as simple as could be. You never learn so well as when you yourself write the manual.

The trial of the labyrinth had undoubtedly turned me into a participant with considerable knowledge and full commitment to all the investigations of my absent hosts. Having lost his trusted friend, Dr. Paolo Paltini, the Duke had promoted me from the very start to the rank of governor of the Atlantean island. Perhaps he had seen in Alexander Jacob Wills, the wanderer who did not know his calling, the presence of an authentic vocation. Perhaps.

I fell asleep, happy, in the moment in which I was repeating that it was time for me to investigate the chapel. Far from being a mere piece of advice that I was blindly following, it was the decision taken by none other than the anonymous Venetian in Master Bartolomeo's painting. There, at the boundary between waking and dreaming, it seemed to me, for a brief but intense moment, that I was he . . .

Chapter 8

Journey to the Center of the Volcano

More than a week had passed since that night in which I had felt the icy draft of death insinuating itself between the blasts of the hurricane that shook the ocean and all that was on it in this region of the world. The *éminence grise* of all catastrophic events, usually detested with horror, desired only by saints and by those in despair—its touch had given me a lesson that was completed by the worthy end of the Nameless One. I recalled all too well the words uttered by Socrates before he died: that philosophy is nothing other than preparation for death and the passage into the state that follows it. During the night, I sometimes touched my forehead, my face, my cheeks, to convince myself that I was really alive. I had survived.

As an involuntary spectator of my own progress along the tortuous path through the labyrinth of the Atlantean island, I continued to write out of the desire to record, from the position of a witness of my own life, the meanders of a quest whose conclusion remained veiled in mystery. Relieved that the cabin had suffered only minor damage, I spent a few hours clearing away the branches and various plant remains that lay scattered all around. I also gathered the remains of the dead birds in a hollow at the foot of a rock, and then covered them with a thick layer of earth and stones. The cries of the flocks of winged survivors could be heard everywhere. Life went on. The sky remained brooding, but the wind had died down, with only sporadic short gusts, as in my first days on the island.

After managing to set down on paper all that had happened so far, I realized that a visit to the island's chapel was a pressing necessity. Once again, following the guiding thread had got me caught up in the whirlpool of unanswered questions. I fell asleep with my head buzzing with hazy memories and various hypotheses. Every time, without exception, I arrived at the same conclusion. I had to investigate the brigantine to establish the meaning of the words "IN MENSA" that had been transmitted to me in such uncommon circumstances.

In the midst of such restless thoughts, the rapid drumbeat of the raindrops caught my attention. The needle of the barometer by the door pointed at the boundary region between "Rain" and "Changeable." The memory of the hurricane from which I had only narrowly escaped returned vividly to my mind. I calmed myself with the thought that here, unlike on the little island of the hermitage, I was safe. Sitting on the chair in front of the desk, I examined the forest through the tear-spattered window. Through the thin curtain of rain, I could just make out the banks of the River Atl.

Without haste, I ate my frugal lunch and watched the curls of mist rolling above trees whose shaken crowns still bore the marks of the storm. More powerful than usual, the noise of the waves mixed with the pattering of the rain. The mixture produced a monotonous symphony that heightened my feeling of loneliness. A state of somnolence came, along with an overpowering sense of exhaustion—not the consequence of any exceptional physical effort, but rather an inner weariness that was no more than the sign that the perpetual state of stress that for years and years had deprived my inner double of profound rest was now gone. Freed from all this extreme tension, I could feel myself sinking into the depths of my soul, beyond which lay another world. The world from which the Nameless One had sent the words that were meant to guide me.

*   *   *

After a few hours of restful sleep, I slowly opened my eyes. I looked in the direction of the tricorne on the desk. The sunlight was drawing clearly defined shapes on the floor of the cabin. The cries of the albatrosses seemed more intense than usual. I got up. Still feeling numb, I did a few torso and arm rotations. Then I opened the door and looked out on a sky covered by thousands of white birds. Most of them were flying toward the ocean. Here and there against the vast expanse of blue, I could see clouds, their forms rapidly changing under the cold touch of the high-altitude currents of air. The sun had triumphed. The barometer now indicated, unequivocally, "Fair." Without delay, but at the same time without haste, I wrapped the precious volume of Plato and placed it in my rucksack. I left on the desk only the anonymous captain's hat and his Spanish book of meditations. I realized that the text of the dialogue *Critias* edited by Henricus Stephanus was the silent witness of my explorations. Its content, the fabulous world of Atlantis, was the source that cast ahead of me the light necessary for my quest.

I set out wishing to see again the beach where I had landed on my first day, and decided to follow the course of the River Atl till it flowed out into the ocean. When I got to the shore, I looked at the water, which was covered with seagulls swimming, flying, and landing with deafening cries. Not too far away, the backs of a few dolphins glittered along the shoreline in the orange sunlight. Everything was reborn.

The number of tree trunks and branches lying around was astounding. Even some rocks of medium size had been dislodged by the fury of the hurricane and now lay flat a good few yards from their original locations. The landscape was completely changed compared with what I had seen on my first excursion, almost three weeks earlier. I approached the pontoon and rediscovered it with the same joy with which one greets an old friend.

Wrenched from its place in front of the wooden steps, the mailbox lay on its side against a heap of seaweed. It was the white ribbon with which Gilbert Newman had marked it—to attract my attention on my arrival to the letters it contained —that enabled me to find it. I put down my rucksack by the steps and did my best to fix it in a vertical position again. As I climbed back after completing this action, I noticed that all the balustrades along the platform leading to the mooring point had gone. Everywhere there were shells and pebbles left behind by the gigantic waves.

The leaves of the palm trees round about hung feebly down toward the green water at their feet. The special elasticity of this species had saved the great majority of young trees from being uprooted. Only two tall palms, so close they seemed almost stuck together, lay flat on the ground like dandelions discarded after their clocks had been half blown away. The shrubs that dominated the wide stretch of ground close to the rocky wall of "The Mandible" had been devastated mercilessly. And yet now the traces left by the hurricane were fading under the infusion of freshness from the sky, whose late shades, tending toward mauve, contrasted with the white or light grey of the countless birds that crossed it ceaselessly.

After a while, I headed toward the end of "The Mandible" plateau, to the left from the pontoon. The vegetation-covered slope allowed access to the higher ground beyond the rocks, which it would be difficult to climb anywhere else. When I reached its base, I saw at close quarters the briers and bushes that before the storm had formed an impenetrable curtain. Now all the vegetation was very much thinned. Leaning on my walking stick, I began to climb, often getting caught on the stalks of young and elastic offshoots or dwarf bushes. Scratched and sweating, I finally managed to reach the lip of "The Mandible." To the west, the megalithic ruins that I had already visited could be clearly seen. To my right, in the direction where I ought to be able to see the chapel, a cluster of tall rocks blocked what would otherwise have been a wide view of the whole north-eastern part of the plateau. I headed toward them.

I climbed up and down slopes and crossed gulleys full of long grass and numerous stones. The first stars were beginning to come out. The moon appeared on the horizon. The ocean breeze blew through the grass, turning the plateau into a land replica of the ocean surface ceaselessly furrowed by waves. Only when I had slipped between the rocks that rose up like huge teeth was I finally able to see the chapel.

The light-colored stone of its walls made it easy to spot from a distance. I estimated that it could be no more than three hundred yards away. I could see that it was a building in Gothic style and surmounted by a black *pinnaculum*. It was framed by some trees much taller than any I had seen so far. Their crowns, too, were shaken and contorted. Around the paved platform where it stood, I could see a parapet of stone blocks, which continued on either side of the steps leading up to the chapel.

I climbed toward it with my eyes fixed on the massive door. On either side there was an ogival window covered with wire mesh. Above, a Spanish cross was carved directly in the stones of the façade. When I stood before the door, I stopped. I put my rucksack down and took a few steps on the platform. The moonlight revealed an unexpected presence: stock still, an iguana held up its head as though sniffing the scents of the night. Its wrinkled, ageless appearance transformed it into a variant on the imperishability of the stone from which it seemed to have broken away. Only the rhythmic beat of the membranes by its ears showed that it was alive. Without turning its reddish eyes in my direction, it disappeared through a gap between the stone supports of the parapet.

I continued my exploration, advancing along the left-hand side of the platform. Behind the chapel, the plateau came to an end just a few yards beyond the parapet. The full extent of the beach, which was surprisingly long and covered for its entire width with palm trees, could now be appreciated. To the north, the island of the Nameless One had the appearance of a sharply defined dark shadow. All around, the ocean looked as though it were made up of tens of thousands of mobile mirrors, constantly reflecting the brilliance of the full moon in a mysterious play of light. Surrounded by such a landscape, it seemed to me that I was dreaming. Only after a few minutes did I pull myself together and return with measured steps to the area in front of the entrance.

The chapel was at the most thirty feet long, and was built, like a Gothic cathedral, in the shape of a cross. I took in my right hand the metal ring, which was at the height of my chest, leaned my shoulder against the door, and pushed, slowly, with my full weight.

The door began to move with a deep, dull, scraping sound that it seemed would never end. Only by giving it a second shove with all my strength did I manage to open it wide. In the middle of the wall facing the door, three tall rectangles ending in pointed arches allowed the rays of moonlight to enter through monochrome glass as blue as the night sky. Through the openings giving access to the two side extensions, windows of the same form could also be seen, set in each of the exterior walls. Even once my eyes had got accustomed to the semi-darkness, I continued to look in from the threshold.

The enclosed, dry air was as one might expect in a space lacking any invisible vibration that might have given away the presence of an occupant, even one dead for hundreds of years. In the center, I could make out a massive parallelepipedal form, an object that absorbed the light without revealing its identity to prying eyes. I switched on my torch. The floor was covered with large mosaic plaques, their geometric designs colored in shades of brown and beige. The walls were plain, without any decoration, and supported only four black torches, the smoke of which had left traces of an undeterminable age. Under each of these old sources of illumination, there was a stone bench, fixed to the wall close to the corners of the space. Thick timber rafters supported the steep roof. A single low step had to be climbed to stand before the cenotaph. Although I knew very well that it was empty, I approached it timidly to examine the sculpture, whose details could be clearly seen.

Conferred on the conquistador by Emperor Charles V of the Holy Roman Empire, the armorial device told, in the language of heraldry, about the life of its bearer. I ran my fingers over the images carved in the stone, seeking to amplify my capacity to penetrate the story enciphered in the four quarters into which the shield was divided. In the upper left, the two-headed eagle of the House of Habsburg, which watched over the unity of the Holy Roman Empire, looked both to the East and to the West. To its right, three crowns evoked Cortés's victories over the Aztec emperors Moctezuma II, Cuitláhuac, and Cuauhtémoc. In the lower left, continuing the zoomorphic sequence, there was a lion, symbolizing the warrior virtues of the bearer. And to the right of the ferocious feline, a castle recalled the conquest, on August 13, 1521, of the Aztec capital Tenochtitlán—the final episode of the terrible clash.

Surprised at the multitude of details that I would not have imagined I could remember after so many years, I took pleasure in going over the lessons on the history of the New World that Paolo Paltini had never hesitated to offer me. All these improvised classes had taken place during our long walks along the corridors of museums in Rome, Venice, or Genoa. Without any concession to my tender age, my grandfather had provided me with details that had remained imprinted with remarkable clarity in the folds of my deep memory.

Much as I would have enjoyed reflecting on these fragments of the past, however, I could not forget the mystery of the absence to which the stone construction bore witness. The number of unresolved questions grew. Awakened to reality, I walked round the massive stone monument and approached its left-hand side, where the heavy lid had been sufficiently pushed away to allow me to see inside.

Astonished at what I saw, I spent several minutes examining the contents of the sarcophagus, following with my eyes the cone of light cast by my torch into its dark interior. I felt the need to close my eyes tight to check the veracity of the improbable vision. When I opened them, embarrassed at my own lack of trust in the train of events that mercilessly smashed through the banality of everyday life, nothing had changed. Calmly, yet at the same time feverishly, I rummaged through the corners of my memory in search of any possible explanation. I hesitated to move—indeed I was afraid to tear the web of another implausible dream. For what could be more bizarre in such a place that what was in front of my eyes?

Leaning against the inside of the right-hand wall of the cenotaph was a diving suit. Yes, an old-fashioned diving suit, of the sort that can be seen in museums dedicated to the history of marine exploration. It bore a striking resemblance to those on French engravings of the nineteenth century showing Captain Nemo and Professor Pierre Arronax venturing into the ocean depths. The principal element was the massive spherical copper helmet with its corselet shaped to rest on the diver's shoulders. From either side of the round faceplate, which reflected the torchlight like a silvery disk, two tubes of the same material as the helmet itself descended to meet a rectangular container, the reservoir for the explorer's vital breath. This element proved that it was an autonomous diving suit, as used in the first decades of the twentieth century.

The suit itself was of a color that recalled that of the sacks of merchandise one sees at the docks and was large enough to be worn by a person already wearing thick clothing, who need have no fear of soaking his garments. The wearer could have squeezed into such a suit not only fully dressed but even with his shoes on. Two huge boots could be seen, made of the same waterproof material as the suit, with rope in place of shoelaces and thick lead soles, the weight of which was easy enough to imagine.

Numbed, I took a deep breath. Finally, I moved the hand in which I held my torch. The trembling beam fell on a small white rectangle, no larger than a visiting card. Its presence, to the left of the diving suit, unleashed all my undecided emotions, in whose mesh there could be detected, firm and inescapable, a huge question mark. I turned my head and blinked a few times, frowning as I peered thoughtfully. Finally edified, I smiled. It was an expression of joy at the thought of the unpredictable friend who never failed to send me guiding messages.

I bent over the edge of the sarcophagus. I touched first the copper helmet, then the two tubes, the suit, and the oxygen tank. Finally, I began to fumble for the little white card. When I lifted it to my eyes, the words written on it made me smile again: "A gift more precious than air." I turned my eyes for a moment to the container whose contents were so essential for explorers of the deep. On the other side of the little card was, as I had expected, the Newman coat of arms.

Slightly tired, though perfectly lucid, I sat down, one more experience the wiser, on one of the pews in the chapel. I switched off the torch. I felt a great need to immerse myself in the dark silence of the night in order to gather my thoughts. I went over all that I knew about the place where I was sitting. A chapel built centuries ago in a style that recalled French Gothic; a solemn sarcophagus, silent and empty, carved with the arms of the celebrated conquistador Hernán Cortés; inside it, a diving suit—the unusual gift of the Duke of Kirkwell. And right in the middle of the island at that, as far as possible—no matter what direction one might take—from the waters of the ocean. What was the point, here, of a suit designed for submersion in the aquatic sky below?

In the depths of the night, the moon offered itself to me as a guide. Fascinated, I watched how its rays passed delicately through the blue glass of the chapel windows. My eyes fell on one of the two side wings of the building: in the middle of the stone-paved floor, I could see what seemed to be a well, covered by a massive iron grille. Built from the same light grey blocks of stone as the walls of the chapel, this exoteric end of a connection with the subterranean world took the form of a plain cylinder, with no ornament, rising about three feet above the paving stones. From the depths of my memory rose the image, long forgotten till then, of a similar construction in the Lower Church of Saint Mungo's Cathedral in Glasgow, which I had visited during my Scottish holidays. The chain of questions was now longer by one more link.

I approached the well, switched on my torch, and directed its beam down into the depths of the shaft, which was more than six feet across. My reserves of astonishment had dried up, and, dominated apparently by a cold, dispassionate spirit of scientific objectivity, I noted the existence of a staircase, whose spiraling steps concealed the depths of the mysterious pit. Determined to follow immediately the guiding thread of my questions, I put the torch down on the ledge of one of the windows. With both hands now free, I wrenched the grille from the opening of the well with one vigorous movement that met no significant resistance. The only difficulty came when I had to oppose the tendency of the metal structure to fall due to its own weight. Once that obstacle was overcome, I shook my hands, picked up the torch, and began, with careful steps, to go down. I had ascended into the vault of the heavens to investigate the mystery of the constellation Orion; now it was time for me to explore the unsuspected depths of this lost island.

On the stone steps, which seemed not at all worn, the sound of my boots was dry and echoless. I descended the spiral in a state of concentration that kept my mind off all my past confusions. The constant sound of the ocean waves, distant but always perceptible, now gradually diminished until it faded away completely. I stopped in fear when I became aware of the utter silence that surrounded me. The torrent of astonishment that had been growing unnoticed as my count of the steps approached a hundred now flooded over me like the tides that I had admired from the pontoon platform. I had already lost count when, in a manner as surprising as all my experiences on the island, the surface of a perfectly polished mirror marked the end of the abyssal staircase, reflecting back at me the orangish light of own torch. The unexpected flash that met my eyes made me blink. I lifted the torch beam a little, and half opened my eyes again to peer cautiously through my eyelashes.

As I examined the surface of the water, a thought came to me that offered a simple answer to the questions raised by the contents of the sarcophagus: the diving suit was to be used to continue the journey. Only now did I understand the true purpose of the underwater torch that I had been using ever since I found it, together with the precious journal, in my grandfather's cabin. I crouched over the motionless mirror and lowered the torch. The cluster of rays shone under the water, illuminating particles, large and small, that floated below the surface.

Excited at the prospect of such an exploration, I got thoroughly splashed when I abruptly pulled my light source out of the water and set off again up the spiral staircase. The ascent seemed shorter than the way down.

As soon as I managed to get the diving suit out of the sarcophagus, I immediately saw the difficulties that lay before me. Putting it on single-handed was no easy matter. After turning the components in all directions, I realized that if it had not been for the exceptionally simple locking system by which the spherical helmet was fixed impermeably to the ring attached to the suit, I would never have been able to put it on without assistance. To get all the equipment down near the shiny surface of the subterranean water, I had to make several trips, carrying a limited weight each time.

Irritated by the sweat that covered me as I prepared to carry down the last component of the suit, the oxygen tube, I stepped out through the huge door, which had remained open, and cooled myself by walking along the platform. In a small necropolis, surrounded by a wall that had subsided in places, I found some stone crosses, nine in number, simple in form and light grey in color, with no signs or names carved on them. Worn by the passage of the years, they exposed the precarity of our human plans, all too often conceived without taking into account the finite nature of our lives. How many of us think, even from time to time, of the severe exigencies that Socrates captured in his words whenever he spoke of preparation for death and for the passage to the state that follows?

Assailed as I was by such thoughts, it was clear to me that the identity of those buried here remained impenetrable. Beyond their little resting place, protected by the crown of an exceptionally tall tree, I could see a few bushes and, a little further on, the ridge that rose to the highest point in this part of the island. The silvery light of the moon gave the landscape a ghostly aura. The smell of rotting seaweed and of the remains of the various creatures killed by the hurricane was as distinct as if I had been right beside the water. From time to time, the odd bird-cry rang out against the background noise of the waves. Otherwise nothing disturbed the night that enveloped this lonely little piece of land.

It was perhaps precisely this nocturnal peace that heightened both the sharpness of my perceptions and the sense of mental clarity that goes with great discoveries and intuitions. I looked toward the shadow of the volcano in the southern part of the island, some two miles away. The thought of the vessel sheltered in its hidden opening took possession of me. I had before me the most important moment in my unlikely expedition. Enveloped in the ethereal body of an uncommon lucidity, totally determined not to postpone a moment longer my underwater exploration, I entered the chapel, shut the door, and descended the shaft of the well.

When I reached the mirror surface of the water, I began to equip myself, but not before hanging at my chest, like a breastplate, the leather folder that concealed the volume of Plato without which I now never went anywhere. I put on the diving suit and closed the huge zip, specially designed to be held in gloved hands. I pulled the boots over the crude paws of the suit that now covered my clothes. Their lead soles must have weighed over twenty pounds each. I observed in passing that inside all these heavy accessories, I felt terribly dry.

After studying the locking system, I placed the helmet over the circle around my neck, but not without first opening the viewport. By a simple rotation, I sealed it without any difficulty. Having completed the circular movement, it only remained to screw in place, on the right-hand side, the end of the stiff tube from the oxygen tank that was riveted to the suit over my chest. Everything went smoothly, as though I were an experienced diver. I had grasped the details of the suit and their functions with remarkable clarity. It only remained to open the tap of the oxygen installation and to close the little round viewport.

I took a few steps. With great difficulty I dragged my feet onto the first submerged step, breaking the mirror surface of the water. Then I continued downward, step after step. Only when the water reached my chest, half covering the oxygen tank, did I turn the key that released the vital gas into the suit, making me look like an astronaut fallen from the sky. I felt a gentle draft caressing my throat. Calculated and prudent, only now did I turn the butterfly screw that sealed the viewport. Holding the handle of the torch in my right hand, I submerged myself in the unknown.

The first minutes of immersion were filled with my amazement at the absence of any clue to the liquid character of the aquatic environment. I understood how absurd it had been to imagine that as I dived deeper I would feel the cold of the water. In fact nothing changed in my sensorial register.

The same dryness that I had felt when I had finished putting the suit on continued to reign in its watertight interior. The only difference I could detect was the temperature of the oxygen from the tank, which was slightly colder than normal air. Nothing else, and above all nothing liquid could be felt inside my amphibious carapace.

I continued to descend until, after a few dozen more steps, I found myself at the foot of the staircase. I rotated the torch and saw that the smooth masonry further up had disappeared, replaced by a wall of irregularly shaped light brown porous stone. The steps led into a cavity in whose side I could see an opening wide enough to allow the passage of three divers shoulder to shoulder. I tried to make my way toward it. I expected I would be able to walk as naturally as in any other circumstances involving horizontal displacement. It was only now that I fully appreciated the real difference between descending vertically step by step and advancing in a straight line through the liquid that filled the whole space.

I had to lean forward and make a sustained effort to move my feet in the desired direction. Lacking the necessary training, I lost my balance. For a moment, I feared that I was going to fall. I pushed as energetically as I could with my hands against the direction of my descent. Fortunately, all my movements underwater were much slower than on the surface. To steady myself and regain my initial posture, all I had to do was to wave my hands in the opposite direction to the trajectory of my fall. I stopped the movements just in time to avoid falling on my back.

After this involuntary initiation in the art of underwater movement, I leaned forward little by little, first lifted my right foot and then, after bending my body forward, took a step. By repeating the movement a few times, I managed, with some effort, to reach the mouth of the passage. The beam of light, whose brightness was amplified by the white of the porous stones through which the corridor advanced, revealed a tunnel of an approximately oval form, sometimes as much as fifteen feet across. Considering its chaotic forms and contours, I concluded that it could be nothing other than a tunnel cut by the stormy waters that had once passed through it, in times immemorial, and not the work of human hands. Leaning forward, I strode like a convalescent learning to walk again after some terrible accident.

I continued to advance toward the destination that sorely tried the limits of my patience. Apart from walking, my only concern was to test the ground in order to avoid any impediments. At quite long intervals, an extreme disturbance of the water and a reduction in visibility indicated places where rapid flows of water entered the tunnel through little channels coming from who knows where. I also discovered that other tunnels absorbed the liquid, helping to maintain a constant change of the contents of the cavity. None of this posed any obstacle to my progress, which lasted almost half an hour.

Insidiously, my concern about the limits of the reserves in my oxygen tank showed its viper's head and bit mercilessly. At once, as in the moments of panic attack described by those who have had such experiences, I felt trapped in my protective suit. I was imprisoned, chained with no hope of escape. My friend had become my enemy. I stopped and closed my eyes. I sought within myself some image, some memory, some reassuring thought. But no. As soon as I identified something, the whispers about the imminent exhaustion of my vital reserves became even louder. I tried to continue on my way, walking with great difficulty and at half my previous speed. I felt cornered, unable to make correct decisions. What if the way ahead were much longer? Or if the oxygen were insufficient? The image of the little visiting card ought to have calmed me—Gilbert Newman would not have left me such a sign without adding a warning if it was required.

In the midst of my state of increasingly acute agitation, out of the depths of my memory the image of the anonymous Venetian painted by Master Bartolomeo burst through to the surface. Calm and serious, he held the hilt of his sword with serenity. His direct gaze transmitted to me once again that strengthening aura that could only be the result of his supreme inner peace. How must he have felt before the life and death confrontation with his martial adversaries—whoever they might have been? A sword worn and held like that was not a mere decorative object. Somewhat reinvigorated by my inaccessible friend, I set off again, determined to advance with all my energy. There was no need. When I pointed the light upward, I saw a dark oval. The submerged part of the tunnel ended here. I had only to step through the mirror of water.

Once on dry land again, I took off the diving suit in perfect peace and set the helmet down. The noise when it made contact with the rock produced prolonged echoes. Giving no more attention to the shadows of fear that I had gone through under the water, I kept by me the torch and the leather folder containing the volume discovered on the brigantine.

I continued on my way with renewed enthusiasm. After a climb of no more than ten minutes, I sensed a slight but definite change of route. The direction of my advance was quite different. I was descending—descending toward the roots of the volcano. Relieved of the weight of the diving suit, I strode on with an agility that gave away my growing enthusiasm.

Joy flooded over me when, on one of the walls, I spotted an eloquent inscription scribbled in white chalk by a benevolent hand: "100 m." That was how far I had to go to the end of the road. I strode through the bowels of the earth faster and faster. Then in the distance I saw an opening much wider than the submarine one at the other end. What it was granted to me to see when I passed through it was beyond the limits of imagination.

I was in a vast cavern, comparable in length to a large park, whose roof could barely be touched by the torch beam, which faded into the darkness above. Massive rocks lay scattered all around. Among them, pools of water sparkled when the bright rays touched them. I examined this abyssal territory, convinced that my emotions, tempered by the ever awake and observant vigilance of reason, were identical to those experienced by Gaspar de Carvajal and Francisco de Orellana on their expedition along the Amazon. I was in the heart of darkness.

I advanced in a zig-zag, with no precise aim. I was trying to grasp, to see all that surrounded me. I passed between rocks that resembled huge black stalagmites reaching up toward the invisible ceiling. In such a place, the shadows had consistency. In the center of the great cavern, I found a small lake whose undisturbed mirror surface amplified the rays from the torch. It was within the bounds of this modest seascape that I saw, for the first time, the brigantine.

It lay on its side like a beached whale. Its sails, of which only a few stiffened rags remained, conveyed an acute sense of decrepitude, as did a number of sizeable holes that pierced its wooden hull. Its distance from the shining water could not prevent me from imagining how it had floated on the much wider and deeper waters that had once occupied the whole space of the cave. Now, however, I could walk round the wrecked vessel on the rocky ground without meeting any obstacle. At the same time, I discovered in the wall of rock more than fifty yards behind it a huge opening, whose pointed top was close to the ceiling of the cavern.

Propelled by curiosity, I headed immediately for this tunnel and advanced carefully into it. I did not have to go far before the light revealed the reason for the absence of the water on which, at one time, the ship had been able to sail into its hiding place. A heap of rocks and boulders completely blocked the way. A massive portion of the ceiling had collapsed—who knows why or when. This explained the diminished volume of water: the underground basin had been deprived of its main source, the ocean, which had previously filled it at high tide.

Having solved the mystery of the presence of the brigantine in the heart of the extinct volcano, I concentrated on the aim of my journey, seized with intense enthusiasm. I had to get into the captain's cabin, with the minimum risk. From a careful examination of the naval plan in the observatory I had learned that the location of the cabin was under the poop deck. Although I had walked round the vessel several times, I had found nothing that would help me to get onto the deck. I was convinced that those who had been there before me had found a way of entering the ship without the help of a ladder. A look at the largest of the holes that pierced the centuries-old wood suggested a simple way of continuing my exploration. Situated no more than three feet above the ground, the gap exposed the lowest deck, where coils of decaying rope and a few barrels with broken heads could be seen. Taking all due precautions, and especially careful not to injure myself on the splinters that stuck out in all directions, I put my right foot on the lower edge of the hole and took hold of the right-hand edge. The ancient timber creaked as I transferred the whole weight of my body inside.

I shone the torch all around. Immediately, I spotted a flight of steps, only a few of which were still in place. The rest hung broken. I pressed down with all my strength on the first of the intact steps. Surprisingly, it took my weight. An acrobat for the day, I clambered gracelessly onto the next one, perspiring abundantly from effort and nerves. I tested the fourth step with my foot, then, avoiding the fifth and the sixth, I stretched up to the seventh. Gradually I made my way up, at the risk of breaking some of the precarious steps along the way.

With great difficulty, I managed to climb to the first level of the ship. I found myself in quite a wide space, bounded by two wooden walls. In the nearer of the two, there was a door hanging on a single hinge. In the other, an opening through which I could make out an almost intact staircase. I climbed up to the second deck and pushed the door that hung at a slant. With a dull noise, it collapsed, raising a cloud of dust that kept me coughing for some time. My curiosity was disappointed: two rusty cannons and the capstan in the middle of the room were the only items to be seen.

I shook off the dust, and after testing each step, I climbed the stairs at the other end. Knowing that I was on the level below the main deck—in other words, exactly where the captain's cabin would normally be found—I was sure that the long-awaited moment could not be far off.

I emerged into a room longer than the one from which I had just come, guarded by four cannons and with a few barrels stacked along the walls. With the same lucidity and attention with which I had put on the diving suit, I made my way to the poop of the ship.

Through an empty space with no door, I entered a small hall with countless cobwebs hanging between its walls, I crossed it in a few steps. At its end there were three doors. The one facing me was half open, while those on either side stood wide open, allowing a view of two cabins only slightly larger than the beds of worm-eaten wood that they contained, each with an empty cupboard at its foot. This was where the captain and the first mate had slept.

I took note of all the details, although I knew that their value consisted only in the nostalgic charm of recalling those who had lived there hundreds of years before. Had I found the way out of the labyrinth? I pushed the door in front of me. This is where it was granted to me to discover what proved to be the very gateway of my dream. It was the cabin of the Nameless One. I stood stock still and looked for a long time. I took short, abrupt breaths: it seemed to me to be the only way to avoid any noise that would break what seemed a phantasmatic vision. I almost refused to believe what was evident. And yet I was here, in the room where, in my dream, I had been present in the last moments of the unknown captain.

I could see that table, a *secretaire* with numerous drawers, all open, where the anonymous occupant had written his message and had scribbled those two words on the edge of the volume of Plato. Between the blind windows, the crucifix, white with dust and the passing of the years, hung in the same place. A lamp on the left-hand wall, a support favored by spiders for their meticulously constructed webs, awaited the hand that would relight it. The ink-pot and quill could be seen on the table. They still bore the marks of dried ink. Even the sword stand, empty, was in its place. The wool of the carpet was decayed and no longer hid the rough wooden boards beneath it, whose brown color was distinct from the tarred black of the walls. Trying with all my might to preserve the absolute silence in which this place was submerged, lost outside time, I began to make my way, hypnotized, toward the table.

"IN MENSA." What could these two words mean? I looked without seeing anything that might perhaps have soothed the agitation of my restless mind. I was afraid. Might I not be the sport of a stupid game, the caprice of a dream without meaning, as most dreams are? A spider's web as fragile, as ephemeral, and as insubstantial as those whose remains hung from the lamp. I looked carefully around one more time, and then I definitively rejected all the doubts that were assailing me in waves. All these things were real. I was here. Only a few steps separated me from the table on which there was nothing to be seen but an unusable pen and an inkpot dried up by the passage of time. The drawers were open. Void, lacking any content or sense, like everything that surrounded me. What more could I do? Where should I seek the point of those two words— "IN MENSA"—from my dream? Worn out with so many emotions, I approached the table. I laid my torch on its top and let my right arm passively rest all its weight on it, through the hand that still gripped the torch's handle. With a reflex gesture, I ran my left hand through my hair. I sighed deeply, and then shifted my weight from one foot to the other. At that moment, several things happened simultaneously.

There was a crack and a sound of scraping metal, followed by the collapse of the floorboards under my left foot, causing me to lose my balance. I dropped, partially but very rapidly, through the floor, which could no longer support my body. The falling movement was totally unexpected, and made me utter a stifled exclamation as, completely unprepared, I tried to support my left elbow on the table, desperately seeking a point of support.

Under this pressure, both legs on the left-hand side of the *secrétaire* suddenly broke with a dry crack. Left with nothing to hang onto, I slid, raising my right hand to protect the torch from possibly fatal shocks. The next thing I knew, I was on the floor, lying on my left side. My elbow was stinging from the impact with the floorboards. I had discovered at first hand the considerable risks involved in any exploration of a ship whose timber was largely rotten. I breathed deeply as, with the most cautious movements I was capable of, I tried to pull my left leg, which was folded under me, out of a gaping hole in the broken floorboard. I prayed that the floor would not give way completely.

Once freed, I dragged myself over to the nearest wall. Exhausted, I supported my back against it. I sat there for a good few minutes before my pulse returned to normal. When I found that the torch was still working, I examined the consequences of the little catastrophe. There was nothing significant. A few scratches, not very deep, two legs of the table broken, the inkpot and pen thrown to the ground, one floorboard broken loose, and a cloud of dust particles gravitating around me. That was all.

When I pointed the beam of light at the little table, I noticed a detail that did not fit the existing picture. Intrigued, I began to look more carefully. At the same time, I gradually changed the position of the beam. When it came to a particular angle, I noticed a silvery flash from a point at the upper end of one of the two broken legs. Such a reflection could not come from wood. Suddenly I understood that the expression "IN MENSA" did not refer, as I had learned from Hans Ørberg's Latin manual, just to the objects that were *on* the table. It could equally indicate something that was *in* the table.

I dragged myself slowly to the place where I had detected the point of brightness, carefully avoiding any sudden movement. I ran my fingers over the stump left after the leg of the table had been broken off. Among the fragments of wood, I felt something round and cold—the end of a metallic tube. I decided to lift the table a little, using both hands. A slender silvery cylinder, polished as smooth as a mirror, began to slide out of the wooden leg, which remained on the floor. Intensifying my effort, I raised myself to my knees and continued to lift the table. A metallic ring announced that the cylinder had fallen. It rolled toward the wall, and then stopped. I left the table in its place, sat down again, and then took the curious object in my hands to wipe it gently with my handkerchief. It was about ten inches long, and seemed to be a rolled-up mirror, closed at both ends. If it was to this object hidden *in* the table that the Nameless One had wanted to lead me, I could not understand for what purpose.

I took the volume from the leather wrapping that hung at my chest, and put the torch down. Placing it on my outstretched legs, I convinced myself one more time that the two words really were scribbled on the edge of that page. Mute in the face of my disappointment, they could not, in the absence of their author, confirm the value of my discovery. Nonplussed, I let my eyes wander from the silvery tube to the unintelligible signs surrounding the little empty space into whose nothingness I felt myself absorbed. I blinked repeatedly, not grasping the value of a thought that insistently demanded a very simply action: I placed one end of the tube in the little empty circle. It fitted perfectly. I turned the torch beam onto the cylinder, which sparkled where I held it carefully, in the middle of the yellowish page.

For a few interminable seconds, I looked at the Latin words that appeared as clear as could be, reflected on the shiny surface of the tube. In a barely restrained grimace, I held my mouth tightly shut and turned the ends of my lips down. It was the only sign that I had been released from a burden that had almost crushed me. I bent my head till my chin touched my chest, keeping my eyes fixed from under my eyebrows on the cylindrical text. What I had in front of me was one of those wonders that fascinated the royal and princely courts of the Baroque period: an anamorphosis!

It was an anamorphosis containing a Latin text, which appeared reflected on the metal tube. Without the cylinder and light correctly directed, the words were no more than mere meaningless scribbles. No one could have read anything of what had been written in the mirror. I stood up slowly, looked around, and thanked the Nameless One out loud. As in my dream, my regret at not knowing his identity cast a momentary shadow over my intense feeling of fulfillment. With my last reserves of strength, I carefully placed the cylinder alongside the book in the leather wrapping, and then set off on my return journey, seeing nothing else around me. I do not know how I made my way home, underwater and on dry land. All I noticed, when I arrived in front of the library, was the brilliance of the stars fading with the approach of the dawn. It was morning.

* * *

When I woke up, I noticed that I had slept curled up on the carpet in the middle of the office beside the great hall with the armillary sphere. I recalled the times when, while I was working on my post-doctoral dissertation, I had often slept on the floor in the reading room of the university library, where I had sat writing till after midnight. Without moving, I looked from this unaccustomed angle at the carpet and at the empty space under the desks, tables, and armchairs. When I woke up, I told myself that after all the tiring efforts of the last few days I ought to sleep for a few more hours. The uncomfortable position of my neck, however, prevented me from putting this plan into practice. I got up with difficulty and turned my head from side to side to restore the flexibility of my muscles. The freshness of the light entering through the stained glass suggested the first hours of the day, which seemed at the very least odd to me, as I had arrived at dawn. Could I have slept so little?

I looked at the date on my wristwatch—a habit that I had almost completely given up since I came to the island. August 27. The time, 6:50. Although the idea was hard to accept, I had to face reality: I had slept through a whole day and a night. Coming back to my senses, I took a few hesitant steps. I stopped as if struck by lightning when, lying on Dr. Paltini's desk, I saw the folder containing the volume of Plato. In addition to its usual contents, it should now also contain the metal cylinder that enabled the reconstruction of the anamorphosis. Pushing aside any thought that might have suggested the illusory character of our investigations, I sat down and opened the leather wrapping.

There could be no doubt that my discovery had been real. One end of the tube glinted timidly in the morning light. At once the spirit of enthusiasm, aroused by the prospect of deciphering a mysterious text, took hold of me. After a short pause for the sake of personal hygiene, I returned to the office with my face cooled by the water that I had allowed to run freely over me. Without more ado, I pulled the lamp toward the center of the table and placed the book under it, open wide at the page with the indecipherable characters. I opened my notebook, ready to record in it the message coming down from the mists of history, and took my pen in the fingers of my right hand, resting the palm on the page where I was about to write. At the same time, taking one end of the cylinder between the thumb and index finger of my left hand, I held it still on the circle in the middle of the strange disc covered with signs. The light of the lamp, projected onto the book, was strong enough to make a decisive contribution to the clarity of the reflections on the silver-plated surface of the tube.

The metaphor expressed through such an instrument was perfectly clear. Like our limited minds, the cylinder represented the irreducible key of understanding, the only means by which, in the presence of the right light, an otherwise indecipherable text could be made intelligible. In the absence of this context in which the three elements—the distorted writing, the cylinder, and the light—came together in harmony, our knowledge became a play of phantasms, a fraud, or perhaps even a mere self-deception. An illusion, I mean. Now, everything had become clear: I had before me a text written in small letters in Latin. Reading the first lines made me start abruptly:

> *And the god of gods, Zeus who reigns by law, and whose eye can see such things, when he perceived the wretched state of this admirable stock decided to punish them and reduce them to order by discipline. He accordingly summoned all the gods to his own most glorious abode, which stands at the center of the universe and looks out over the whole realm of change, and when they had assembled addressed them as follows . . .*

These were the last lines of the unfinished dialogue *Critias*. No one has given a satisfactory answer as to whether Plato really stopped writing at this point or whether the continuation has, for some obscure reason, been lost. The extent of the text that followed stunned me. There were a few blank lines after the ellipsis marking the end of the known fragment of the dialogue, and then another text followed, much longer, and opening with a similar ellipsis. Everything suggested that this was a continuation of the lines read previously. It was the unwritten part of the dialogue *Critias*.

Lost, recovered, and then lost again. And now rediscovered. A vague sensation of dizziness came over me, accompanied by a pulsating headache. The best course of action was clear: to transcribe the text and leave the task of understanding it for later. And so I turned myself into the calligraphic instrument of transcription of the concluding part, hitherto completely unknown, of the story of Atlantis. The cold shivers that passed through me at intervals could not divert me from my tenacious activity. Occasionally, I made brief pauses, just enough to ease the numbness in my hands, which were tightly gripping the cylinder and the pen. Unconscious of my growing hunger, I continued to transcribe one of the most disturbing stories that has ever been read.

Concentrating exclusively on the form, I did not give the slightest attention to the content. Soon three pages of the notebook were filled with Latin sentences handwritten with all the care of a medieval scribe. As I carried out my duties as a copyist, in my imagination I went over each moment of my walk through the tunnel, and then of my investigation of the brigantine in the cave of the volcano. In this way, I managed to set to one side my capacity to understand the significances of the text I was transcribing.

I was already copying the fourth page, and was pleased to see that I was approaching the end of the written text revealed by anamorphosis. Only two more paragraphs awaited transcription. I stopped, put down my instruments, and moved my arms, my shoulders, my back. I was about to resume my activity, when I became aware of a noise that was quite unexpected in such a place cutting clearly through the distant roar of the waves. Though muffled, the sound of someone steadily climbing the steps up to the building could be heard without any effort. Surprised and tense, I held my breath when the footsteps stopped suddenly. At once, the creak of the entrance door pierced the silence of the hall, filling it with echoes. The footsteps could be heard again, this time with the specific intonation of the wooden floor on which they were falling heavily. A clear, slightly elderly voice rang out:

"Alexander?"

Incapable of answering immediately because of my surprise, I rose to my feet, my eyes open wide with astonishment. A tall male figure, upright, but not necessarily grand, appeared in the doorway. My lips were dry, but I managed to utter two words:

"Your Grace . . ."

The grey-headed face, adorned with its unmistakable completely white moustache, covered with wrinkles and harmonious features forming a whole that you might say was at once incredibly simple and terribly complex, sketched a smile that in no way changed the lively look in eyes that seemed capable of reading one's thoughts.

"Alexander, I rejoice with all my heart that we meet again."

Awkwardly, I managed to mutter a few words, wondering myself at what I was saying without thinking:

"I've almost finished, sir . . . I've almost finished transcribing the text inscribed in the Stephanus volume. It's an anamorphosis. I'll finish the transcription, and then I'll try to translate it."

Not very edified, Gilbert Newman looked at me out of his dark eyes with their silvery glint. He kept that same smile intact, barely sketched on his thoughtful face. Without the slightest haste, he spoke:

"I was worried, Alexander. As long as it has been in my ownership, this island has never been at the mercy of a Category 5 hurricane. I almost find it difficult to believe that the damage is so slight. But what am I saying? All that is nothing compared to the value of a life, of a soul. I was afraid, Alexander. I was afraid for your life. I hope you will recount to me how you got through the storm, here on your own."

"Actually I wasn't here. I was on the little island to the north. And I believe I was not completely alone."

Visibly surprised, the duke turned his gaze inward. I had the impression that he was looking through me. Obviously he could not, for the time being, penetrate the full meaning of the words I had uttered. After a few indecisive moments, he added, with his inimitable air of self-possession:

"You will tell me later. Please carry on with your work. I hope the smell of tobacco doesn't bother you."

He took out a simple, straight pipe of black wood, sat down in one of the armchairs, and began to fill it carefully with tobacco from a goatskin pouch that bore the marks of long use. The calm in his bearing transmitted an energy to me that made me double my calligraphic efforts. While I continued my sustained philological work, Gilbert Newman left the room, only to return with a thermos flask of cold water and two glasses adorned with the same hieroglyphs that I had seen on the coffee cups in his Oxfordshire residence. From that moment, the dryness that had remained with me was overcome. I finished the transcription and began to go through the text, attentive, this time, to all the nuances and details of its meanings. When I had read and re-read it several times, I brought my state of excitement under control and stated, in the most neutral tone that I could manage, a conclusion for which I do not believe the right words exist:

"It is the *Critias*. Plato's *Critias*. However, there is something here that no one has ever seen before. Apart from the captain of the brigantine, that is. It's the missing part. Zeus's whole speech and all that follows."

After a short pause, caused by a tremor in my voice that I could not sufficiently control, I added with some haste:

"I believe I can read . . ."

Resting the hand in which he held his pipe on the right-hand arm of his chair, and enveloped in the thin smoke that perfumed the room as it rose, Gilbert Newman gave his assent with a barely perceptible motion of his head. Forgotten for centuries, the continuation and conclusion of the dialogue *Critias* was heard once more, recounting the end of Atlantis.

And the god of gods, Zeus who reigns by law, and whose eye can see such things, when he perceived the wretched state of this admirable stock decided to punish them and reduce them to order by discipline. He accordingly summoned all the gods to his own most glorious abode, which stands at the center of the universe and looks out over the whole realm of change, and when they had assembled addressed them as follows . . .

. . . "O gods and goddesses! Troubled by harsh thoughts, I have often wanted to summon you here, to the peak of Olympus where mortal feet never trod, to share with you my decision, long ago taken, but always postponed.

"None of us was wronged then, at the dawn of the world, when we each, according to our rank and our wishes, received a portion of the earth together with the mortals who dwelled in it. By drawing of lots it was decided again, as before, when I, Zeus received the heavens, Poseidon the sea, and Hades the subterranean realms of darkness. According to the same ancient custom, it was decided which portions we should each receive on the fertile plains or on the islands of the great Okeanos that encircles the world. We all had and still have earthly dwelling places befitting us. For only thus could the mortals live at ease within the boundaries of the lands whose rulers we are: honoring

us with unfeigned worship, in temples, as befits the difference that separates all that is perishable from all that is imperishable. It is we who guided them in the way of law and virtue, of decency and measure, punishing lawlessness, repaying just deeds. Skilled helmsmen that you are, I believe that none of you can say that you have hidden all this from those entrusted to you. And above all, you have not hidden from them the penalty for disregarding virtues and for that sin of rebellion whose name is not to be uttered lightly here, on heavenly Olympus. It is about this that I desire to speak to you, today, after not only skilled Hephaistos and wise Athena, but others among you have repeatedly brought to my attention deeds such as have not been heard of before in the world of humans.

"First of all, I will address you, Poseidon, and I will command you to hold back your hand from any hasty action and to guard yourself strictly. Only remember how I saved your life—and those of our other brothers—from all-devouring Chronos. Be sure that I will do nothing to harm or dishonor the name you bear. On the contrary, although your mission will be one of the hardest and will bring you no small distress, by your fulfilling the task that I shall entrust to you, our whole heavenly world will honor it beyond measure, and you will give the world of humans an example that will last forever.

"O gods! Although many rumors had reached my ears, and some of you had told me of dark deeds, bright-eyed Athena has shocked me with her testimony. She, the goddess of the city that bears her name, has spoken to me of the unjust armed rising of those who are the descendants of King Atlas, on the island of Atlantis, which honors Poseidon. Had it been only greed that drove them to such an act, their punishment would be lighter. But no! A crazed desire for power, for power beyond measure, drove them to rebel not just against the earth but against the sky itself. . . . They went to war with the city of Athena, planning with a single attack to conquer all the lands this side of the Pillars of Herakles. All teachings about virtue were forgotten, and true philosophy was replaced by a great and arrogant praise of the imagined power of their poor mortal bodies. So greatly was the ruling part of their souls darkened, there where we dwell as skilled coachmen, that they came to consider themselves to be like us, the immortal gods! This is what our virtuous maiden, the wise Athena, has brought to my knowledge.

"Becoming drunk on the measureless growth of their riches, the Atlanteans began to dabble in the infamous art that Circe revealed to some of her lovers. They began to construct mechanisms and artefacts designed to give them divine powers. I speak not only of the flight of Apollo or of the swiftness of Hermes, but of our very immortality, the privilege of those who can at any time taste of the divine ambrosia. The secret of

life without death they seek to reveal through the means of the deceiving craft. As for sacrifices and the duties of worship, they perform them only as a façade, measuring the virtue of their religion by the number of animals sacrificed, and not by the obedient heart that they owe to their lord Poseidon, and indeed to all of us Olympians. In this way, they have become boastful and have begun to destroy all that they find in their way. Likewise, they have committed sacrileges that it is not fitting even to mention, here at the center of the world. The Athenians, fighting with fierce tenacity, have suffered heavily from the attacks of these beasts whose presumption knows no limits. To the Atlanteans, I once gave the priceless orichalcum that they might create the most beautiful adornments. They came to boast so much of their skill and their riches that a dark shadow descended over their faith. Almost all of them now doubt our very existence as immortal gods, and even that of the unseen world about which the lovers of wisdom have taught them.

"Enough is enough! Their sins have reached the heavens. Let those be punished who have betrayed the religion of their ancestors, by which was preserved the delicate bond between things seen and things unseen. Let none of you dare to oppose me! As I once said before, if you were to hang a golden chain from heaven, you would never shift me, even if all of you were to pull on it, striving with all your strength, while I, if I should once frown, could pull you all up to myself like nothing. So listen, and hasten to fulfill my just command.

"Atlantis will perish! Let its example thus remain for the peoples who will come after until the end of this perishable world. All those who dare to repeat the deeds of the Atlanteans, learning Circe's art of sorcery or founding cities and settlements where the virtues are no longer known, should know what awaits them.

"Poseidon! You will bring upon them waves the like of which have never been seen. All the power of the waters, subject to your rule, you will bring down on the home of lawlessness, after which, at my command, your earthquakes will shake the earth as far as Tartarus. Nothing will remain of that island of rebellion!

"Hephaistos! Rivers of fire you will release from the depths of the mountains to scorch all that stands in their way. You will receive the signal when I, the Thunderer, throw from these heights the lightning shafts of my unleashed rage.

"A single sign of our mercy toward the few faithful Atlanteans will be permitted. Athena, the most wise, will guide ten of the descendants of the kings of Atlantis, with all their households, to far off shores and islands lost in the sea of Okeanos. But you,

Poseidon, their ruler, will be able to choose them. Let them be among those who have loved true wisdom! There, in the world across the sea, they will keep both the memories of the terrible punishment and the ancient customs of their ancestors. If they value wisdom, they will raise up a new world together with those whom the Power that is higher than me will send after many centuries to their aid."

Thus spoke the great king of Olympus, Zeus, the heavenly master of the merciless lightening. With a grim face, Poseidon left the terrible assembly where the fate of his Atlantean people had been sealed. The privilege granted by Zeus, of choosing for himself the worshipers destined for exile, calmed his wrath and the distress that troubled his divine blood. Athena followed him, to carry out his wish without delay and to guide his chosen survivors. Hephaistos set out at once to the hearts of the volcanoes to work the bellows that belch fire and smoke. The other gods departed in silence, waiting for the fulfillment of the terrible judgement.

During this time, down below, on earth, the Atlanteans, sure of victory, were celebrating the gains of their lawless war. Although the Athenian soldiers were still resisting on their shores across the sea, countless festivities were held on the rings that surrounded the island, the birthplace of the ten Atlantean kings borne by Cleito. Around the temple at the center, the celebration was beyond all imagining. Wine flowed in rivers and bulls were greedily slaughtered one after the other, without offering the appropriate parts to Zeus. A single old man, Mneseas, named in memory of one of the twins of the third generation of kings, retired with tears in his eyes into the temple of Poseidon. There, he looked with sadness at the huge marble statue whose head almost touched the ivory ceiling of the temple. A curious unease had troubled him since the dawn of that day. Now, in the peace of the temple, assailed by the lewd songs and cries outside, it seemed to him that a strange tremor was coming from the statue of Poseidon itself.

With his ears pricked and his heart beating faster and faster, Mneseas waited. A resounding crash made him turn white with horror. Pieces of the roof collapsed under the furious blows of the lightning thrown by Zeus Palamnaios. Immediately, a rain of thousands more fiery arrows fell down on the whole territory, to the applause of the Atlanteans, who in the intoxication of their madness thought themselves blessed with a glorious rain of stars. But the shouts and cries of the celebration turned to yells of horror. Mneseas saw the statue of Poseidon and all the other statues fall to the ground, crushing all that was in their way. Miraculously, a gentle breath of wind protected him from all that might have harmed him. None of the huge pieces of stone so much as touched him. He got up, with all the weight of his almost ninety years. His back bent, his robe and mantle wrapped tightly around his body, the old man set out, driven by the urgings of an unseen being, toward the harbor of the island. A voice that both frightened and encouraged him could be heard as clearly as the murmur of an untainted spring: "Do not stop!"

He kept going. He did not understand how he could go anywhere when he saw around him the waves of the devastating earthquake throwing everyone to the ground and rolling them around like knucklebones. Huge cracks opened everywhere. Out of them burst flames that scorched everything around. Houses, temples, storehouses, farms collapsed under a sky from which the sun had disappeared as though blown away by the wind. Mneseas passed through the disaster unharmed. He continued on his way with his heart burning, with tears streaming down his shocked face. It took hours for him to cross the three great rings of the island, between piles of bodies and trees burning like torches, constantly swaying as earthquakes shook the land with greater and greater force. Down below, he saw the harbor. The sea was bubbling like a cauldron of boiling tar. A single long boat could be seen, with twelve pairs of oars, looking as tiny as a patch of coral. Only a divine intervention could explain its existence. Mneseas had long understood that a secret divine presence was guiding him toward some saving shore.

Once on board, he was not surprised to meet a few members of minor branches of the old Atlantean families. Some, like him, even came from the stock—once so vigorous—of the royal houses. Children, grandchildren, servants, and also some womenfolk accompanied them. As soon as he climbed on board, led by the unseen hand, the vessel left the shore. A night as black as the depths of ravenous Hades fell over the island of Atlantis. Sitting on a bundle of rope, resting his hands on his knees, Mneseas found it hard to breathe.

He looked back toward the island. Higher and higher waves were sweeping its shores. They twisted like great furious dragons, devouring and carrying off all in their path. The waters were full of the corpses of people—men, women, children, young and old alike—who had died without having time even for a prayer. His eyes dry from suffering, Mneseas shook his head. With unspeakable pain, he assented to the judgement of heaven. Who would have opposed it? Who would have dared to cast doubt on its justice? When he had seen the lack of piety with which the old rites were celebrated and disfigured, he himself had tried long ago to warn the ringleaders of the danger they were courting. Only his age and lineage had saved him from their wrath. But not from their mockery. "Storm crow," they called him, and sometimes asked him rudely, "Cawing again today, old man?" He was silent and swallowed the knot of the pain of not being able to make himself heard. He continued to bring fiery brands to Athena, without forgetting always to mention that unknown god beyond the bounds of the heavenly world watched over by the Olympians.

As he thought about all these things, he felt a new earthquake that made the water of the ocean rise in gigantic waves, such as no one could have imagined. With blurred eyes, almost blinded by the brilliance of the infernal flames, the people on the boat saw huge cracks yawning wide in the island, whose hills and forests were burning like a torch, giving off clouds of steam whenever the waters touched them. The cracks turned into bottomless crevasses into which everything around fell. The earth was collapsing, falling bit by bit into the yawning abyss in Okeanos. With an unearthly crackling sound, burning forests and temples alike sank into the depths. Darkened, the sea and the sky united like a hideous monster whose jaws of cosmic dimensions were consuming Atlantis. Now some leagues away, the last descendants of the line of King Atlas watched in horror as its remains disappeared under the water.

As the first glimmer of dawn appeared, the still raging ocean swallowed the last spur of the island, on which the ruins of a temple dedicated to Poseidon looked like a horse's skull thrown by the wayside. Weeping abundantly, the Atlanteans chosen by Poseidon called out between sobs the names of their lost loved ones. Only Mneseas, his face like marble, moved his lips in silence. He was uttering prayers known only to himself. Unseen, Athena continued to guide the vessel, until, far out to sea, where the sky was starting to clear, they saw, rising out of the mist, beyond the most distant waters ever sailed by their people, the outline of an island.

Chapter 9

The French Captain's Last Confession

As the shadows of evening enveloped us, we reflected on what we had heard. Only the desk and the books on it, together with my hands, were vividly illuminated. The rest of the room was sunk into a darkness that grew denser and denser the greater the distance from the single source of light. I could guess at, rather than see, the figure of the Duke of Kirkwell, as he refilled his pipe while I tried to set down in my journal the key points of the story of the sinking of Atlantis. Worked into the fabric of the tale without being insistently underlined, the thoughts of the author shone out like diamonds in the dark mass of coal. However, the question of the authenticity of the text cast shadows that caused all other question to fade. Regardless of whether the text was or was not the work of Plato, the mere reading of it had transformed the library into a place of obscure hypotheses. I recalled all too well the Athenian philosopher's warning in another dialogue, *Phaedrus*. There, through the mouth of Socrates, he warns us that in the absence of the author, the text is incapable of speaking on its own. Indeed.

After the stress of the last few days, the anxiety of the test of the labyrinth took possession of my pilgrim soul once again. I felt as though the butterflies in the shadows of the cases around us had come to life and were flying in ever decreasing circles around my head, brushing against my face, my neck, the crown of my head with their velvety wings. No matter how many times I tried to catch one of the delicate winged creatures, thought without body, idea without materiality, it immediately vanished into the air and left me nonplussed, prey to the uncertainties aroused by this text that spoke of the end of a world. With its deep timbre, far from the characteristic tone of expressions of astonishment, the steady voice of my host broke the silence. He gave voice to the most pressing question, only to set it in the less disturbing perspective of the near future.

"If this is indeed the ending of the dialogue written by Plato himself, then we have here a notable discovery in the field of classical studies. In any case, according to the author, at least one key issue in the mystery of Atlantis seems to be clarified: the existence of descendants of the inhabitants of the island who were allowed to emigrate. The search for the Atlanteans who survived would thus be fully justified."

This was how Gilbert Newman categorized the ending, perhaps authentic, perhaps not, in any case hitherto unknown, of one of the most discussed texts in the history of ancient Greece: "a notable discovery." Opposed to any form of facile enthusiasm, he immediately jumped to another subject.

"But how did you reconstruct the anamorphosis? If I'm not mistaken, this is impossible without a cylinder whose mirror surface enables one to restore the correct angle of vision."

My interlocutor waited, in a manner that would have appeared solemn, if it had not rather been delicate. The feeling of inner freedom, doubled by the perception of a perfect courtesy, helped me to regain clarity of mind. As calm as the anonymous knight in Bartolomeo the Venetian's painting, I began to recount all the ups and downs of the last few days, not forgetting to include as many details as I could remember. My visit to the island and my discovery of the remains of the Nameless One aroused the Duke's interest to the maximum. For minutes on end, he listened without even puffing on his pipe, which finally went out. He watched me intently, making evident his desire to take in as fully as possible, to contemplate faithfully the experiences I had gone through. When, after more than an hour, I concluded my narration, he stood up and struck the calves of his boots, a military gesture marking a conclusion, or perhaps a decision. With no further introduction, he addressed me in a cordial tone filled with a warmth that made me blush, just as when, as a teenager, I received praise for a successful translation from Greek or Latin.

"Where to begin? What should I say first? I heartily congratulate myself for the trust I put in you. When the news of the hurricane reached me, you can scarcely imagine how much I reproached myself. Day and night I accused myself of pushing you into such a journey. I told myself thousands of times that all my research and your grandfather's had been no more than mere manifestations of elegant but risky passions, perhaps even groundless. That I should have given up our dreams rather than ask such a sacrifice of you. But now everything has changed . . ."

After a short pause, he continued in a tone that, if not commanding, was certainly impetuous: "Could you show me the page with those charcoal marks?"

I turned round the volume of the Stephanus edition, which still lay open, and pushed it slowly toward the edge of the desk. Before approaching the book, he went over to the switch panel that controlled the electrical installations. The yellow light of the standard lamps and the lights hanging from the ceiling and on the walls spread through the whole room like a golden web. The motionless butterflies metamorphosed into signs of a waiting full of promises, zoomorphic symbols of thoughts that were going to rise in their myriads under the impact of the unseen currents welling out of the pages of an ancient book.

Gilbert Newman stopped by the desk, standing with his head slightly inclined, and looked at the two words "IN MENSA," while at the same time touching the page with the fingers of his right hand as if wishing to convince himself of its substantiality. Then he directed his attention to the silver tube. He picked it up and studied it at length. Then he positioned it right in the middle of the disc of distorted letters. With the index finger of his left hand on the upper end of the cylinder, he held it pressed against the page. When he turned toward me, his face was lit up by the bare sketch of a smile. His eyes shone, reflecting his preoccupation with what had just been discovered.

"Alexander, it's time for a rest. We need clear heads if we really want to understand all these remarkable discoveries and to sketch out the next steps in our research. For someone of my age, sleep is no longer an inevitable necessity. I shall go to Dr. Paolo Paltini's cabin, while you will be able to rest in the room upstairs. We shall meet again tomorrow, here in this office." Without allowing me to react in any way, he continued in a lower tone, but as cordially as before: "I assure you that it is not a question of the rules of hospitality, but simply of my irrepressible curiosity. The tricorne . . . the Spanish book . . . Do you imagine that I could sleep without seeing everything? To you, on the other hand, I wish a most refreshing sleep."

He shook my hand in the same ceremonious manner with which he had greeted me on the threshold of his family residence in Oxfordshire. Then with a slight nod of his head, he left the room. The sound of the door closing was followed by that of footsteps descending the stairs in the same steady rhythm as when he had come. Leaning on the edge of the desk, I felt a sense of exhaustion in every fiber of my body, in every fold of skin, in every muscle. Convinced that I was about to fall asleep on the spot, I strove with all my power to keep my eyes open. I put out the lights, and then, as though in a trance, followed the labyrinthian trail to the bedroom, where I collapsed on the bed, fully clothed, incapable of thinking, dreaming, or planning anything at all.

* * *

Lacking any fixed time reference, I lay immersed in the warm darkness of sleep. I could detect, somewhere, far off, a man's voice chanting the Gregorian *Credo* that I had not heard for some days. The sounds were as clear as the light of an autumn morning, bright and cool. Not only could I hear the music, but I could perceive—first vaguely, and then more and more clearly—a disturbing vision. The image of a great Gothic cathedral, in which the vibration of the music rebounded from majestic walls, alternated with that of a terrible cataclysm in which the same cathedral was destroyed by an earthquake that made the ground fold in waves like the water of a river whose bed was a cradle swung by an invisible giant. For a fraction of a second it seemed to me that behind the ruins I could see a giant woman dressed in regal garments, as sad as she was beautiful, the top of her head touching the sky. The music stopped. The image gradually darkened until it finally disappeared completely. I was left sunk in an unsettled sleep, from which I woke in a state of confusion.

In the office, a generous breakfast was laid out on the little table between the armchairs. There was no one in the room. A visiting card, placed on the edge of the tray, displayed a message of encouragement: "Bon appétit!" I ate with sufficient appetite for the traces left in my memory by the dream of catastrophe to be almost completely wiped away. I still wondered what all these images could have meant, but a much more worldly concern with bread and jam and the shelling of boiled eggs put an end to such questions.

I was already pouring my coffee when, announced by the creaking of the stairs, Gilbert Newman appeared in the doorway. He held in his right hand a little volume with gold-edged pages. I stood up attentively, as in my childhood when my mother taught me how to salute my father. The elderly aristocrat, the perfect embodiment of a man in his place, turned toward me with a look that seemed to hide an inextinguishable joy that was ready to burst forth at any moment. Although serious, the sober expression of his Roman face was not discordant with this hidden cheerfulness. With a slight modulation in his voice, he greeted me: "Alexander! I was hoping you had already eaten. We have much to do. Or, more precisely, to discuss."

"Thank you, sir, for this breakfast. I'm sure that we shall be able to talk all day now. I have never had such a substantial subject to talk about as the anamorphic text."

While he seemed to be weighing his answer, the Duke looked out in that way that made clear the determined direction of his attention toward the unsuspected depths of his own thoughts. Seated at the desk where, the previous evening, I had transcribed the mysterious text that completed the dialogue *Critias*, he prepared his pipe with the same slow, firm, and precise gestures that characterized his whole bearing. He took a few puffs just to follow the curls of smoke that took flight toward the ceiling. Then, after a pause, he asked me a question that made me remember who I was: Alexander Jacob Wills, holder of a PhD in the history of ancient Greek philosophy. "Tell me, you spent a good few years studying the classical Greek texts, and I've no doubt you've read and reread Plato's dialogues many times. Has your attention ever been caught by anything odd in the whole Atlantis story?"

Eager to put to use the vast panorama of the Greek world that I had charted in detail, I was excited at the chance, so rare in recent years, that was offered to me: I could share my knowledge. It seemed to me that this too was an occasion to get closer, to settle again in my own place. After moistening my throat with a single invigorating gulp of the bitter black liquid, I tried to answer in the most level tone possible.

"I'll try to get to the essential. I mean, to that point that has always seemed to me to have a potential that has been insufficiently exploited by interpreters of the dialogues. It is mentioned explicitly just once, toward the end of the known part of the *Critias*. It is where Plato reveals the profound reason for the fall of the Atlanteans: the demeaning mixture of the part resembling the divine in their souls with that which is mortal.

"Every time I read these lines, one fatal question comes back to my mind again and again: did there exist on this earth whole peoples whose souls, for generations, were in a state of purity 'resembling the divine,' as described in the *Critias*? I have never had any doubt about the excellence of some individual members of the various peoples. No one could cast doubt on that. However, here it seems that the whole Atlantean people is characterized by features beyond the normal limits of mortals. And then, what is the meaning of that 'admixture with mortal stock' that Plato speaks of? What sort of human condition was that of the inhabitants of Atlantis?

"Much more appropriate to the tragic experiences of humanity seems to me the account of the Alexandrian Christian philosophers Origen and Clement, or that of the scholastic doctors, among whom Albertus Magnus, Thomas Aquinas, and Bonaventure still shine today: after that mysterious event at the beginnings of history, humanity 'falls' into the miserable condition characterized by death, by sickness, in other words by the corruption of human nature. Of course, this involves precisely the mixture of the part that Plato says 'resembles the divine,' the intellect, with that which is transient, evanescent, mortal. Humanity 'drowned' in this flow that carries it through history without stopping, without rest, without peace. We are specters floating inert under the troubled waves of

Heraclitus's becoming. Dreams of shadows . . . living dead, buried in the vault of our own body. But what place can there be for the Atlanteans in such a picture? And how could someone—someone who enjoys a spiritual and moral state such as theirs—fall in such a way? This is something that I cannot understand. Something essential, yet at the same time so obscure. It is this, not the question of the existence of Atlantis, which I have always considered to be resolved by Socrates, that troubled me and continues to trouble me even now."

The Duke gently challenged me. "Your determination to maintain the historicity of Atlantis would be at the very least debatable in the absence of a solid argument. What is the decisive proof that you would propose to those who raise objections?"

Encouraged by my interlocutor's openness to discussion, I continued my exposition, not before noticing that the silvery cylinder had taken the place of the already extinguished pipe between his long fingers.

"Plato's text itself. But not any statement in the *Critias*. This time it's a line in the *Timaeus*. Where Socrates himself insists that 'it is not a fiction but true history.' Why should we doubt his word? The expression he uses to characterize all that is narrated in the *Critias*, 'true history,' leaves no room for doubt. If we add to that the opinions of his successors—including the greatest of these, Aristotle and Proclus—then I believe that the discussion should not be about *whether* Atlantis existed, but rather about *where* the traces of the sunken island are to be found."

Although he was listening to me with visible concentration, Gilbert Newman continued to roll the silvery cylinder between his fingers. Then he held it gently in his right palm, as though he wanted to feel the coldness of the whole polished surface. He pressed one end with his thumb, while at the same time turning his face toward me, as though about to add something. Just at the moment when I was expecting his comments, I saw the smile on his face give way to a look of concentration and enquiry.

He held the cylinder up to his eyes and looked at it attentively. Although from where I was sitting I could not make out his focal point, I could see that he was examining the end of the tube while at the same time feeling it meticulously with the tip of his index finger. Without a word, he stood up and looked for a few moments in one of the drawers of the desk. Then, armed with a little screwdriver, he picked up the tube again. My curiosity was heightened when I saw the operation he was carrying out, not with the blade but with the handle of the tool: he was carefully pressing in the center of one of the extremities of the cylinder. I watched without understanding, infected with the intensity with which the Duke kept pressing.

Suddenly, surrounded by the same explosive silence, he lifted the cylinder and in a low voice uttered a single word: "Look!"

What I saw made me turn pale. At the opposite extremity to where he was pressing with all his strength, another, even more slender, tip had appeared. After a few seconds, enough for me to grasp the purpose of his action, as he continued slowly but firmly to push the end that had already disappeared inside the silvery tube, another cylinder was emerging, telescopically into full view. Its surface was broken by a long slit, sufficiently wide to allow me to see what it was that Gilbert Newman now extracted after first putting on a pair of thin cotton gloves, of the sort used for handling old books.

It was two pages. Two thin pages, improbably white, covered with very small and orderly black handwriting. As he held them between his long fingers, it seemed to me for a few moments that his hands were slightly trembling. An experienced commander, the venerable aristocrat resumed his attitude of constant restraint. I, on the other hand, found myself covered in great drops of sweat and unable to speak a word.

On the Duke's desk, now illuminated also by the lamp that he had switched on after extracting the contents of the tube, lay the two cylinders and, beside them, the two pages, each with writing on one side only. He invited me to sit down on the chair next to the desk. I hurriedly conformed, eager to see everything close up. The light that fell on the two leaves revealed a detail that made the corners of my mouth drop. Although scattered in just a few places, the grains of a fine white powder could be clearly seen. After several failed attempts, I managed to articulate feebly a few words:

"The writing on the desk! The writing in my dream! This was one of the last acts of the Nameless One before the end: he sprinkled talcum powder over the two pages. . . ."

The Duke lifted the pages to look at them in the light of the lamp at an angle that allowed him to examine their whole surface. He was trying to detect every detail. Indeed, the remaining powder could still be seen, like tiny excrescences stuck to the white paper. Calm and precise as a professional archivist, he looked at the pages for a few moments and then turned to me:

"Traces of powder used to dry the ink. However, as to whether or not it's the letter in your dream, that we cannot know. But let's first see what it's all about."

A minutes of silence passed before he gave his verdict: "The French is that of a native. More than that, it seems to me that we have here the French of the eighteenth-century royal court. So not just *any* French, but the French specific to those brought up in the ranks of the high aristocracy."

He adjusted his glasses with the aid of his right index finger, and began to read the most fascinating confession I have ever had the privilege of hearing.

Monsieur,

If you are reading these lines, you will, undoubtedly, also have found the conclusion of the Athenian philosopher's dialogue Critias. *You have not been tried and tested in vain. The symbol used to read the story of the end of Atlantis will reveal all to you. The captain asks that you do not forget to pray for his soul. He wants only to transmit the teaching that he has acquired all the length of his life. He dares to hope that you will be able to meet the writer of these lines, after the final judgement ordained by the Most High. Until then, it will suffice for you to know that, as a humble servant of the forces of His Serene Majesty Louis XV, he governs the vessel where you have found the volume of the master printer Stephanus and the key of light. The captain assures you that it is not from any lack of respect toward your rank that he refrains from revealing his name, but out of the desire to follow the way of humility by which he hopes to atone for the sins of his youth.*

Before being sent, at the age of fourteen, into the military career in which he served His Majesty, the captain often took delight in the stories told by his good and learned mother. One of these stirred him to such an extent that he made the decision to follow the way of a life at sea. Heard countless times, the tale of the sinking of the royal island of Atlantis was read by the captain at the very time when he began his apprenticeship in the handling of the sword and of other weapons. Never, however, did he believe that all he read might somehow be true. Not, at least, until the day when a Spanish knight told him about his comrades who had set out on the trail of Christopher Columbus—he who discovered lands where no one had ever set foot. The life of the captain, at that time a mere foot-soldier of nineteen years, was changed. He began to seek out and to read all the books about the waters of the Atlantic ocean and about the voyages of the Spanish and Portuguese navigators. In his mind there took root the most sinful idea conceivable: he began to believe that in Plato's Atlantis lay hidden the secret of immortality . . . of youth without age and life without death. He was led to this conception by the description in the Critias, *in which it may be seen that the Atlanteans had, at first, had souls untainted by mixture with those subject to mortality.*

Troubled by such thoughts, the captain joined His Majesty's Navy as navigator on a small ship, where in a short time he became commander. For twenty years, he scoured the seas and oceans seeking the lost island. His convictions were strengthened when, reading the chronicles of Father Francisco López de Gómara, he saw that this learned man, as associate of Hernán Cortés, said that the remains of Atlantis had been found in the New World. From that time on, the captain began to seek the trail of Cortés's expeditions. He wondered if the conquistador might not have known more than Father Francisco had written in his chronicles.

He consumed another seven years of his life on the trail of Cortés and his secretary. In the course of one of his voyages, he discovered a little known island where he found strange constructions that might be monuments erected by the last survivors of Atlantis. In order to examine them properly, he commanded that a chapel be built right here—thus fulfilling the mission of honor with which he had been entrusted by the Franciscan friars in Ciudad de México. It was while he was on this island that the meditations of the Venerable Luis de Granada and the reading of the treatise De Paradiso *by the holy doctor Ambrosius of Milan illumined his heart. He recognized a quite different sense to his searches. For the first time, he understood what blindness had struck him ever since he had deluded himself with the possibility of obtaining everlasting life here on mortal soil. The Atlanteans had never possessed such a miraculous elixir. When he realized the sinfulness of his fleshly understanding, he renounced the madness of his searches in order to dedicate himself to penitence and mortification in the hope of obtaining forgiveness.*

The way to eternal life is quite different.

In this state, Monsieur, knowing that the dreadful hour of his death approaches, the captain has written these lines to explain what you have found. Although he has not fulfilled the mission for which the chapel was built, he places his hopes in the mercy of Heaven—at least at the end of the years of Purgatory which he is ready to suffer beyond the bounds of this world.

And to you, Monsieur, he sends the request that you pray for his soul, deceived as it was for so many years by an unworthy dream. Although he is not acquainted with you in person, the captain assures you that he feels bound to you more than to anyone else on this earth, for only one sent by Holy Providence would ever have read these lines.

You most humble and obedient servant,

A. L. D. de Ch.

It was well past midday when the Duke finished reading. He placed the second page on the table, next to the two cylinders, of which only the outer one was shiny. He looked at the clock and then began to clean his pipe. This activity was merely the pretext that channeled his attention, permitting him a complete meditative withdrawal into the world of his own visions and ideas.

As for myself, I was pleased to note the last piece of information provided by the French captain's letter. The identity of the Nameless One was no longer completely unknown. The mere fact that we had established his allegiance was a significant step forward. Then his initials—A. L. D. de Ch.—made it possible that sometime, probably after meticulous archive research, the full name of their bearer would be discovered.

All that remained unclear was the origin of the missing part of the dialogue *Critias*. The confession contained no revealing detail. I was profoundly troubled by the sin denounced with such pathos by the author, the sin generated precisely by those claims of Plato's that had always intrigued me: the Atlanteans were described, in the first period of their history, as having souls unmixed with those of a mortal nature. However, I confess that it had never occurred to me that the subjects of the god Poseidon might have possessed some elixir of immortality.

A man of arms, totally dedicated to the active life, the captain must have carried out operations that took him on the trail of the pioneers of the New World. How else could he have reached Ciudad de México? What mission had he received from the Franciscans? And why had he built the chapel containing the cenotaph bearing the arms of Cortés? All these questions found their places in the pages of my journal dedicated to the problems—as yet, insoluble—arising from our reading of the texts discovered on the brigantine.

Numb after hours of tense expectation, I got up and took a few steps. Surrounded by a cloud of smoke, Gilbert Newman was looking thoughtfully at the pages on his desk. Without taking his eyes off them, he addressed me with a voice that produced echoes that seemed to come from the reflection of the sound waves off the massive armillary sphere in the hall of the library.

"What would you say to a walk? A breath of sea air would change our vision of the world. I should tell you that Dr. Paolo Paltini liked nothing better than a conversation on the shores of the island. The endlessness of the aquatic abyss inspired him."

"A walk would be more than welcome."

As usual, I walked to the Duke's right, and at least half a pace behind him—the same distance at which I used to follow my father whenever I accompanied him on our long walks in the vicinity of Cambuskenneth Abbey.

Outside the library, I noticed in passing the large number of birds that whitened the surface of the water. The loud noise of the waves testified to the strength of the winds that blew around the island, throwing my hair in all directions. The sun still shone brightly against the intense blue sky behind the library building, but already it was beginning its westward descent. We strode out in silence in the direction of the electric generator. I was waiting for the Duke to share with me his first impressions after reading an unexpected text. However, when he broke the silence, it was on a completely different subject.

"Sometimes we are surprised by the mysteries that appear in our path, while we do not notice those in our immediate proximity. Routine, habit, familiarity stand in the way of the clarity of a fresh examination. We easily discover unusual things, but we would never have noticed them if we had lived a long time among them."

Breaking off this meditation spoken aloud, the elderly nobleman stopped. His face seemed to me to be covered by an imperceptible white powder. He turned toward me, leaning with both hands on his silver-headed walking stick.

"Alexander, do you know why your grandfather was searching for Atlantis?"

I had to confess that I had never asked myself that simple but unanswerable question. While I rummaged through the deepest corners of my memory in search of some illuminating recollection, I answered somewhat tentatively, "No, I don't think I ever understood what his deep motives were. With a little effort, I could at best tell you why he was *not* searching for Atlantis . . . but his real, positive motives are unknown to me."

"You see," said the Duke, "that and that alone was precisely what determined me to support his research with such enthusiasm. I hope that you now understand rather better what exactly I mean by enthusiasm."

I looked at him enquiringly.

"It's not a matter of being in a state of manifest exaltation or exuberance, of a revelation with strong affective implications, so much as a durable, serious commitment that pursues a well-defined end with the same tenacity as that of the hunter who watches night and day the paths where at any moment his prey may appear. Right from the beginning, I recognized in Dr. Paolo Paltini exactly this knightly state of mind. Although we did not immediately have a chance to discuss the fundamental aim of the research he was embarking on, the seriousness, the enthusiasm with which he dedicated himself to it convinced me from the start. I was sure that we were dealing with a crucial subject, which he presented to me in detail right here, on the island. The motive for Dr. Paltini's prolonged explorations was political, Alexander. Political."

I stopped still and directed toward the trees that descended to the shore beyond the generator a look that became terribly intense. My creased brows almost caused me a slight headache. Nonplussed by this revelation, I squeezed out—through lips tensed with puzzlement—a reply that I tried to utter as gently as possible: "My grandfather was never interested in politics. Rather I would say that he had a sort of reserve, a very strong one, regarding any discussion that tended in that direction. He never voted, never read the papers, and I never heard him mentioning the name of any politician. What you are telling me is incomprehensible."

I was met with a clear gaze. Leaning on the head of his stick with just the palm of his right hand, the Duke continued his explanations after first cutting the air, at chest level, with his left hand, an eloquent gesture that signified his rejection of any common understanding of the notion that had occasioned my consternation. He set off along the path that led straight to the beach, still speaking with the same even tone, free of any asperities.

"Indeed, Dr. Paolo Paltini never displayed the least interest in a field that remained, till the end of his life, alien to him. But this did not prevent him being interested, in an essential way, I would say, in the fate of the *polis*, of the city, of the world in which he lived. Your grandfather wanted, in fact, to demonstrate that Atlantis had disappeared as the result of a divine judgement. That was why he desperately sought evidence that would attest to its tragic end. For him, as he revealed to me in several conversations that I remember as though they were yesterday, the consequences of substituting the vice of power for the virtues of the descendants of King Atlas were proven, decisively, by the fate of Atlantis. 'In the *Critias*, we have the most valuable lesson in political philosophy.' These are his words. In a world such as ours, avid for the concreteness of what is perceived through the senses, superficially identified with the real, only such a discovery could bring back to the foreground the significance of the fate of that civilization. And it might perhaps awaken a heightened attention to the imminent end of all history. Dr. Paltini was convinced that this was the significance of the story of the rise and fall of the island beyond the Pillars of Herakles: its *hybris* had been punished by a power that transcended the boundaries of the visible world. When vices are substituted for virtues, the denouement becomes just a matter of time. *Nemesis* acts implacably not just in individual cases, but also in cities, peoples, continents, and at the end of history, even of the whole world. This is the *thema*, the guiding thread that directed your grandfather's research. It seems to me that our French captain was no stranger to this subject either."

The orbit of the ideas that gravitated around us was appreciably modified. Everything acquired hitherto inaccessible significances. The Duke paused, allowing me the necessary time to take in statements that had expanded my understanding.

The peace of the Atlantic afternoon was filled with the loud noise of the waves, tirelessly pounding the shore with their transparent fingers. Hemlines of foam dissolved, covering the sand with little silvery spheres that burst with a sound like that of a pen sliding over the surface of absorbent paper. For all that, no message remained on the surface of those millions of particles, which exhausted every possible shade of brown and grey.

We made our way toward the boathouse from which I had set out, just a few days before, on my reckless expedition to the island of the Nameless One. A fine dust touched my face, cooling me. I looked toward the ocean, impressed and attracted by the endless expanse of water. At home, in Umbria or in Scotland, such an open prospect had been possible only vertically, on days when the sky was free of clouds. Leaning back, I would direct my gaze upward, so that no earthly object entered the field of my peripheral vision. After a few minutes of contemplation, I felt the whole prospect undergoing a mutation that influenced my very way of thinking. Here, looking out to the ocean, a similar experience could be attained just by seeing the great immensity of water stretching out before me. The aquatic boundlessness corresponded to the aerial infinity that again and again reminded me of my creaturely limits. I reflected on the words of Plato, of the French captain, and of the Duke of Kirkwell. I shuddered every time I imagined the moment when the island of King Atlas sank:

The earth was collapsing, falling bit by bit into the yawning abyss in Okeanos. With an unearthly crackling sound, burning forests and temples alike sank into the depths. Darkened, the sea and the sky united like a hideous monster whose jaws of cosmic dimensions were consuming Atlantis. Now some leagues away, the last descendants of the line of King Atlas watched in horror as its remains disappeared under the water.

As the first glimmer of dawn appeared, the still raging ocean swallowed the last spur of the island, on which the ruins of a temple dedicated to Poseidon looked like a horse's skull thrown by the wayside.

The conclusion of the dialogue *Critias*, passed down to us by the Nameless One, became, more and more acutely, the inner film that showed the consequences of the *hybris* committed by the Atlanteans. I would have liked to reject this vision, to place it among the fabulations of an era in which natural catastrophes took on legendary proportions. What could all this mean for us, who pride ourselves on our ability to predict floods and earthquakes? I wanted to pull myself out of a nightmare that was made possible only by my grandfather's interpretations. I would have preferred a cold, objective analysis of all the texts discovered on the island. Determined to proceed along that path, I prepared my voice to utter the proposal I had already assumed.

"What do you say to a recapitulation of the main ideas in the French captain's letter? And after that, we could continue our discussion about the final part of the *Critias*."

"A recapitulation, you say? Clear and precise."

In the silence that followed, like an unspoken invitation, I began, in a tone as neutral as possible, to present all the information we knew.

"First, a basic characterization. We are not dealing with someone thoroughly acquainted with Greek and Latin antiquities, but rather with a lover of certain ancient texts, among which Plato's *Critias* occupies an important place. His reading led to that 'error' that resulted not only in a mistaken understanding of the dialogue, but also in his painstaking search for the traces of Atlantis: he believed that the inhabitants of the island possessed the elixir of everlasting life. Although the passage in the *Critias* remains obscure and we cannot, for the time being, establish its precise significance, it is clear to us that it cannot be interpreted in this sense. The originary purity of the divine part in their souls does *not* imply immortality. As indeed the captain himself came to realize, under the influence of the two authors mentioned in his confession, the Venerable Luis de Granada and Saint Ambrose of Milan. In his testimony, he seems convinced that he has identified the remains of Atlantis on this island. This was made possible by Father Francisco López de Gómara, whose interpretation he followed literally, embarking on expeditions along the coast of the New World. At the same time, we learn that he was entrusted by the Franciscan monks in Ciudad de México with a mission that involved building the chapel on the island. After the revelation of the fundamental error that lay at the origin of his search for Atlantis, the captain spent the last years of his life, without completing his mission, in the hermitage on the small island where his bones were found. He makes no statement that would elucidate the provenance of the continuation of the *Critias*."

"I would just add a single observation regarding our man's identity," responded the Duke. "We don't know who he is. However, incontestably his family belonged to the French aristocracy, whose male members, with the exception of those who chose the call of the Church, followed the path of arms. In addition, the initials with which he signs offer us another significant detail. The last letters do not indicate his own name, but his title and the land held by his family. Very probably, 'D.' is for 'duc' and "de Ch.' indicates the region to which he belonged: 'de Chartres.' So he is A.L., duc de Chartres. Of course it could be another duchy beginning with 'Ch.' For example, Châtellerault. However, the other initials will help us to narrow down the possibilities. What is remarkable is the humility of the man who is confessing. Although he speaks about himself, he does so exclusively in the third person. A style that reminds me of the journal of Christopher Columbus, with which an explorer of the New World must have been familiar."

Gilbert Newman stopped to draw my attention to the construction that sheltered the two remaining boats. I had not seen the boathouse since the day of the storm, when I had taken out the third boat. A huge tree trunk, brought down by the hurricane, had dislodged one of the doors, which lay half inside the tin-walled shelter. Blackened seaweed, the carcass of a dolphin, pieces of timber, and a lot of other debris lay scattered around. Only one of the three wooden rollers for dragging the boat to the water's edge was still to be seen, stuck under a rock and almost completely buried in sand. Impressed, the Duke shook his head.

"Let's go on. We'll visit the observatory."

To my surprise, instead of turning to the right, along the deep gulley that led to the ruins, he continued along the beach toward the end of the plateau. After a few minutes, the building became visible. The round window reflected the light of the sun as it rolled down toward the horizon. Most of the surrounding trees, battered by the storm, had not yet regained their vertical position. Likewise, the richness of the foliage was much reduced. Otherwise, nothing seemed to have changed.

Instead of advancing further, Gilbert Newman headed straight toward the slope, which was so steep that I could not imagine how we might scale it. It was only when we reached its foot that I saw the thin line of a winding path, hitherto invisible, marked by stones set in the sandy soil. On it, treading carefully, it was possible to climb up to the plateau. I observed the balanced way in which my guide proceeded, step by step, sizing up as he went, but without stopping, the distance to the next stone. I followed him with care. The path took us to the edge of the little depression from which the metal staircase led up toward the door of the observatory. The hollow was full of pieces of wood brought by the hurricane. One balustrade of the metal staircase had been bent by the powerful impact of broken branches. On the other hand, the windows, protected by metal grilles, were intact. The entrance to the building was partially covered by branches from which leaves hung lifelessly. It took some effort to clear them away before we could enter.

We left the door open. Gilbert Newman claimed the tall armchair and turned it with a short and unexpectedly energetic gesture toward the central table. I sat down on the chair near the door, so as to avoid the rays of sun coming in through the huge windows facing the desk. My host lit his pipe, whose smoke was immediately dispersed by the light breeze coming in through the wide open door.

Together with the smoke, the last traces of my inner turmoil were also carried away by the wind. The peace of this place was beyond all imagining. A single glance at the Duke's face gave me the certainty of a unique intuition: he *knew*. It was something as sure as my previous uncertainty about my own vocation. And just as surely, the moment had come for him to share this knowledge with me.

I waited. My whole being felt the gravity of the moment, although, at the same time, I was delighted at this restful pause.

"Alexander, don't you find the content of this message—in association with the end of the *Critias*, with Dr. Paolo Paltini's research, with our research—perfectly coherent?"

Hesitantly, I again confessed to my ignorance: "I can see some resemblances. However, so far, I don't detect any great coherence."

"And yet I believe you will easily manage to identify it. Here is my own summary. Deceived by a chimera, the French captain searches for Atlantis. Perhaps he even found it. Time, our future investigations, will help us to find out. Especially as we have, right here on the island, the ruins that led him to make such a claim. At the same time, he sends us a text of uncertain authorship, the conclusion of the dialogue *Critias*, which confirms his discovery. Yes, Atlantis existed. However, the discovery of its remains cannot offer him the key to everlasting life. Then, he redirects his search. In the end, he discovers the correct answer. The title of the learned doctor Ambrose of Milan's book, *De Paradiso*, is telling. Only in Paradise can there be eternal life. Is that not so? The road to the Eden of our origins . . . One might say that he found what he had spent a lifetime seeking. It only remains for us to establish the nature of this road and to locate its destination. In any case, I believe we know what motivated this anonymous sage: the fear of death. The fear of the end. Preoccupied with finding again a world that had, tragically, experienced its own extinction, he wanted to discover how this could be avoided. How we can stand in the face of the end of all history. How we can stand in the face of the end of our personal history. Paradoxical, isn't it? Sometimes, those who flee from death meet it, against their will, while others, who seek it, find that it passes them by again and again. Socrates is just one of the many examples that confirm the enigmatic hieroglyph carved in the material of our lives."

"So you would argue that even the French captain's error fits perfectly into the logic of his whole quest. A quest for life."

"Exactly. I would argue even more than that. Our presence here fits into the same blurred picture. All your discoveries are essentially part of the same story, whose totality, for the time being, escapes us. Just one thing seems to me more obvious than anything else: the vanishing point of the perspective of the whole picture merges with your essential vocation. It is that call which, in spite of the frustrations that my little charade must have caused you, led you onward. Without it, you would never have continued your journey."

The short pause that followed allowed his words to penetrate deep into the corners of my mind. I saw again succinctly various episodes in the course of my own life, and realized, with uncanny insight, that they were no more than moments that anticipated my being placed in this point of the universe, in this point of the novel, face to face with my author. With my *Author*. I recalled all the dreams, by day or by night, in which I used to glimpse myself, for a fraction of a second, on an island, seated before a mysterious interlocutor who revealed to me the secret of my own life, the mystery of my own vocation. Without any doubt, right now, as I set down these words, I am in the right place, at the right time. Placed, somehow, outside time, I grasped the connections between all past and present moments of my apparently pointless life. Only the voice of Gilbert Newman, addressing without pathos Alexander Jacob Wills, plucked me from the contemplation of an intuition that, otherwise, I could not have seized on my own.

"You see, Alexander, your vocation is precisely that of transmitting what lovers of wisdom like Plato and Ambrose knew very well—that not just people, but even worlds can know the bitterness of death, of punishment. Punishment which is always the result of the most terrible sin: *hybris*. You will ask me, perhaps, what is the name of such a vocation. Bard? Prophet? Chronicler? Perhaps something of each of these. How can you fulfil such a calling? You already know. From the moment when you began to set all your investigations down in writing, you have done no more than fulfil your destiny. This is the mission that awaits you: to find out everything about the French captain and his discoveries, to evaluate them, to draw conclusions, to write. The essential thing is not to stop. The fact that you are treading not only in his footsteps and in those of Francisco López de Gómara, but also in those of your grandfather, Paolo Paltini, cannot be sheer accident. Just as this conversation of ours is not the result of chance."

The Duke's words seemed as natural to me as the twilight sky outside. Probably anyone who saw the readiness with which I accepted his words would have regarded me, condescendingly, as frivolous. For me, however, the time had come to enjoy the quiet waters in which I had docked after passing through the terrible Atlantic storm, a pale reflection of the inner hurricane that had haunted me in recent years. I fully assented to his verdict regarding my calling. Precisely for this reason, without further alluding to the subject, I concentrated on those unknown aspects of our discoveries that still waited to be solved.

"Sir, I shall honor your invitation to continue the research. I have no doubt as regards the historical existence of the island of Atlantis. Its identification is just a matter of time. However, another question seems to me more urgent. The French captain speaks of the 'symbol' used to read the anamorphic text. And about the 'key of light.' Obviously, he means the silvery tube. But why 'symbol'?"

The Duke looked at me and said: "Because that is exactly what it is: a symbol that indicates the motives for which the captain chose, with the help of an optical illusion, to camouflage the ending of the *Critias*. It is significant that the text is written in the same volume in which the tetralogy including that particular dialogue is to be found. Then we have those unintelligible signs. Unintelligible to anyone who is not so placed as to have the right perspective and who lacks the appropriate optical instrument. Do not for a moment forget that we are dealing with a person to whom the notion of allegory was very familiar. I think this is how the French captain's words are to be understood: anamorphosis itself is a symbol, an allegory."

"So the text," I responded, "written in the proximity of the Platonic dialogue, is invisible to the reader who lacks the appropriate instruments. The 'key of light' would indeed seem to be the perfect metaphor for the human intellect endowed with its own light. The natural light of reason. Which cannot decipher the strange characters unless the reader is so placed as to have the right perspective. And yet, there is something else that I can't understand. Not regarding the French captain's confession, but regarding something you yourself said. You somehow suggested that there might be more involved than the end of *a* world? Were you perhaps thinking of the end of more than one world? Of all worlds? I mean . . . of *the* world?"

Almost in a whisper, I had dared to formulate the question that had been troubling me throughout our conversation. For a historian of today, there is nothing unusual in studying the beliefs and ideas of the ancients *as if* they were true. In the case of Gilbert Newman, however, I had observed to my astonishment that there was no question of "as if." For him, all these things *were* true.

"Alexander, the list of readings I proposed in the labyrinth has already answered your question. All these texts, without exception, from Hesiod and Thrasyllus to Bellarmino, Solovyev, and the Holy Scriptures, present a vision that permits the interpretation of history. It is a matter of that 'deciphering of signs' that you mentioned earlier. And of the end of the world, the end of history. For what is an epochal event like the sinking of Atlantis if not the mere prefiguration of the great final conflagration—the *ultima conflagratio* of the scholastics? As for signs, we should not let ourselves be deceived by the would-be prophets who point to all sorts of natural catastrophes and announce the fulfillment of Mayan or Biblical predictions. It is not to the catastrophes of the physical world that we should look, but into the souls of those who become guilty of *hybris*. This is Plato's lesson. Forgetting, ignoring, even denying that way of life that is based on the practice of the virtues is always the prelude to the greatest catastrophe imaginable. That is why it is worth our while continuing the research of Dr. Paolo Paltini, of the French captain, and also of Father Gómara. Three lives whose threads are interwoven in a fabric whose final form as yet remains to be revealed. It is on you that the discovery of the whole depends.

"Perhaps now is the moment to ask you if you will remain on the island to investigate the ruins. In a few days, a university team will arrive. A good friend of mine, a historian specialized in Meso-American cultures, is waiting only for a confirmation. You would be directly involved in coordinating the whole archaeological project. At the same time, I have another piece of news, at least equally gratifying: our family's chaplain, Father Rafael del Val, will be arriving on Saturday. In addition to attending the daily liturgy in the chapel, we shall be able to give the bones of the Nameless One a fitting burial."

At this point, the elderly sage stopped. No sign suggested that he might have more to add. Without haste, he refreshed the tobacco in the bowl of his pipe.

The sun had reached the line of the horizon. Now orange toward red in color, its disc shed waves of light like the flames of a colossal fire burning up the surface of the ocean. The distant islands, a few scattered clouds, the shore and the trees that came within the frame of the whole vision—in a word, all that was not water—seemed mere silhouettes, like the figures in the shadow theater, where the opaque characters are set against a luminous background. As the long minutes passed, for as long as it took for the solar disc to sink into the waters of the Atlantic, the fantastic spectacle seemed to confirm a terrible truth in all its simplicity: humanity, indeed the world, grows old and dies. Like a body destined for the ritual of purification by fire, silent and cold, the whole landscape seemed ready to be engulfed by incandescent heat that would ignite even the water. Never had I believed that such a cosmic denouement was conceivable. Now it seemed not only conceivable, but perfectly plausible.

With the disappearance of the sun, the fire was extinguished. Soon all was enveloped in thick darkness. Only the embers in the Duke's pipe glittered in the night. The only words I was able to articulate were sufficient to close that evening in which the secret of my own calling had been revealed to me: "I'll stay on the island."

I then murmured, in a whisper, the last words written in Paolo Paltini's journal: "*Nella lontana isola dove regna una sola stagione . . .*"

Before he answered me, it seemed to me that a discreet smile blossomed on Gilbert Newman's lips, a smile almost imperceptible in the semi-darkness of the observatory, but still clearly defined.

"How could it be otherwise, Alexander?"

Os Justi Press specializes in reprinting Catholic classics and new works that support the Roman Church's traditional Faith. Check out some of our other titles:

Os Justi Studies in Catholic Tradition

John Joy, *Disputed Questions on Papal Infallibility*

Fr. Réginald-Marie Rivoire, *Does "Traditionis Custodes" Pass the Juridical Rationality Test?*

Joseph Shaw, *The Liturgy, the Family, and the Crisis of Modernity*

Translations of Dr Kwasniewski's tract True Obedience

La Verdadera Obediencia en la Iglesia

A Verdadeira Obediencia na Igreja

Wahrer Gehorsam in der Kirche

Dogmatic Theology

Lattey (ed.), *The Incarnation*

Lattey (ed.), *St Thomas Aquinas*

Pohle, *God: His Knowability, Essence, and Attributes*

Pohle, *The Author of Nature and the Supernatural*

Scheeben, *A Manual of Catholic Theology* (2 vols.)

Scheeben, *Nature and Grace*

Spiritual Theology

Doyle, *Vocations*

Guardini, *Sacred Signs*

Leen, *The True Vine and Its Branches*

Swizdor, *God in Me*

Liturgy

The Life of Worship

A Benedictine Martyrology

The Roman Martyrology (Pocket Edition)

Chaignon, *The Sacrifice of the Mass Worthily Offered*

Croegaert, *The Mass: A Liturgical Commentary* (2 vols.)

Kwasniewski (ed.), *John Henry Newman on Worship, Reverence, and Ritual*

Parsch, *The Breviary Explained*

Pothier, *Cantus Mariales*

Language & Literature

The Little Flowers of Saint Francis (illustrated)

Brittain, *Latin in Church*

Farrow, *Pageant of the Popes*

Kilmer, *Anthology of Catholic Poets*

Walsh, *The Catholic Anthology*

www.ingramcontent.com/pod-product-compliance
Lightning Source LLC
Chambersburg PA
CBHW030822210726
48290CB00002B/719